D0560847

SEROTONIN

SEROTONIN

MICHEL HOUELLEBECQ

Translated from the French by Shaun Whiteside

FARRAR, STRAUS AND GIROUX

NEW YORK

Farrar, Straus and Giroux
120 Broadway, New York 10271

Printed in the United States of America
Originally published in French in 2019 by Flammarion, France, as *Sérotonine*
English translation originally published in 2019 by William Heinemann, Great Britain
Published in the United States by Farrar, Straus and Giroux
First American edition, 2019

Library of Congress Control Number: 2019947078
ISBN: 978-0-374-26102-3

www.fsgbooks.com
www.twitter.com/fsgbooks • www.facebook.com/fsgbooks

1   3   5   7   9   10   8   6   4   2

SEROTONIN

It's a small, white, scored oval tablet.

I wake up at about five o'clock in the morning, sometimes six; my need is at its height, it's the most painful moment in my day. The first thing I do is turn on the electric coffee maker; the previous evening I filled the water container with water and the coffee filter with ground coffee (usually Malongo, I'm still quite particular where coffee is concerned). I don't smoke a cigarette before taking my first sip, it's an obligation that I impose upon myself, a daily success that has become my chief source of pride (here I must admit, having said this, that electric coffee makers work quickly). The relief that comes from the first puff is immediate, startlingly violent. Nicotine is a perfect drug, a simple, hard drug that brings no joy, defined entirely by a lack, and by the cessation of that lack.

*

A few minutes later, after two or three cigarettes, I take a Captorix tablet with a quarter of a glass of mineral water – usually Volvic.

I'm forty-six, my name is Florent-Claude Labrouste and I hate my first name, which I think was inspired by two members of my family that my father and my mother each wished to honour; it's all the more regrettable that I have nothing else to reproach my parents for, they were excellent parents in every respect, they did their best to arm me with the weapons required in the struggle for life, and if in the end I failed – if my life is ending in sadness and suffering – I can't hold them responsible, but rather a regrettable sequence of circumstances to which I will return, and which is, in fact, the subject of this book; I have nothing to reproach my parents for apart from the tiny – irritating but tiny – matter of my first name; not only do I find the combination 'Florent-Claude' ridiculous, but I find each of its elements disagreeable in itself, in fact I think my first name misses the mark completely. Florent is too gentle, too close to the feminine Florence – in a sense, almost androgynous. It does not correspond in any way to my face, with its energetic features, even brutal when viewed from certain angles, and which has often (by some women in any case) been thought virile – but not at all, really not at all – as the face of a Botticelli queer. As to Claude, let's not even mention it; it instantly makes me think of the Claudettes, and the terrifying image of a vintage video of Claude François shown on a loop at a party full of old queens comes back to mind as soon as I hear the name Claude.

It isn't hard to change your first name, although I don't mean from a bureaucratic point of view – hardly anything is possible from a bureaucratic point of view. The whole point of bureaucracy is to reduce the possibilities of your life to the greatest possible degree when it doesn't simply succeed in destroying them; from the bureaucratic point of view, a good citizen is a dead citizen. I am speaking more simply from the point of view of usage: one needs only to present oneself under a new name, and after several months or even just several weeks, everyone gets used to it; it no longer even occurs to people that you might have called yourself by a different first name in the past. In my case the operation would have been even easier since my middle name, Pierre, corresponds perfectly to the image of strength and virility that I wished to convey to the world. But I have done nothing, I have gone on being called by that disgusting first name Florent-Claude, and the best I have had from certain women (Camille and Kate, to be precise, but I'll come back to that, I'll come back to that) is that they stick to Florent. From society in general I have had nothing; I have allowed myself to be buffeted by circumstances on this point as on almost everything else, I have demonstrated my inability to take control of my life, the virility that seemed to emanate from my square face with its clear angles and chiselled features is in truth nothing but a decoy, a trick pure and simple – for which, it is true, I was not responsible. God had always disposed of me as he wished but I wasn't, I really wasn't; I have only ever been an inconsistent wimp and I'm now forty-six and I've never been capable of controlling my own life. In short, it seemed very likely that the second part of my life would be a flabby and painful decline, as the first had been.

The first known antidepressants (Seroplex, Prax) increased the level of serotonin in the blood by inhibiting its reabsorption by the 5-HT_1 neurones. In early 2017, the discovery of Capton D-L opened up the way to a new generation of antidepressants that operated more simply by encouraging the liberation through exocytosis of serotonin produced at the level of the gastro-intestinal mucous membrane. By the end of that year, Capton D-L was on sale commercially under the name Captorix. It proved to be surprisingly successful overall, allowing patients to perform afresh the major rituals of a normal life within a developed society (washing, good neighbourliness, simple bureaucratic procedures), and unlike previous generations of antidepressants it did not encourage suicidal tendencies or self-harm.

The most undesirable side effects most frequently observed in the use of Captorix were nausea, loss of libido and impotence.

I have never suffered from nausea.

The story starts in Spain, in the province of Almería, precisely five kilometres north of El Alquián, on the N340. It was early summer, probably about mid-July, some time towards the end of the 2010s – I seem to remember that Emmanuel Macron was President of the Republic. The weather was fine and extremely hot, as it always is in southern Spain at that time of year. It was early afternoon, and my 4x4 Mercedes G350 TD was in the car park of the Repsol service station. I'd just filled up with diesel, and I was slowly drinking a Coke Zero, leaning on the bodywork, prey to a growing sense of gloom at the idea that Yuzu would be arriving the next day, when a Volkswagen Beetle pulled up by the air pump.

Two girls in their twenties got out, and even from a distance you could tell that they were ravishing; lately I'd forgotten how ravishing girls could be, so it came as a shock, like a fake and overdone plot twist. The air was so hot that it seemed to vibrate slightly, so that the tarmac of the car park created the appearance of a mirage. But the girls were real, and I panicked slightly when one of them came towards me. She had long light-chestnut hair, very slightly wavy, and she wore a thin leather band covered with coloured geometrical patterns around her forehead. Her breasts were more or less covered by a white strip of cotton, and her short, floating skirt, also in white cotton, seemed as if it would lift at the slightest gust of wind – having said that, there was no gust of wind; God is merciful and compassionate.

She was calm, and she smiled, and didn't seem afraid at all – I was the one, let's be honest, who was afraid. Her expression was one of kindness and happiness – I knew at first sight that in her life she had only had happy experiences, with animals, men, even with employers. Why did she come towards me, young and desirable, that summer afternoon? She and her friend wanted to check the pressure of their tyres (the pressure of the tyres on their car, I'm expressing myself badly). It's a prudent measure, recommended by roadside assistance organisations in almost all civilised countries, and some others as well. So that girl wasn't just kind and desirable, she was also prudent and sensible; my admiration for her was growing by the second. Could I refuse her my help? Obviously not.

Her companion was more in line with the standards one expects of a Spanish girl – deep black hair, dark brown eyes, tanned skin. She was a bit less hippie-cool, well, she was certainly cool, but a bit less of a hippie, with a slightly sluttish quality. Her left nostril was pierced by a silver ring, the strip of fabric over her breasts was multicoloured, with very aggressive graphics, run through with slogans that might have been called punk or rock, I've forgotten the difference – let's call them punk-rock slogans for the sake of simplicity. Unlike her companion, she wore shorts, which was even worse; I don't know why they make shorts so tight, it was impossible not to be hypnotised by her arse. It was impossible, I didn't do it, but I concentrated again quite quickly on the situation at hand. The first thing to look for, I explained, was the desirable tyre pressure, taking into account the model of the car: it usually appeared on a little metal plate soldered to the bottom of the driver's seat door.

The plate was indeed in the place I suggested, and I felt their admiration for my manly abilities growing. Since their car wasn't very full – they even had surprisingly little luggage, only two light bags that must have contained a few thongs and the usual beauty products – a pressure of 2.2 kbars was easily enough.

All that remained was the pumping operation itself. The pressure of the front offside tyre, I observed, was only 1.0 kbars. I spoke to them seriously, indeed with the slight severity afforded to me by my age: they had done the right thing in coming to me, it was only a matter of time and they might have unwittingly put themselves in real danger: under-inflation could lead to a loss of grip, or veering, and in time an accident was almost inevitable. They reacted with naive emotion, and the chestnut-haired girl rested a hand on my forearm.

It must be admitted that those contraptions are tedious to use, you have to check the hiss of the mechanism, and you often have to fiddle about to fit the nozzle over the valve. Fucking's easier; in fact, it's more intuitive – I was sure that they would have agreed with me on that point but I couldn't see how to broach the subject; so in short I did the front off-side tyre, then the rear offside tyre, while they were crouching beside me, following my movements with extreme attention, trilling '*Chulo*' and '*Claro que sí*' in their language; then I passed the task to them, instructing them to attend to the other tyres, under my paternal surveillance.

The darker girl – I sensed she was more impulsive – started off by attacking the front nearside tyre, and it became very hard; once she was kneeling – her bottom swelling in her mini-shorts, so perfectly round, and moving as she tried to control the nozzle – I think the chestnut-haired girl was aware of my unease, and briefly put an arm around my waist, a sisterly arm.

At last the time came for the rear nearside tyre, which the chestnut-haired girl took charge of. The erotic tension this time was less intense, but an amorous tension was gently superimposed upon it, because all three of us knew that it was the last tyre, and now they would have no choice but to continue on their journey.

But they stayed with me for several minutes, twining words of thanks and graceful movements, and their attitude wasn't entirely theoretical – at least that's what I tell myself now, a few years on, when I find myself remembering that I did, in the past, have an erotic life. They talked to me about my nationality – French, I don't think I'd mentioned it – about whether I liked the area, and they particularly wanted to know if I knew of any nice places nearby. In a sense, yes: there was a tapas bar that also served large breakfasts, just opposite my residence. There was also a nightclub a little further off, which one might at a pinch have called nice. There was my place, I would have put them up for at least a night, and I have the feeling (but I may be inventing this in retrospect) that that could have been really nice. But I didn't say anything about any of that; I gave them a summary, explaining broadly that the region was pleasant (which was true) and that I felt happy there (which was false, and Yuzu's imminent arrival wasn't going to make things any better).

They left at last, waving broadly; the Volkswagen Beetle did a U-turn in the car park and then headed down the slip road to the motorway.

At that moment several things could have happened. If we'd been in a romantic comedy, after a few seconds of dramatic hesitation (important at this stage is the actor's art, I think Kev Adams could have pulled it off), I would have leapt to the wheel of my Mercedes 4x4, and quickly caught up with the Beetle on the motorway, overtaking it while making slightly idiotic hand gestures (as rom-com actors do). The car would have pulled up on the hard shoulder (in fact, in a classic rom-com there would probably have been only one girl, probably the chestnut-haired one), and various touching human acts would have taken place, in the blast of the lorries that rushed past us a few metres away. It would have been in the screenwriter's interest to crank up the dialogue for that scene.

If we'd been in a porn film, what happened next would have been more predictable, but with less emphasis on the dialogue. All men want fresh, eco-friendly girls who are keen on threesomes – or almost all men, me at any rate.

But this was reality, so I went home. I found myself with an erection, which was hardly surprising given the afternoon's events. I gave it the usual treatment.

Those girls, particularly the chestnut-haired one, could have given meaning to my stay in Spain, and the disappointing and banal conclusion of my afternoon cruelly stressed something obvious: I had no reason to be here. I had bought this apartment with Camille, and for her. It was a time when we were making plans together: a family base, a romantic mill in the Creuse or somewhere, perhaps the only thing we hadn't imagined was having children – and even that hadn't mattered at a particular point. It was the first time I had bought a house, and it remained the only one.

She had taken an immediate liking to the place. It was a little naturist colony, quiet and far away from the huge tourist complexes that stretch from Andalusia to the Levant, whose population essentially consisted of pensioners from Northern Europe – Germans, Dutch, sometimes Scandinavians, with the inevitable English, of course; curiously, on the other hand, there were no Belgians even though everything in the resort – the architecture of the buildings, the running of the shopping centres, the furniture in the bars – seemed to cry out for their presence: in fact it was a really Belgian neck of the woods. Most of the residents had had careers in teaching, public service in the broadest sense of the term, intermediate professions. Now they were finishing their lives peacefully; they weren't the last to turn up for an aperitif, and they cheerfully strolled about with their drooping buttocks, their redundant breasts and their inactive cocks from bar to beach, beach to bar. They didn't make a fuss, they didn't start any neighbourhood squabbles: they civically spread towels over the plastic chairs in the *No Problemo* (in the colony it was an accepted politeness to put down a towel as a way of avoiding contact between furniture that was intended for collective use, and the private and possibly moist parts of the guests) before immersing themselves with exaggerated attention in the study of a menu, albeit a rather short one.

Another clientele, smaller in number but more active, consisted of Spanish hippies (adequately represented, it pained me to realise, by those two girls who had asked me for help in pumping up their tyres). A brief detour through the recent history of Spain may be of use here. With the death of General Franco in 1975, Spain (more precisely Spanish youth) found itself facing two contradictory trends. The first, which was a direct outcome of the 1960s, placed great stress on free love, nudity, the emancipation of the workers and that kind of thing. The second, on the other hand – which took centre-stage in the 1980s – valued competition, hard-core porn, cynicism and stock options; well, I'm simplifying, but you have to simplify sometimes or you end up with nothing. The representatives of the former, whose defeat was programmed in advance, gradually retreated towards nature reserves, like this modest naturist resort where I had bought an apartment. Had that programmed defeat been definitive? Some phenomena long after the death of General Franco, such as the *indignados*, might suggest the contrary. As did, more recently, the presence of those two girls at the Repsol filling station at El Alquián, on that grim and unsettling afternoon – was the feminine of *indignado* an *indignada*? Had I therefore been in the presence of two ravishing *indignadas*? I would never know – I hadn't been able to bring my life anywhere near theirs; though I could have suggested that they visit my naturist colony, they would have been in their natural environment there, and perhaps the dark one would have left but I'd have been happy with the chestnut-haired one. Well, at my age, promises of happiness became a bit vague but for several nights after that encounter I dreamt of the chestnut-haired girl coming and ringing my doorbell. She had come to look for me, my wandering in this world had come to an end, she had come back to save my cock, my being and my soul all at once. 'Come into my house, and be my lovely mistress.' In some of my dreams she specified that her dark friend was waiting in the car, wondering if she could come up and join us; but that version became more and more infrequent, the scenario grew simpler and in the end there wasn't even a scenario; immediately after I had opened the door we entered a luminous and indescribable space. These ramblings continued for just over two years – but let's not get ahead of ourselves.

*

The following afternoon, I would have to go and collect Yuzu from Almería airport. She had never been here, but I was sure she would hate the place. She would have nothing but disgust for the Nordic pensioners, and nothing but contempt for the Spanish hippies, as neither of those two groups (which coexisted without great difficulty) had anything to do with her elitist vision of social life and of the world in general – all of those people definitely lacked *class*, and besides I had no *class*, I just had money, quite a lot of money (the result of circumstances which I will perhaps relate when I have time), and with that said, basically everything that there is to say about my relationship with Yuzu has been said. Of course I had to leave her, that much was obvious, and we should never even have moved in together, except that it took me a long time, a very long time, to regain control of my life, as I have said before, and I was mostly incapable of doing even that.

I easily found a space at the airport, the car park was enormous – everything in the region was enormous in fact, in preparation for a huge wave of tourists that had never arrived.

It was months since I had slept with Yuzu, and I certainly didn't plan on starting again, not under any circumstances (for reasons that I may explain later). I had no idea why I had organised this holiday, and I had already thought, as I waited on a plastic bench in the arrivals hall, of cutting it short – I had planned for two weeks, but one week would be quite enough. I would lie about my professional obligations, the bitch wouldn't have an answer to that when she depended entirely on my money, and that gave me certain rights.

The plane from Paris-Orly was on time, and the arrivals hall was pleasantly air-conditioned and almost entirely deserted – tourism rates were clearly at crisis point in the province of Almería. When the arrivals board announced that the plane had landed, I nearly got up and headed for the car park – she had no idea of the address and would be absolutely unable to find me. I reasoned quickly: one day I would have to go back to Paris, if only for professional reasons; in any case I was almost as fed up with my job at the Ministry of Agriculture as I was with my Japanese companion – I was going through a very difficult time, there are people who kill themselves for less.

As usual she was ruthlessly made-up, almost painted: the scarlet lipstick and violet eyeshadow stressed her pale complexion – her 'porcelain' skin as it says in the novels of Yves Simon. I remember that at that time she never exposed herself to the sun – a bit of pallor (or porcelain skin, to use Yves Simon's term) being viewed by Japanese women as the height of distinction – and yet what were you supposed to do at a Spanish seaside resort if you refused to expose yourself to the sun? My holiday plan was decidedly absurd, that very evening I was going to change the hotel reservations on the way back, even a week was too much – why not keep a few days in spring for the blossoming cherry trees in Kyoto?

With the chestnut-haired girl everything would have been different; she would have stripped off at the beach without resentment and without contempt, like an obedient daughter of Israel; she wouldn't have been troubled by the rolls of fat on the old German women (that was the fate of women, she knew, until the coming of Christ in his glory); she would have offered the sun (and the male German pensioners, who wouldn't have missed a second of it) the glorious spectacle of her perfectly round buttocks and her frank but depilated pussy (for the Lord is bountiful); and I would have got another hard-on, I would have had a hard-on like an animal, but she wouldn't have sucked me off right there on the beach – it was a family naturist colony after all. She would have avoided shocking the old German women doing their hatha yoga on the beach at sunrise, and yet I would have sensed her desire to do so, and my virility would have been fundamentally regenerated, but she would have waited until we were in the water, about fifty metres from the shore (the slope of the beach was very gentle) to offer her moist parts to my triumphant phallus, and later we would have dined on *arroz con bogavantes* in a restaurant in Garrucha, romance and pornography would not have been strangers to one another, the Creator's munificence would have manifested itself most powerfully; in short my thoughts were going in all directions but I still managed to summon a vague expression of satisfaction when I spotted Yuzu entering the arrivals hall in the middle of a dense horde of Australian backpackers.

We mimed a kiss – at least our cheeks brushed against each other – but that in itself was probably too much and she immediately sat down, opened her vanity case (the contents of which conformed strictly to the rules imposed on hand luggage by all airline companies) and began reapplying her powder without paying any attention to the luggage carousel – clearly it was going to be up to me to lug her bags about.

I knew them very well, they were from a well-known brand that I'd forgotten the name of, Zadig & Voltaire maybe, or Pascal & Blaise; the concept, such as it was, had been to reproduce on the fabric one of those Renaissance maps in which the terrestrial world was represented very approximately, but with vintage inscriptions along the lines of: 'Here be Tygers'. They were smart cases, their exclusivity reinforced by the fact that they were not equipped with wheels, unlike the vulgar Samsonite bags made for middle-management, you had to actually *lug* them, just like the trunks that well-to-do women owned in the Victorian age.

Like all countries in Western Europe, Spain, engaged in a deadly process of increasing productivity, had gradually rid itself of all low-skilled jobs that had previously helped to keep life a little less unpleasant, and in doing so had condemned the majority of its population to mass unemployment. Such bags, whether they were branded Zadig & Voltaire or Pascal & Blaise, only made sense in a society where the role of *porter* still existed.

That was apparently no longer the case, but on the other hand maybe it was, I said to myself, taking Yuzu's two bags one after the other (a suitcase and a travelling bag of almost identical weight – together they must have weighed about forty kilos) off the carousel: the porter was me.

I also fulfilled the function of chauffeur. Shortly after we reached the A7 motorway, she turned on her iPhone and plugged in her headphones before covering her eyes with a strip of fabric soaked in aloe vera exfoliating lotion. The motorway heading south, towards the airport, could be dangerous, and it was not unheard-of for a Latvian or Bulgarian lorry driver to lose control of his vehicle. In the opposite direction, the flotillas of trucks feeding Northern Europe with vegetables cultivated in greenhouses and picked by illegal Malians were setting off on their journey. The lack of sleep had not yet caught up with their drivers, and I overtook about thirty trucks without encountering a problem before approaching the 537 turn-off. The safety rail was missing for a stretch of just over five hundred metres at the start of the long curve leading to the viaduct that loomed above the Rabla del Tesoro; all I had to do to deal with it was avoid turning the wheel. The slope was very steep at that spot and taking into account the accumulated speed, one could expect a perfect trajectory: the car wouldn't even have bounced off the rocky slope, it would have crashed directly one hundred metres further down. A moment of pure terror and then it would be over, I would give the Lord my uncertain soul.

The weather was clear and calm again and I quickly reached the start of the bend. I closed my eyes and clamped my hands on the wheel; there were a few seconds of paradoxical balance and absolute peace, certainly less than five, during which I felt as if I had stepped out of time.

In a convulsive and entirely involuntary movement, I swung violently to the left. It was about time, and the front nearside wheel briefly touched the stony hard shoulder. Yuzu pulled off her mask and tore out her headphones. 'What's happening? What's happening?' she repeated, furious but a little bit frightened too, and I began playing with her fear. 'It's all fine . . .' I said as gently as I could, with the unctuous intonation of a civilised serial killer. Anthony Hopkins was my model, inspiring and almost unimprovable, the kind of man you need to meet at a certain stage in your life. I said again, even more gently, almost subliminally: 'It's all fine . . .'

As far as I was concerned, I wasn't fine at all; in fact, I had just failed in my second attempt at liberation.

As I expected, Yuzu reacted calmly, although she struggled to hide her feeling of satisfaction at my decision to reduce our holiday to a week, and my professional explanations seemed to be immediately convincing; the truth was that she really couldn't have given a shit.

In any case, it had been little more than a pretext: the fact was that I'd left before delivering my report on the apricot producers of the Roussillon, revolted by the pointlessness of my task. As soon as the free-trade agreements currently under negotiation with the Mercosur countries were signed it was clear that the apricot producers of the Roussillon would no longer stand a chance; the protection offered by the AOP status 'red Roussillon apricot' was merely a derisory joke and the surge in Argentinian apricots was inexorable, the apricot producers of the Roussillon were effectively all dead – there wouldn't be any left, not a single one, not even a survivor to count the corpses.

I was, I don't think I've mentioned this, employed at the

Ministry of Agriculture, my essential task consisting in writing notes and reports for negotiating advisers usually within European bureaucracies, sometimes within the context of broader commercial negotiations whose role was to 'define, sustain and represent the positions of French agriculture'. My contractual status allowed me to attain a high salary, far higher than that a civil servant would have been allowed under prevailing rules. This salary was justified in a sense: French agriculture is complex and diverse, few can master the challenges of every branch, and my reports were generally well thought-of. I was praised for my ability to get to the essentials; not to lose myself in a multitude of numbers, but rather shed light on certain key elements. On the other hand, my defence of France's agricultural policies was nothing but a long list of failures, failures that were not down to me; they were more directly those of the negotiators: a strange, vain species whose record of defeat showed no signs of abating. I had had dealings with some of them (quite rarely, as a rule we communicated by email) and had emerged from those meetings with a sense of disgust. As a rule, they weren't agronomic engineers but former business school students – since the outset I had felt nothing but revulsion for business and all that it involves, and the idea of 'graduate business studies' was in my eyes a desecration of the very idea of study, but after all it was normal to hire young business studies graduates as negotiators. A negotiation is always the same thing: whether you're negotiating apricots, almond biscuits, mobile phones or Ariane rockets, negotiation is an autonomous universe which obeys its own laws, a universe that will always be inaccessible to non-negotiators.

Still, I picked up my notes about the apricot producers of the Roussillon and went and sat in the top room (it was a duplex), and in the end I barely saw Yuzu for a week; for the first two days I made an effort to join her downstairs, to maintain the illusion of a conjugal bed, and then I gave up and developed the habit of eating on my own in the tapas bar, which was actually quite pleasant and where I had missed the opportunity to share a table with the chestnut-haired girl from El Alquián. As the days passed, I resigned myself to spending all my afternoons there, in that commercially tone-less but socially incompressible space which, in Europe, separates lunch from dinner. The atmosphere was restful and there were people a bit like me but even worse off: they were twenty or thirty years older than me and their verdict had been delivered – they were *beaten*. There were a lot of widowers in this tapas bar in the afternoon – naturists know widowhood too – or, rather, there were a lot of widows, and quite a few homosexual widowers, whose frailer companions had fluttered off to gay heaven. Distinctions of sexual orientation seemed to have evaporated, in this tapas bar manifestly selected by pensioners as a place to end their lives, in favour of flat national divides: by the terrace tables you could easily tell the English corner from the German corner; I was the only Frenchman; as to the Dutch, they were really a bunch of slags and sat down anywhere at all, a race of opportunist polyglot tradespeople it can't be said often enough. And they all sat getting pleasantly stupid on *cervezas* and *platos combinados,* the atmosphere generally very calm, the tone of the conversations measured. From time to time, however, a wave of *indignados* crashed down, straight from the beach, the girls' hair still damp – and the noise level in the restaurant went up a notch. I don't know why Yuzu gave a damn about not exposing herself to the sun; she was probably watching a Japanese TV series on the Internet; even now, I still wonder what she made of the situation. A simple *gaijin* like me – not even from a remarkable background, just capable of bringing in a comfortable but not stupendous salary – should normally have felt infinitely honoured to share the existence of a woman who was not only Japanese, but also young and sexy and from an eminent Japanese family, and who also mingled with the most advanced artistic circles in both hemispheres. The theory was unimpeachable: I was barely worthy to untie her sandals – that went without saying – but the problem was that I was showing an increasingly vulgar indifference to her status and mine. Once, when I was going to get some beers from the downstairs fridge, I bumped into her in the kitchen and couldn't help saying: 'Get out of the way you fat slut,' before grabbing my pack of San Miguel and a half-eaten chorizo. She probably felt a bit thrown during that week: it isn't easy pointing out the eminence of your social status when the other party threatens to belch in your face or fart by way of reply. There were certainly a lot of people she could have informed about her concerns – not her family, who would immediately have investigated the situation before concluding that it was time for her to return to Japan, but certainly girlfriends, friends or acquaintances, and I think that she used Skype a lot during those few days when I was busy resigning myself to abandoning the apricot producers of the Roussillon as they began their descent towards annihilation. Today my indifference at the time towards the apricot producers of the Roussillon seems a warning sign of the indifference that I showed towards the milk producers of Calvados and Manche at the crucial moment, and also of the more fundamental indifference that I would go on to develop towards my own fate, which at that moment made me eagerly seek out the company of pensioners, something that was not, paradoxically, all that easy; they were quick to unmask me as a fake pensioner, and in particular I suffered rebuffs from the English (which wasn't very serious, you're never well received by the English – they are almost as racist as the Japanese, like a lite version of them), but also from the Dutch, who obviously didn't reject me out of xenophobia (how could a Dutch person be xenophobic? That's an oxymoron: right there: Holland isn't a country, it's a business at best), but because they refused me access to their world of pensioners, I hadn't sat the tests and so they couldn't open up to me easily about their prostate problems or their heart bypasses. Surprisingly enough, I was much more warmly welcomed by the *indignados*; their youth went hand in hand with real naivety, and during those few days I could have changed drastically, and I would have had to change; it was my last chance and at the same time I had a lot to teach them. I was perfectly familiar with the abuses of the agro-industry; their militancy would have developed, all the more so since Spain's policy towards GM food was more than questionable. Spain was one of the most liberal and most irresponsible European countries where GM was concerned: it was the whole of Spain, the whole of the Spanish *campos*, which risked turning into a genetic bomb from one day to the next. It would only have taken a girl – it only ever takes a girl – but nothing happened that could make me forget the chestnut-haired girl from El Alquián, and in retrospect I don't even blame the *indignadas* who were there. I can't even really remember their attitude towards me; I have a sense when I think about it of superficial benevolence, but I imagine that I myself was only superficially accessible. I had been destroyed by Yuzu's return – by the obvious fact that I had to get rid of Yuzu and do it as quickly as possible – and I had become unable to really notice them, and even if I had noticed them, to believe in the reality of their charms; they were like a documentary about the waterfalls of the Bernese Oberland captured on the Internet by a Somalian refugee. My days passed, increasingly painfully, in the absence of tangible events and of reasons for living – in the end I had even completely abandoned the apricot producers of the Roussillon and had stopped going to the café often for fear of being confronted by a bare-breasted *indignada*. I watched the movements of the sun on the tiles, I knocked back bottles of Cardenal Mendoza brandy, and that was more or less it.

In spite of the unbearable emptiness of the days, I dreaded the return journey, those few days I would have to sleep in the same bed as Yuzu. There was no question of us booking separate rooms, I didn't feel I could collide so violently with the *Weltanschauung* of the receptionists and of the whole hotel staff, so we would be permanently glued to one another, twenty-four hours out of twenty-four, and that ordeal would last for four whole days. When I had been with Camille, that journey only took me two days, firstly because she could drive as well as me and so we took turns, but also because speed limits weren't respected in Spain yet – they didn't even have a system of points on licences – and the coordination of European bureaucracies was less perfectly organised in any case, hence a general laxity about minor infractions committed by foreigners. Not only did driving at 150 or 160 kilometres per hour – rather than the ridiculous limit of 120 kilometres per hour – obviously reduce how long the journey took, but it also allowed you to drive for longer, and under

safer conditions. On those interminable Spanish motorways –
straight lines leading all the way to infinity, almost empty;
crushed by the sun and passing through an entirely boring landscape, particularly the part between Valencia and
Barcelona: not that crossing the interior really helped, the
stretch between Albacete and Madrid was also perfectly
deadly – on those Spanish motorways, even the consumption
of strong coffee, even chain-smoking one cigarette after
another, didn't help you combat sleepiness. After two or three
hours of that tiresome itinerary your eyes inevitably closed,
only the discharge of adrenalin induced by speed would have
helped to preserve your vigilance. In fact that absurd speed
limit was the direct reason why fatal accidents returned to
Spanish motorways, and unless I wanted to risk a fatal
accident – although I admit that might have been a solution –
I was now obliged to limit myself to journeys of five or six
hundred kilometres a day.

Even during my time with Camille, it wasn't easy to find
hotels that accepted smokers, but for the reasons I've already
stated, it only took us one day to cross Spain and another to
reach Paris, and we had discovered some dissident establish-
ments: one on the Basque coast; the other on the Côte
Vermeille; a third also in the Pyrénées-Orientales but further
inland, in Bagnères-de-Luchon to be precise – already in the
mountains, it's probably the last of those – the Château de
Riell, which left me with the most magical memory of the
improbable kitschy, pseudo-exotic decoration in all the rooms.

Legal oppression was less perfect in those days – there
were still a few holes in the mesh of the net – but also I was
younger and hoped I could stay within the limits of the law;

still believing in the justice of my country, I trusted in the generally beneficial character of its laws and hadn't yet acquired the skill of the guerrilla fighter that would later let me treat smoke detectors with indifference: once you'd unscrewed the cover of the device, you only needed two good clips with the wire cutter to deactivate the power circuit of the alarm and that was that. It's harder to get around housekeepers, whose sense of smell – over-trained in detecting the scent of tobacco – is usually flawless. The only solution in that situation is to keep them sweet: a generous tip always helps to buy their silence, but obviously it makes your stay more expensive, and you're never quite safe from betrayal.

I had planned our first stop in the *parador* at Chinchón, an uncontroversial choice. *Paradores* in general are an uncontroversial choice, but this particular one was charming, based in a sixteenth-century convent. The walls opened on to a tiled patio with a flowing fountain and there were magnificent dark wooden Spanish armchairs that you could sit on in all the corridors and even at reception. So she did, crossing her legs with her usual blasé hauteur and, without paying the slightest attention to the decor she immediately turned on her mobile, preparing to complain that there was no network. There was network, in fact, which was quite good news as it would keep her busy throughout the evening. She still had to get up again, not without some signs of irritation, to present her own passport, as well as her French residence permit, and to sign in the places marked on the different forms presented to her by the hotelier, three in all. The administration of the *paradores* still had a strangely bureaucratic and pernickety side, absolutely inappropriate to what the reception of a *hôtel de charme* should be like in the imagination of the Western tourist. Welcome cocktails were not their style but photocopies of passports were; things probably hadn't changed since Franco. Perhaps *paradores* were in fact *hôtels de charme*: they were their almost perfect archetype, every medieval fortress or Renaissance monastery still standing in Spain had been converted into a *parador.* This visionary policy, first put in place in 1928, had assumed its full scale a little later on, with the arrival of one man. Francisco Franco, regardless of other – sometimes questionable – aspects of his political activities, could be considered the genuine inventor, on a global scale, of *gracious tourism.* But his work didn't stop there: this same universal spirit would later lay the foundations of an authentic *mass tourism* (think of Benidorm! think of Torremolinos! was there anything like it in the world in the 1960s?). Francisco Franco was in fact a real giant of tourism, and it was by that standard that he would ultimately be re-evaluated; several Swiss hotel training schools had already begun to re-evaluate him and, in more general economic terms, Francoism had recently been the subject of interesting studies in Harvard and Yale, showing how the *caudillo* – sensing that Spain would never catch up with the train of the industrial revolution (which, let's face it, it had completely missed) – had boldly decided to burn its bridges and invest in the third and final phase of the European economy, the tertiary sector: tourism and services, giving its country a crucial advantage at a time when salaried workers in newly industrialised countries, having achieved greater purchasing power, wanted to spend their money in Europe on gracious or mass tourism, in accordance with their status. Having said that, for now there was not a single Chinese person at the *parador* in Chinchón. An extremely ordinary English academic couple waited their turn behind us, but the Chinese would come, they were bound to come, I had no doubt that they were on their way. But the welcome formalities needed simplifying, however much respect we can or must feel for the *caudillo*'s contribution to tourism things had changed; it was unlikely now that spies from colder climates would slip among the innocent cohort of ordinary tourists, as the spies from the cold countries had themselves become ordinary tourists, like their boss Vladimir Putin, the first of them.

Once the formalities were out of the way and all the hotel forms filled in and signed, I experienced one more moment of masochistic jubilation when I caught the ironic, if not contemptuous, look that Yuzu darted at me as I held out my *Amigos de Paradores* card to the receptionist to collect my points: she'd be saving that one up. I headed towards our room, pulling my Samsonite behind me; she followed me, head boldly raised, having left her two Zadig & Voltaire (or maybe Pascal & Blaise, I don't remember) bags right in the middle of the reception hall. I pretended not to notice, and as soon as we got to our room I poured myself a Cruzcampo from the minibar while lighting a cigarette – I had nothing to fear, past experiences had convinced me that the smoke detectors in the *paradores* also dated from the Franco era, from the end of the Franco era actually, and nobody cared. Regardless of whether it was a late and superficial concession to the norms of international tourism – based on the illusion of an American clientele who would never come to Europe anyway, let alone visit the *paradores* – only Venice could still boast a vague presence of American tourists in Europe. It was now time for the European tourist industry to turn towards rougher and newer countries for whom lung cancer represented only a marginal and relatively undocumented inconvenience. For about ten minutes nothing happened, or hardly anything; Yuzu walked around a little, checked that her mobile was still picking up a signal and that there was no drink in the minibar appropriate to her status – there were beers, ordinary Coke (not even Diet Coke) and mineral water. Then, in a tone that didn't even sound like a question: 'Aren't they bringing the luggage?' 'I don't know,' I replied before opening a second Cruzcampo. The Japanese can't really blush, the psychological mechanism exists but the result tends towards a shade of ochre, and I must acknowledge that at last she swallowed her outrage – it took a moment of quivering but she did swallow her outrage – then she turned around without a word and made for the door. She came back a few minutes later, dragging her suitcase, while I was finishing my beer. When she came back again five minutes later with her travelling bag, I had started on a third drink – the journey had made me really thirsty. As I expected she didn't address a word to me all evening, which allowed me to concentrate on the food – since the very beginning, part of the package at *paradores* has included an emphasis on regional Spanish gastronomy, and in my eyes the result is often delicious, albeit usually a bit greasy.

For our second stop, I had upped the ante further still by choosing a Relais & Châteaux, the Château de Brindos, in the commune of Anglet, not far from Biarritz. This time there was indeed a welcome cocktail, numerous hurried waiters, *canelés* and *macarons* lay ready for us in porcelain bowls, and a cold bottle of Ruinart awaited us in the minibar. It was a really terrific Relais & Châteaux on that terrific Basque coast, and everything could have gone brilliantly if I hadn't suddenly remembered – just as I was passing through the reading room where deep wing chairs surrounded tables covered with piles of *Figaro Magazine*, *Côte Basque*, *Vanity Fair* and various other publications – that I had come to this hotel before, with Camille, before we split up, at the end of our final summer together. The minimal and very temporary revival of goodwill that I might have felt for Yuzu (who, in this more favourable environment, had perked up again, who had to some extent started to purr again, and who had already begun to spread outfit choices out on the bed, with the obvious intention of being *dazzling* at dinner) had immediately been cancelled out by the comparison I was inevitably led to make between their reactions. Camille had strolled through the reception rooms open-mouthed, studying the framed paintings, the bare stone walls, the elaborate chandeliers. Stepping into the bedroom she had stopped, impressed, by the immaculate mass of the king-size bed before sitting down shyly on its edge to test out how springy and soft it was. Our junior suite had a view of the lake; she had immediately wanted to take a photograph of the two of us, and when, opening the door of the minibar, I had asked her if she wanted a glass of champagne she had exclaimed: 'Oh yeahhh . . . !' with an expression of total joy, and I knew she was savouring every second of that joy accessible only to the upper-middle classes. It was different for me because I had had access to this category of hotel in the past; these were the hotels where my father stopped off when we were going on holiday to Méribel, at the Château d'Igé in Saône-et-Loire, or the Domaine de Clairefontaine in Chonas-l'Amballan – I myself belonged to the upper-middle classes while Camille was a child of the middle-middle classes, who to tell the truth had been rather impoverished by the financial crisis.

I no longer even wanted to go for a walk on the shore of the lake while waiting for dinner-time; the very idea was odious to me, like a violation, and I only reluctantly put on a waistcoat (after finishing the bottle of champagne, however) to go to the hotel restaurant, *one star* in the Michelin Guide, where John Argand *creatively revisited* the Basque *terroir* through his menu *'Le marché de John'*. These restaurants might have been bearable if the waiters hadn't recently acquired the habit of announcing the composition of every last *amuse-bouche*, their tone inflated with an emphasis that was half-gastronomical and half-literary, studying the customer for signs of complicity or at least of interest – with a view to making the meal a shared convivial experience, I imagine, while their way of bellowing: 'Enjoy!' at the end of their culinary sermon was generally enough to take away my appetite.

Another even more regrettable innovation since my visit with Camille was the installation of smoke detectors in the rooms. I had spotted them as soon as I entered, but at the same time had noted that, given their height on the ceiling – three metres at least, more probably four – it would be impossible for me to put them out of action. After hesitating for an hour or two, I discovered additional blankets in a cupboard and settled down to sleep on the balcony – luckily it was a mild night; I had experienced much worse during a conference on the pig-farming industry in Stockholm. I used one of the porcelain bowls holding the pastries as an ashtray; I would just have to clean it in the morning, and throw the butts into one of the hydrangea pots.

The third day of driving was interminable; the A10 motorway seemed almost entirely given over to roadworks, and there were two hours of traffic jams at the Bordeaux exit. I was in an advanced state of exasperation when I reached Niort, one of the ugliest towns I have ever had the misfortune to see. Yuzu couldn't conceal an expression of alarm when she realised that our stop for the day was leading us to the Hôtel Mercure-Marais Poitevin. Why inflict such humiliation on her? Humiliation that was also in vain because, as the receptionist told me with a visible hint of malicious satisfaction, the hotel had very recently, 'at the request of the clientele', become 100 per cent non-smoking – yes, it was true, the website hadn't yet been changed, she was aware of that.

*

In the middle of the afternoon the following day, and for the first time in my life with relief, I saw the foothills of Paris. Every Sunday as a young man I left Senlis, where I had had a very protected childhood, to come back and continue my studies in the centre of Paris; I passed through Villiers-le-Bel, then Sarcelles, then Pierrefitte-sur-Seine, then Saint-Denis; I saw the population density and the rows of buildings rising around me, and the violence of conversations increasing on the bus, and the level of danger growing visibly; each time I had the clearly characterised sensation of coming back to hell, and a hell built by human beings at their convenience. Now it was different; a social trajectory without any great verve, but which none the less had allowed me to escape – I hoped once and for all – the physical and even visual contact of the dangerous classes; I was now in my own hell, which I had built to my own taste.

We lived in a big three-bedroom flat on the twenty-ninth floor of the Totem Tower, a kind of honeycombed structure of concrete and glass resting on four enormous raw concrete pillars, which looked like those mushrooms that have a repugnant appearance but are apparently delicious – I think they are called morels. The Totem Tower was located in the heart of the district of Beaugrenelle, just opposite Swan Island. I hated that tower and hated the district of Beaugrenelle, but Yuzu loved that gigantic concrete morel; she had 'immediately fallen in love with it', that was what she announced to all our guests, at least at first. Perhaps she still did announce it, but I'd given up meeting Yuzu's guests a long time ago – I shut myself away in my room just before they arrived and wouldn't come out for the rest of the evening.

We had had separate rooms for several months; I had left the 'master suite' (like a bedroom, but with a dressing room and a bathroom, I mention this for the benefit of my working-class readers) to occupy the 'friends' room', and I used the adjacent shower room. A shower room was all I needed: a brush of the teeth, a quick shower and that was me done.

Our relationship was in its terminal phase – nothing could save it, and besides that wouldn't even have been desirable; however I have to agree that we had what people call a 'superb view'. Both the sitting room and the master suite overlooked the Seine, and beyond the sixteenth arrondissement to the Bois de Boulogne, the Parc de Saint-Cloud and so on; on fine days you could make out the Palace of Versailles. From my bedroom, you had a direct view of the Novotel, only a stone's throw away, and beyond that most of Paris; but that view didn't interest me, I always left the double curtains closed, I didn't just hate the district of Beaugrenelle, I hated Paris; that city infested with eco-friendly bourgeois repelled me. Perhaps I was a bourgeois too but I wasn't eco-friendly; I drove a diesel 4x4 – I mightn't have done much good in my life, but at least I contributed to the destruction of the planet – and I systematically sabotaged the selective recycling system put in place by the residents' association by chucking empty wine bottles in the bin meant for paper and packaging, and perishable rubbish in the glass collection bin. I was rather proud of my lack of civic spirit, but I was also taking revenge on the indecent price of rent and service charges – once I had paid rent and the service charges, given Yuzu the monthly allowance she had asked me for to 'cover household expenses' (essentially, ordering sushi), I had spent exactly 90 per cent of my monthly salary; in short, my adult life consisted of slowly gnawing away at my inheritance, and my father didn't deserve that; it was definitely time for me to put a stop to this nonsense.

*

Since I'd known her, Yuzu had worked at the Japanese House of Culture on Quai Branly, which was only five hundred metres from the apartment and yet she still cycled there on her stupid Dutch bike that she had to bring up in the lift afterwards and then park in the living room. I suppose her parents must have pulled strings to get her that sinecure. I didn't know exactly what her parents did, but they were undeniably rich (with the only children of wealthy parents, you get people like Yuzu, whatever the country, whatever the culture), probably not extremely rich – I couldn't imagine her father as chairman of Sony or Toyota, more like a civil servant, a high-ranking civil servant.

She explained to me that she had been employed to 'rejuvenate and modernise' the programme of cultural events. They weren't high-end events: the flyer that I picked up the first time I visited her at her office gave off a sense of deadly boredom: workshops in *origami, ikebana* and *tenkoku*; lectures on playing Go and tea ceremonies (the Urasenke school and the Omotosenke school). The few Japanese guests they had were living national treasures, but most of them were at least ninety years old – they could appropriately have been called dying national treasures. In short, to fulfil her contract she only had to organise one or two manga exhibitions, or a couple of festivals on new trends in Japanese porn; *it was quite an easy job.*

I had given up going to exhibitions organised by Yuzu six months previously, after the one devoted to Daikichi Amano. He was a photographer and video artist who showed images of naked girls covered with different repugnant animals like eels, octopuses, cockroaches, earthworms . . . In one video a Japanese girl caught the tentacles of an octopus coming out of a toilet bowl with her teeth. I don't think I'd ever seen anything so disgusting. As usual, unfortunately, I had started on the buffet before taking an interest in the works on display; two minutes later, I hurried to the toilets at the cultural centre to throw up my rice and raw fish.

The weekends were always torture, but otherwise I could almost go for weeks without meeting Yuzu. When I set off for the Ministry of Agriculture, she was still fast asleep – she rarely got up before midday. And when I got back in the evening at about seven o'clock she was hardly ever there. It probably wasn't her work that made her keep such long hours – this was perfectly normal after all, she was only twenty-six, I was twenty years older and the desire for a social life fades with maturity, you end up telling yourself you're over it. I had also installed an SFR box in my room so I could access the sports channels and follow the French, English, German, Spanish and Italian national championships, which represented a considerable number of hours of entertainment – if Pascal had been aware of the SFR box he might have sung a different tune – and all that for the same price as other operators; I couldn't understand why SFR didn't put more emphasis on its marvellous sports package in their advertising, but each to his own.

What was probably more deserving of criticism, from the point of view of generally accepted morality, is that Yuzu went, I was convinced, to 'swingers' parties' quite often. I had attended one of these with her at the very beginning of our relationship. It took place in a town house on Quai de Béthune, on the Île Saint-Louis. I had no idea how much a house like that could cost, perhaps twenty million euros – anyway, I'd never seen anything like it. There were about a hundred participants, roughly two men for every woman, and as a rule the men were younger than the women, and of a clearly less elevated social class – most of them even had a frankly inner-city look about them, it occurred to me for a moment that they probably got paid, but then again probably not, for most men a free fuck is a bonus in itself, and there was also champagne and canapés, served in the three interjoining reception rooms, which is where I spent the evening.

Nothing sexual happened in those reception rooms, but the extremely erotic outfits of the women and the fact that couples or groups headed regularly towards the stairs that led to the bedrooms or the basement, left no doubt about the spirit of the assembly.

After almost an hour, when it became apparent I had no intention of exploring what was being hatched or swapped away from the safety of the buffet, Yuzu called an Uber. She didn't tell me off on the way back, but she didn't show any regret or shame either; in fact she didn't allude to the evening at all, and would never mention it again.

That silence seemed to confirm my hypothesis that she hadn't given up those distractions, and one evening I wanted to know for certain; it was absurd, she could come back any minute and there's nothing very honourable about going through your partner's computer. The need to know is a curious thing, though 'need' is perhaps a bit strong – let's say the matches that were on that evening were a bit uninspiring.

By sorting her emails by size, I easily isolated the ten or so with videos attached. In the first, my partner was at the centre of a classic gang-bang; she was masturbating, fellating and being penetrated by about fifteen men, who were unhurriedly waiting their turn, and using condoms for vaginal and anal penetrations; no one uttered a word. At one point she tried to take two cocks in her mouth, but couldn't quite do it. Another time the participants ejaculated on her face, which was gradually covered with sperm, and later she closed her eyes.

That was all very well – in fact let's just say that I wasn't overly surprised – but there was one other thing that grabbed my attention more: I immediately recognised the interior design; the video had been shot in my apartment, more precisely in the master suite, and I wasn't very happy about that. She must have taken advantage of one of my trips to Brussels – and I'd stopped having those over a year ago – so it must have happened right at the start of our relationship, at a time when we were still fucking and even fucking a lot. I don't think I've ever fucked that much in my life. She had been available for sex on a more or less constant basis, and at the time I had deduced that she was in love with me. Perhaps that was an error of analysis, but in that case it was an error common to many men, in which case it isn't an error at all and just how most women work (as they say in popular psychology books), they're programmed to do it (as they say in debates on Public Sénat), and so Yuzu might have been a special case.

And she was indeed a special case, as the second video proved. This time it wasn't filmed at my place, or in the town house on the Île Saint-Louis. While the furniture in the Île Saint-Louis house was high-class, minimalist, black and white, this new location was affluent, bourgeois, Chippendale – it suggested Avenue Foch, a rich gynaecologist or perhaps a successful television presenter. Either way Yuzu was masturbating on an ottoman before sliding on to the floor covered by a carpet decorated with vaguely Persian motifs, on which a middle-aged Dobermann was penetrating her with the vigour normally associated with its breed. Then the camera switched direction, and while the Dobermann went on fucking her (dogs in fact ejaculate very quickly under natural conditions, but a woman's vagina must differ in notable respects from that of a bitch, and he couldn't find his bearings), while Yuzu tugged on the dick of a bull terrier before taking it in her mouth. The bull terrier, which was probably younger, ejaculated in less than a minute before his place was taken by a boxer.

After this canine mini gang-bang I interrupted my viewing; I was disgusted – particularly on behalf of the dogs – and at the same time I couldn't conceal the fact that for a Japanese girl sleeping with a Westerner wasn't far off copulating with an animal (at least from what I had been able to observe of their mentality). Before leaving the master suite, I downloaded all the videos on to a USB stick. Yuzu's face was easily recognisable, and I began to imagine drawing up a new liberation plan, which consisted very simply (good ideas are always simple) of throwing her out of the window.

The practical realisation of this plan presented few difficulties. First of all, I would have to make her drink, on the pretext that the beverage was of astonishing quality, a present from a small local producer of Mirabelle *eau-de-vie* in the Vosges, for example; she was very susceptible to such arguments, because she really had remained a tourist. The Japanese, and Asians in general, cope very badly with alcohol, due to their low level of aldehyde deshydrogenase-2, which transforms ethanol into acetic acid. In less than five minutes, she would plunge into a state of ethylic drowsiness, I'd seen it happen before; then I would only have to open the window and move her body, and as she weighed less than fifty kilos (roughly the same as her bags), I would be able to drag her without difficulty, and twenty-nine storeys are unforgiving.

Of course I could try and convince people that it had been a drunken accident, that seemed quite credible, but I had an enormous and perhaps misplaced trust in my country's police, and my initial plan was to confess: those videos, I thought, constituted mitigating circumstances. The Penal Code of 1810, article 324, stipulates that 'murder committed by a husband on his wife, or by the latter on her husband, is not excusable (. . .) Nevertheless, according to article 336, in the case of adultery, murder committed by a husband on his wife, as well as on the accomplice, at the moment of surprising them in the act in the marital home, is excusable. In short, if I had set off with a Kalashnikov on the evening of the orgy, and we had been living in Napoleon's time, I would have been acquitted without difficulty. But we were no longer living in Napoleon's time, not even in the time of *Divorce, Italian Style*, and a swift Internet search told me that the average sentence for a crime of passion committed in a conjugal context was seventeen years in prison; some feminists wanted to go further and permit the introduction of more serious penalties by introducing the idea of 'feminicide' into the Penal Code, which I found quite amusing; it sounded like insecticide, or raticide. Still, seventeen years seemed a lot to me.

At the same time, maybe prison's not so bad, I said to myself: administrative problems evaporate, you get medical treatment; the chief inconvenience is that you're constantly being beaten up and sodomised by other inmates, but on second thought it was perhaps mostly the paedophiles who were humiliated and raped by the other prisoners, or perhaps pretty young guys with angelic little arses, frail and well-to-do delinquents who gave in stupidly for a line of coke – whereas I was hefty, squat and a bit alcoholic and actually looked more like your average defendant. *Fucked and Humiliated* would have been a good title, a bit of trash Dostoyevsky, and besides I seemed to remember that Dostoyevsky had written about the prison world; it might be transferable, although I hadn't had time to check and needed to make a decision quickly, and it seemed to me that a guy who had killed his wife to 'avenge his honour' might enjoy a certain level of respect among his fellow inmates, or at least that was what my feeble understanding of the psychology of the prison environment suggested to me.

On the other hand, there were things that I liked in the outside world: a little trip to the G20, for example, they had fourteen different kinds of hummus; or a walk in the woods, I liked going for walks in the woods, I should have done it more often – I'd missed the contact with my childhood – so in the end a long time in prison perhaps wasn't the best solution, but I think it was the hummus that made my mind up. Not to mention the moral element of murder, of course.

Curiously enough, it was while watching Public Sénat – a channel from which I didn't expect very much, and certainly nothing like this – that the solution finally came to me. The documentary, entitled *Voluntarily Missing*, told the stories of various people who had, one day, totally unpredictably, decided to sever all connections with their families, their friends, their jobs: one man who, on a Monday morning on his way to work, had abandoned his car in a station car park and taken the first train to a random destination; another who, rather than going home after a party, had found a room in the first hotel he came across before wandering for months from one Paris hotel to another, changing his address every week.

The statistics were impressive: more than twelve thousand people, in France, every year, chose to disappear, to abandon their families and remake their lives, sometimes at the other end of the world, sometimes without changing cities. I was fascinated, and spent the rest of the night on the Internet trying to find out more, increasingly convinced that I was witnessing my own fate: I too would become someone voluntarily missing, and my case was especially simple as I didn't have to escape a wife, a family, a patiently constructed social environment, but merely a simple foreign live-in girlfriend who had no right to pursue me. Having said that, all the online articles on the Internet insisted on a point that had already been put forward by the documentary: in France, any adult was free 'to come and go' – abandoning your family was not a crime. That phrase should have been carved in huge letters on all public buildings: *In France, abandoning your family is not a crime.* They insisted on this point a great deal, providing impressive evidence: if someone who had been reported missing was stopped by the police or the *gendarmerie*, the police or *gendarmerie* were forbidden to communicate that person's new address without their consent; and, in 2013, searches on behalf of families had been terminated. It was startling that, in a country where individual liberties had tended to shrink, legislation was preserving this one, which was fundamental – in my eyes even more fundamental, and philosophically more troubling, than suicide.

I didn't sleep that night, and I immediately put appropriate measures in place. Without a precise destination in mind, it seemed that my path would now lead me towards the countryside, so I opted for the Crédit Agricole. The account was opened immediately, but I would have to wait a week to have Internet access and a cheque book. It only took me fifteen minutes to close my account with BNP, and the transfer of the full balance into my new account was instantaneous.

Moving the direct debits that I wanted to keep (car insurance, health insurance) took only a few emails. The apartment took a bit longer; I thought it would be a good idea to pretend I had a new job waiting for me in Argentina on a huge vineyard in the province of Mendoza and everyone at the agency thought it was wonderful – all French people think it's wonderful to leave France, it's a typical feature among them; even if you're going to Greenland they think it's fantastic, so let's not even mention Argentina – and if I'd been going to Brazil I think the account manager would have drooled with jealousy. I had to give two months' notice and would pay them via direct debit; as to the state of the place when I left I certainly couldn't be present, but that wasn't compulsory.

Which left only the question of my job. I was a contractual worker within the Ministry of Agriculture, and my contract was renewed annually at the beginning of August. My office manager seemed surprised that I was calling him during my holidays, but he agreed to a meeting that same day. It seemed to me that I needed a more sophisticated lie as he was relatively well informed about agricultural matters, although it would have to be one connected to the first lie. So I invented a job offer as an 'agricultural exports' adviser to the Argentinian embassy. 'Ah, Argentina . . .' he said darkly. In fact agricultural exports from Argentina had been exploding for some years, in all fields, and the growth wasn't over; experts estimated that Argentina – which had only forty-four million inhabitants – could feed up to six hundred million people, and the new government had understood that, by devaluing the peso, those bastards were literally going to inundate Europe with their products, and they had no restrictive legislation regulating GM food, which got us off to a bad start. 'Their meat is delicious . . .' I objected in a conciliatory tone. 'If only it was just the meat . . .' he replied, his voice increasingly gloomy. Cereals, soya, sunflower, sugar, peanuts, fruit, meat of course and even milk: these were all industries in which Argentina could do a lot of harm in Europe, and do so very quickly. 'So you're going over to the enemy . . .' he said in a tone that was superficially jocular, but filled with real bitterness; I preferred to remain prudently silent. 'You're one of our best experts; I imagine their offer must be financially interesting . . .' he insisted in a voice that made me anxious that he was on the brink of losing control; on the other hand, I didn't think it a good idea to reply, and attempted a smile which was at once affirmative, regretful, complicit and modest – a smile, in fact, that was hard to pull off.

'Right . . .' he tapped his fingers on the table. As it happened, I was on annual leave, and the end of it coincided with the end of my contractual period; so technically I didn't even need to come back. Obviously he was a little perturbed, caught off guard, but it couldn't have been the first time something like this had happened. The Ministry of Agriculture pays its contractors well as long as they can show enough operational competence, and broadly speaking it pays them considerably more than its civil servants; but it is clearly no match for the private sector, or even for a foreign embassy whose budget is almost limitless, once they decide to put a real plan of conquest in place. I remember a fellow student who had been offered a fortune by the United States Embassy and completely failed in his mission; Californian wines were still very poorly distributed in France, and beef from the Midwest struggled to work its charm while Argentinian beef remained successful; go figure why that might be – what an impulsive little creature the consumer is, more impulsive than cattle, anyway – although some communication advisers had reconstructed a plausible scenario and in their view the cowboy had been greatly over-exploited as an icon, these days everyone knew that the Midwest was really a vague anonymous territory covered with meat factories; there were too many burgers to serve every day and it wasn't possible any other way; you had to be realistic, and catching animals with a lasso was no longer a viable option. But the image of the *gaucho* (was there some Latin magic at work here?) still fed the dreams of the European consumer, who imagined vast prairies as far as the eye could see, and animals galloping proud and free across the *pampa* (we would have to check whether a cow gallops), but either way a royal road was opening for Argentinian beef.

My former office manager shook my hand, just before I left his office, and he was decent enough to wish me good luck in my new job.

Clearing my office took me a little under ten minutes. It was nearly four o'clock; in less than a day I had reconfigured my life.

I wiped the traces of my previous social life without any real problem; things had become easier with the Internet; all invoices, tax declarations and other formalities could now be dealt with electronically, and physical skill was no longer a requirement, an email address was all that was necessary. But I still had a body, that body had certain needs, and the hardest thing about my flight was to find a hotel in Paris that accepted smokers. It took me a good hundred phone calls, each time enduring the triumphant contempt of the switchboard operator who felt a palpable pleasure in repeating to me, with ill-disguised satisfaction: 'No, sir, that's impossible, our establishment is entirely non-smoking, thank you for your call.' In the end I spent two whole days on that quest, and it was only at dawn on the third day – when I was seriously considering becoming homeless (a homeless person with seven hundred thousand euros in the bank was unusual, even intriguing) – that I remembered the Mercure hotel in the Marais Poitevin, quite recently still a smoking-friendly hotel, and I thought perhaps there was a chance there.

In fact, a few hours on the Internet told me that while almost all Mercure hotels in Paris applied a strict non-smoking policy, there were exceptions. So my freedom would not even come courtesy of an independent hotel but rather from the revulsion of an underling at respecting the orders of his hierarchy, a kind of insubordination, a rebellion of the individual moral conscience, already depicted in various pieces of existentialist theatre immediately after the Second World War.

The hotel was on Avenue de la Soeur-Rosalie, in the thirteenth arrondissement, near the Place d'Italie; I didn't know the avenue or the sister in question, but Place d'Italie suited me; it was far enough from Beaugrenelle, and so I didn't risk running into Yuzu by chance; she hardly went anywhere aside from the Marais and Saint-Germain, and add in a couple of swingers' parties in the sixteenth or the better part of the seventeenth and you had a good picture of her tracks – I would be as safe in Place d'Italie as I would have been in Vesoul, or Romorantin.

I had planned my departure for Monday 1 August. On the evening of 31 July, I sat down in the sitting room and waited for Yuzu to come home. I wondered how long it would take her to grasp reality, to realise that I had left for good and would never be coming back. Her stay in France, whatever else it was, would be directly determined by the two months' rental notice on the apartment. I didn't know exactly what her salary at the Japanese House of Culture was, but it certainly wouldn't be enough to cover the rent, and I couldn't imagine her agreeing to move to a miserable studio flat, since at the very least it would mean getting rid of three quarters of her clothes and beauty products; while the dressing room and bathroom in the master suite were enormous, she'd still managed to fill all the shelves to the brim – the number of things that she needed to maintain her status as a woman was actually startling, and though women don't generally know this, it's a thing that men don't like, that even disgusts them, and gives them a sense of having acquired a tainted product whose beauty can only be maintained by infinite artifice, artifice which one quickly comes to see as immoral (despite the initial indulgence an alpha male might display towards the repertoire of feminine faults), and the truth is that Yuzu spent an incredible amount of time in the bathroom, which I had realised when we went on holiday together: between getting ready in the morning (at around midday), a slightly more basic touch-up mid-afternoon, and the interminable and exasperating ceremony of her evening bath (she had once told me she used eighteen different creams and lotions), I had calculated that she spent six hours on it every day, and it was all the more unpleasant in that not all women were like that, there were counter-examples, and I felt a wave of heartbreaking sadness as I thought of the chestnut-haired girl from El Alquián, with her tiny suitcase; some women give the impression of being more natural and more naturally in tune with the world, sometimes they even manage to seem indifferent to their own beauty – of course this is an additional lie, but in practice the result is there – and for example Camille spent half an hour at most in our bathroom, and I'm sure the same was true of the chestnut-haired girl from El Alquián.

Unable to pay her rent, Yuzu would therefore be condemned to return to Japan, unless she decided to turn to prostitution; she had some of the necessary abilities, her sexual skills were of a very high level, particularly the crucial area of the blow-job; she licked the glans with great determination without ever forgetting the existence of the balls; she fell short only when it came to deep-throating, due to her small mouth, but in my opinion only a small number of maniacs are obsessed with deep-throating – if you want your cock to be entirely surrounded by flesh, well, that's what the pussy is for – the advantage of the mouth, which is the tongue, is useless in the closed universe of the deep throat, where the tongue is ipso facto deprived of any possibility of action. And let's not now descend into controversy, but the truth is that Yuzu was good for a hand-job, and she liked giving them under any circumstance (how many of my flights were improved by little surprising wanks!), and she was also exceptionally gifted at anal: her arse was receptive and easy to access, and she offered it with perfect goodwill; and yet anal always commands a supplementary fee with escorts, so she would even be able to earn much more than a simple prostitute. I estimated her probable rate as around seven hundred euros an hour and five thousand euros a night: her genuine elegance, her limited but adequate level of culture could allow her to become an escort, a woman who could be taken to dinner without any difficulty – even to an important business dinner, or to artistic functions – and prove to be a source of significant conversation, as we know businessmen are very fond of artistic conversations, and I knew that some of my colleagues suspected me of being with Yuzu precisely for those reasons: Japanese girls in any case are always quite classy, almost by definition, but she was, and I may say this without false modesty, a particularly classy Japanese girl. I knew I was admired for that, but I still maintain – and believe me, now that I am close to the end the desire to lie has deserted me once and for all – it wasn't her qualities as a 'top-of-the-range' escort that made me fall for Yuzu, but rather quite simply her skills as an ordinary whore.

Essentially, however, I couldn't really see Yuzu as a prostitute. I'd been with prostitutes a lot, sometimes on my own, sometimes with the women who had shared my life, and Yuzu lacked the essential quality of that marvellous profession: generosity. A whore doesn't choose her customers – that's the point, that's the axiom – she gives pleasure to everyone, without distinction, and that's how she attains greatness.

Yuzu had certainly been at the centre of gang-bangs, but that is a special situation where the multiplicity of cocks placed at her service plunges the woman into a state of narcissistic rapture – the most exciting probably being the one where she is surrounded by men wanking as they wait their turn; well, I'm referring to Catherine Millet's books, which are quite clear on this point – and the fact remains that Yuzu, apart from gang-bangs, chose her lovers and chose them carefully. I had met some of them, generally speaking they were artists (but not bad-boy artists so much, rather the reverse in fact) and sometimes cultural taste-makers, but in any case always quite young men, rather handsome, rather elegant and rather rich, which leaves quite a large number of people in a city like Paris – there are always several thousand men who match that profile, I would say fifteen thousand to name a number – but she had had less than that, probably a few hundred, and a few dozen of those during our relationship, you might even say that she had shone in France, but now it was finished and the party was over.

Never, during the entirety of our relationship, had she gone back to Japan or even planned to do so, and I had overheard some of her telephone conversations with her parents which had struck me as formal and cold, short in any case, I couldn't hold that expense against her. I suspected (not that she opened up to me about it, but the truth had emerged over the course of dinner parties that we had organised at the start of our relationship, at a time when we still imagined that we would have friends, that we would become part of a refined, warm and demanding social network. The truth had emerged thanks to other women, whom she considered as belonging to the same milieu as herself: fashion designers for example, or talent scouts, were present, and the presence of those women was probably necessary for her confessional outbursts), that her parents, back in that vague Japan of theirs, had marriage plans for her, extremely precise marriage plans (there were apparently only two possible suitors, and perhaps even only one), and that as soon as she found herself under their wing once more it would be extremely hard for her to escape – indeed it would be frankly impossible, apart from the chance of creating a *kanjei* and finding oneself in a situation of *hiroku* (I'm making these words up a bit, well, not entirely, I do remember some combinations of sounds during her phone conversations), in short her fate would be sealed as soon as she set foot in Tokyo Narita International Airport.

That's life.

At this stage it might be necessary to provide some clarification about love, intended more for women as women have difficulty understanding what love is for men, and they are constantly disconcerted by their attitudes and behaviour, and sometimes reach the erroneous conclusion that men are incapable of love; they rarely perceive that the very word 'love' signifies two radically different realities for men and for women.

For women, love is power: a generative, tectonic power; love when it manifests itself in women is one of the most imposing natural phenomena and it should be treated with awe; it is a creative power of the same order as an earthquake or a climatic disturbance, its origin lies in a different ecosystem, a different environment, a different universe. Through love, women create a new world; small isolated creatures were bobbing about in an uncertain existence and here comes a woman to create the conditions for life as a couple, a new social, sentimental and genetic entity whose vocation is quite simply to eliminate all traces of the pre-existing individuals of which it is formed; this new entity is already essentially perfect, as Plato had perceived. It may sometimes become more complex with a family but that is almost a detail, contrary to what Schopenhauer thought; in any case women are entirely devoted to this task, they plunge into it, they devote body and soul to it as they say, though they don't differentiate between the two very much, the difference between body and soul is merely masculine hair-splitting. To this task, which as the pure manifestation of a vital instinct is hardly a task, they would sacrifice their lives without hesitation.

Men are initially reserved, they admire and respect this emotional release without fully understanding it; it seems quite strange to them to make such a fuss about it. But gradually they are transformed, they are slowly sucked into the vortex of passion and pleasure that a woman creates: more precisely, they recognise her will, her pure and unconditional will, and they understand that that will is in essence absolutely good, even though she requires frequent and preferably daily vaginal penetration as the normal condition of its manifestation, in which the phallus, the core of men's being, alters its status by becoming the condition under which the manifestation of love is made possible – men having hardly any other means of showing it – and by this strange detour the happiness of the phallus becomes a goal in itself for the woman, a goal that justifies any means employed. Gradually, the immense pleasure given by the woman changes the man: he feels gratitude and admiration; his vision of the world is transformed; and in an unexpected way he attains the Kantian dimension of *respect* and gradually imagines the world in a different way; life without a woman (and, specifically, without this woman who gives him so much pleasure) becomes truly impossible, almost the caricature of a life; in that moment, the man really begins to love. Love for men is therefore an end, an accomplishment, and not, as for women, a beginning, a birth; that's what you need to bear in mind.

Sometimes, however rarely, among the most sensitive and imaginative men, love arrives in the first moment, therefore *love at first sight* is absolutely not a myth; but rather when a man, by a prodigious psychological movement of anticipation, has already imagined all the pleasures which this woman could provide over the years (and, as they say, until death does them part), so the man has already (always already, as Heidegger would have said on one of his good days) anticipated the glorious ending; and it was that infinity, that glorious infinity of shared pleasures, that I had glimpsed in Camille's eyes (but I will return to Camille), and also less randomly (and a little more powerfully, but I was ten years older, and at the time of our meeting sex had completely disappeared from my life; there was no longer any room for it, I was already resigned and already I wasn't entirely a man) in the eyes of the chestnut-haired girl from El Alquián, the eternally heartbreaking chestnut-haired girl from El Alquián – the most recent and probably the last possibility of happiness that life had placed in my path.

I had felt nothing like that with Yuzu; she had conquered me only gradually, and she had done it by secondary means – resorting to what is usually called perversion – with her immodesty above all, with her way of wanking me off (and masturbating herself) in all kinds of circumstances; other than that I didn't know how she'd done it: I'd known prettier pussies, hers was a bit too complicated, too many folds of skin (from certain angles one might even have called it pendulous, in spite of her youth); the best thing about her when I think about it again was her arsehole, the permanent availability of her arsehole, apparently tight but in fact so manageable – I found myself constantly in a situation of free choice between three holes and how many women can you say that about? And at the same time how can you consider them women, those women who don't offer that?

Perhaps I will be rebuked for placing too much importance on sex; I don't think so. Even though I remain aware that other joys can gradually replace it, in the normal course of a lifetime sex remains the only time when we personally and directly engage our organs, so the passage through sex, and through intense sex, remains necessary for the loving fusion to occur; nothing can happen without it, and all the rest, normally, flows gently from it. There is also another thing, which is that sex remains dangerous, the moment *par excellence* when the game becomes interesting. I'm not talking about AIDS specifically, even though the threat of death may add a spicy note, but rather procreation, a much more serious danger in itself; for my own part I gave up using condoms as soon as possible in each of my relationships, to tell the truth not using a condom had become a necessary condition for my desire, in which the fear of multiplying played a notable part, and I knew that if by some misfortune Western civilisation effectively managed to separate procreation from sex (as it has sometimes planned to do), it would thereby condemn not only procreation but also sex, and would therefore condemn itself; Catholics knew that – although their position also involved some strange ethical aberrations, such as their reticence towards such innocent practices as threesomes or sodomy – but I was gradually getting lost by dint of drinking glasses of cognac as I waited for Yuzu, who was in any case not Catholic in any way, let alone a hard-line Catholic. It was already ten o'clock in the evening, I wasn't going to spend the night there, but the idea of leaving without seeing her again still annoyed me a little; I made myself a tuna sandwich while waiting, I had finished the cognac but I still had a bottle of calvados.

My reflections gradually deepened, thanks to the calvados, a powerful and profound spirit, and unfairly ignored. Certainly

Yuzu's infidelities (to be diplomatic) had hurt me, my manly vanity had suffered, and above all I had been filled by doubt: did she love all cocks as much as mine? That is the question that men typically ask themselves at such moments, and I too had asked it of myself before concluding, alas, in the affirmative; it's true that our love had been sullied by it, and I now saw in a different light the compliments about my cock that had been such a source of pride at the start of our relationship (a comfortable size without being excessive, exceptional endurance), I saw them as the manifestation of a coldly objective judgement, the result of regular encounters with multiple cocks rather than the lyrical illusion emanating from the excited mind of a woman in love, which I confess I would humbly have preferred, I had no particular ambition for my cock so it was enough that it should be liked, and then I would like it too, that was where I stood with regard to my cock.

It was not then, however, that my love for her had faded once and for all, but, in an apparently more anodyne and briefer circumstance – conversation had lasted no longer than a minute, and it had immediately followed one of those fortnightly phone calls that Yuzu had with her parents. In it, and it couldn't have been in my imagination, she mentioned going back to Japan, and of course I asked her about it, but her answer was supposed to have been reassuring, that she wouldn't be going back for a long time, and in any case I shouldn't worry about it; it was then that, in a fraction of a second, I understood. A kind of huge white flash obliterated all clear consciousness in me, and I returned to a normal state and engaged Yuzu in a brief interrogation, which immediately confirmed my essential suspicion: she had already planned, in an ideal life, her return to Japan, but it would be in about twenty or thirty years, or, to be precise, immediately after my death; she had already factored my death into her future life, she had taken it into account.

My reaction was probably irrational, Yuzu was twenty years younger than me, everything suggested that she would survive me – and by a considerable length of time – but that is something that unconditional love seeks to ignore and frankly deny, unconditional love is built on that impossibility, that denial, and whether it is validated by faith in Christ or by belief in Google's plan of immortality it makes very little difference for someone who is in love, the loved one cannot die, they are by definition immortal. Yuzu's realism was therefore an absence of love, and that deficiency, that absence, had a definite character, and in a fraction of a second it stopped being romantic, unconditional love and became part of an arrangement, and from that moment I knew it was over, our relationship was over, and it would be even better for me if it ended as quickly as possible, because never again would I have a sense of having a woman beside me, but rather view her as a kind of spider, a spider feeding on my vital fluids which maintained the appearance of a woman: she had breasts, she had an arse (which I have already had the opportunity to praise) and even a pussy (about which I have expressed certain reservations), but none of that counted for anything any more, because in my eyes she had become a spider, a stinging and poisonous spider who was injecting me day after day with a deadly paralysing fluid; it was important for her to leave my life as soon as possible.

It was after eleven and the bottle of calvados was almost finished too, leaving without seeing her again was perhaps the best solution after all. I walked to the bay window: a *bateau-mouche*, probably the last of the day, was turning round the tip of the Île des Cygnes; it was then that I realised I would forget Yuzu very quickly.

I had a bad night, filled with unpleasant dreams in which I risked missing my plane, which led me to undertake different dangerous actions like flying off the top floor of the Totem Tower to try and get to Roissy by air – sometimes I had to flap my arms, sometimes I just had to glide – but I couldn't quite manage, and the slightest lapse in concentration would have made me crash; I had an especially difficult moment above the Jardin des Plantes, where my altitude dropped to only a few metres and I could barely fly over the big cat enclosure. The interpretation of that pathetic but spectacular dream was probably quite clear: I was afraid that I wouldn't succeed in escaping.

I woke up at exactly five o'clock and though I craved a coffee, I couldn't risk making a noise in the kitchen. It was very likely that Yuzu had come home. She never stayed out all night, despite how her evenings might have gone: falling asleep without coating herself in her eighteen beauty creams was unimaginable. She was probably asleep already, but five o'clock was still a bit early; her sleep was at its deepest at around seven or eight, so I would have to be patient. I had chosen the early check-in option at the Mercure – my room would be available from nine o'clock – and I was bound to find a café open somewhere nearby.

I had prepared my suitcase the previous day and had nothing more to do before I left. It was a bit sad to realise that I had no personal memento to take away: no letter, no photograph, not even a book, it was all on my MacBook Air, a thin parallelepiped of brushed aluminium; my entire past weighed 1,100 grammes. It also dawned on me that during the two years of our relationship, Yuzu had never given me a present – absolutely nothing, not one.

Then I realised something even more surprising: the previous evening, stunned by Yuzu's tacit acceptance of my death, I had for a few minutes forgotten the circumstances of my parents' death. There was of course a third solution, for romantic lovers, that was independent of hypothetical transhuman immortality or of the equally hypothetical celestial Jerusalem; an immediately practicable solution, which required neither high-level genetic research nor fervent prayers to the Lord; the very solution that my parents had adopted some twenty years ago.

A notary from Senlis who counted all the local dignitaries among his clientele and a former student at the École du Louvre who settled for the role of housewife: there was nothing about my parents, at first sight, to suggest a passionate love affair. Appearances, I had observed, were rarely deceptive; but in this case they were.

On the day before his sixty-fourth birthday my father, who had been suffering from persistent headaches for several weeks, consulted our family doctor who prescribed him a CT scan. Three days later, the doctor informed him of the results: the scan revealed a large tumour, but it was impossible to tell at this stage whether it was cancerous or not and a biopsy was required.

A week later, the results of the biopsy were perfectly clear: the tumour was in fact cancerous and aggressive, and it was developing rapidly through a mixture of glioblastomas and anaplastic astrocytomas. Brain cancer is relatively rare but very often fatal, the rate of survival for a year is below 10 per cent; its causes unknown.

Due to the placement of the tumour a surgical operation was unthinkable; but chemotherapy and radiotherapy had sometimes produced some kind of results.

It should be noted that neither my father nor my mother saw fit to inform me of these facts; I discovered them only by chance during a visit to Senlis, when I asked my mother about a letter from the hospital that she had forgotten to put away.

The other thing that gave me pause for thought was that, on the day of my visit, they had probably already made their decision, and perhaps even ordered the pills on the Internet.

*

They were found a week later, lying side by side on their marital bed. Always anxious to avoid causing anyone any trouble, my father had alerted the local police by letter, even including a copy of the keys in the envelope.

They had taken the pills in the early evening on the day of their fortieth wedding anniversary. Their death had been quick, the police officer kindly assured me; quick but not instant – it was easy to tell by their positions on the bed that they had wanted to hold hands until the end, but they had suffered from convulsions in their death throes, and their hands had parted.

No one ever discovered how they had got hold of the pills; my mother had deleted her navigation history on the home computer (she would inevitably have been in charge, my father hated computers and anything that might have looked like technological progress more generally; he had held back for as long as possible before giving in and buying equipment for his office, and it was his secretary who dealt with everything – he had never touched a computer keyboard in his life). Obviously, the police officer told me, if I really wanted to they could easily trace the order, nothing is ever totally deleted in the cloud; it was possible, but was it necessary?

I didn't know that two people could be buried in the same coffin, there are so many health and safety regulations about everything that you imagine almost anything is forbidden, but not that, apparently it was possible, unless my father made use of his contacts post-mortem by writing some letters – as I have said he knew all the dignitaries in the town, and even most of those in the *département* – but whatever happened, that was how it was done, and they were laid to rest in the same coffin, in the northernmost corner of Senlis cemetery. At the time of her death, my mother was fifty-nine and in perfect health. The priest had irritated me a little during his sermon, glibly talking about the magnificence of human love as a prelude to the even greater magnificence of divine love; I found it a bit indecent of the Catholic Church to try to *recover* them. When he is faced with genuine love a priest *keeps his trap shut*, that was what I wanted to say to him; what could he have known, the idiot, about my parents' love? I wasn't sure I really understood it myself – I had always sensed in their gestures, in their smiles, something I would never entirely have access to. I don't mean that they didn't love me, they probably did, and from every point of view they were excellent parents: attentive, present but not too much so, generous when they had to be; but it wasn't the same type of love, and I always remained outside the magical, supernatural circle that they formed together (their level of communication was truly astonishing, I'm sure I witnessed at least two clearly demonstrable cases of telepathy). They had no other child, and I remember that the year I went back to the Lycée Henri IV after my *baccalauréat* for the preparatory course in Agriculture, and explained that, given the poor public transport in Senlis, it would be far more practical for me to rent a room in Paris, I clearly remember spotting, fleetingly but indisputably, an expression of relief in my mother; the first thought that had come to her was that she and my father would finally be able to rediscover one another. My father barely tried to conceal his joy; he immediately took charge of things and a week later I moved to an unnecessarily luxurious studio – bigger, I realised straight away, than the attic rooms which my classmates settled for – on Rue des Écoles, five minutes' walk from the *lycée*.

I got up at precisely seven o'clock in the morning and crossed the sitting room without a sound. The front door to the apartment, massive and reinforced, was as silent as that of a safe.

On that first day of August, the traffic in Paris was flowing, and I was even able to park on Avenue de la Soeur-Rosalie, a few metres from the hotel. Unlike the other major roads (Avenue d'Italie, Avenue des Gobelins, Boulevards Auguste-Blanqui and Vincent-Auriol . . .) which begin at the Place d'Italie and drain most of the traffic from the south-eastern arrondissements of Paris, Avenue de la Soeur-Rosalie turned into Rue Abel-Hovelacque after fifty metres, which was a street of only modest importance. Its status as an avenue might have seemed undeserved had it not been for its surprising and point-less width, and for the central strip planted with trees that separated the two thoroughfares, currently deserted; in one direction, Avenue de la Soeur-Rosalie looked more like a pri-vate drive – it called to mind those pseudo-avenues (Vélasquez, Van Dyck, Ruysdael) on the edge of Parc Monceau; in short there was something luxurious about it, and that impression was further reinforced at the entrance to the Hôtel Mercure, which curiously consisted of a large porch that opened on to an inner courtyard decorated with statues: a setting more easily imagined as part of a mid-ranking château. It was half-past seven, and three cafés in Place d'Italie were already open: the Café de France, the Café Margeride (serving specialities from the Cantal, but it was a bit early for that) and the Café O'Jules, at the corner of Rue Bobillot. I opted for the last of these, in spite of the stupid name, because the managers had had the original idea of translating 'happy hours' into French, here rendered as *'les heures heureuses'*; I was sure that Alain Finkielkraut would have approved of my choice.

Overall, the menu of the establishment excited me, and even made me reconsider the negative judgement that I had initially formed about its name: the use of the name 'Jules' had in fact allowed them to develop a deeply innovative menu system, in which the creativity of the names of dishes was combined with meaningful contextualisation; for example, the chapter devoted to salads juxtaposed 'Jules in the South' (lettuce, tomatoes, egg, prawns, rice, olives, anchovies, peppers) with 'Jules in Norway' (lettuce, tomatoes, smoked salmon, prawns, poached egg, toast). For my part, I felt that I would soon (perhaps even this lunchtime) be succumbing to the delights of 'Jules on the farm' (lettuce, ham, Cantal cheese, fried potatoes, walnut halves, boiled egg), unless I fell prey to those of 'Jules the shepherd' (lettuce, tomatoes, warm goat's cheese, honey, lardons).

Generally speaking, the proposed meals did not address an

obsolete controversy, tracing the outlines of a peaceful co-habitation between traditional cuisine (onion soup *gratinée*, fillets of herring with warm potatoes) and innovative *fooding* (panko prawns with salsa verde , bagel *aveyronnais*). A similar desire for synthesis was apparent from the cocktail list which, apart from all the classics, contained some original creations such as 'green inferno' (Malibu, vodka, milk, pineapple juice, *crème de menthe*), the 'zombie' (amber rum, *crème d'abricot*, lemon juice, pineapple juice, grenadine) and the surprising but extremely simple 'Bobillot beach' (vodka, pineapple juice, strawberry juice). In short, I felt that I wasn't going to be spending just happy hours in this establishment, but also happy days, weeks and even years.

At about nine o'clock, having finished my regional breakfast, and having left enough of a tip to ensure the goodwill of the waiters, I made for the reception desk of the Hôtel Mercure, where the welcome I received broadly confirmed my initial hopes. The receptionist confirmed before even asking for my Visa card, exceeding my expectations: a smoking room had been reserved for me, as I had requested. 'You are our guest for a week?' she continued, with an exquisite interrogatory hint; I confirmed as much.

I had said a week as I might have said anything else, my only plan had been to free myself from a toxic relationship that was killing me: my planned deliberate disappearance had been a complete success, and now there I was, a middle-aged Western man, sheltered from need for several years, with no relatives or friends, stripped of personal plans and of genuine interests, deeply disappointed by his previous professional life, whose emotional experiences had been variable but had had the common feature of coming to an end, essentially deprived of reasons to live and of reasons to die. I could take advantage of the possibility to make a new start, to 'rebound', as they say comically on television programmes and in articles about human psychology in specialist magazines; I could also allow myself to slip into lethargic inactivity. My hotel room, I was immediately aware, would guide me in that second direction: it was genuinely tiny, ten square metres in total, I guessed, the double bed occupied almost the whole space, you could move around it but only just; facing it, on a narrow table, were the indispensable television and a courtesy tray (which is to say a kettle, some paper cups and sachets of instant coffee). They had also managed, in that constrained space, to place a minibar and a chair opposite a mirror thirty centimetres square; and that was it. This was my new home.

Was I capable of being happy in solitude? I didn't think so. Was I capable of being happy in general? That's the kind of question, I think, that is best not asked.

The only difficulty with living in a hotel is that you have to leave your room – and therefore your bed – every day so that the housekeeper can do her job. The time when you need to leave is in principle indeterminate, since the chambermaids' timetable is never communicated to the customer. For my part I would have preferred, knowing that the cleaning never took very long, to have been assigned a time to go out; but that was not how things were organised, and in a sense I understood that: it would not have been in line with the values of the hotel trade, it would have been more like how a prison functions, say. So I had to trust in the spirit of initiative and the responsiveness of the cleaning woman, or rather women.

But I could help them, give them a clue by turning over the little information card hooked on the door handle, moving it from the position, 'Shhhh I'm sleeping – Please do not disturb' (symbolised by the picture of an English bulldog asleep on a mat) to the position, 'I'm awake – Please make up the room' (two chickens, photographed against a theatre curtain, in a state of vigorous and almost aggressive wakefulness).

After experimenting for the first few days, I concluded that going out for two hours would be sufficient time. I soon perfected a mini-circuit that began with the O'Jules, which was quiet between ten o'clock and midday. Then I went back to Avenue de la Soeur-Rosalie, which ended with a kind of little roundabout covered by trees; in fine weather I positioned myself on one of the benches arranged under the trees, I was generally alone but every now and again a pensioner sat on one of the other benches, sometimes accompanied by a small dog. Then I turned right into Rue Abel-Hovelacque; on the corner of Avenue des Gobelins I always paused at Carrefour City. I had had an inkling since my first visit that this shop would play an important part in my new life. The oriental food shelf, while not quite reaching the level of variety of the G20 near the Totem Tower where habit had taken me some days before, still displayed eight different varieties of hummus, including abugosh premium, misadot, zaatar and the extremely rare mesabecha; as to the sandwich section, I wonder if it wasn't even superior. Until then I had believed that the minimarket sector was entirely dominated, in Paris and the '*petite couronne*', by Daily Monop'; I should have been suspicious when a brand like Carrefour 'only joined it', as its CEO had pointed out recently in an interview with *Challenges*, 'to make up the numbers'.

The opening hours, which were exceptionally generous,

revealed the same desire for conquest: 7.00 to 11.00 on week-days, 8.00 to 1.00 on Sunday; even the Arabs had never done as well as that. The reduced Sunday hours were the result of a bitter conflict initiated by a process launched by the labour inspectorate of the thirteenth arrondissement a small poster hanging in the shop informed me, which, in breathtakingly virulent terms, stigmatised the 'aberrant decision' taken by the district court that had finally led them to give in, under threat of a penalty 'so exorbitant it would endanger your local trade'. Freedom of trade, and beyond it freedom of the con-sumer, had therefore lost a battle; but the war, one could tell from the martial tone of the poster, was far from over.

I seldom stopped at Bar La Manufacture, directly opposite Carrefour City; some of the micro-brewery beers seemed enticing, but I wasn't keen on the laboriously constructed atmosphere of a 'workers' pub', in an area where the last worker had probably disappeared in around 1920. I would soon discover much worse, in the grim zone of Buttes-aux-Cailles; but I didn't know it yet.

Then I went about fifty metres back down Avenue des Gobelins before turning into Avenue de la Soeur-Rosalie, and that was the only truly urban part of my circuit, the one that would allow me, through the increase in pedestrian and motorised traffic, to feel that we had crossed the barrier of 15 August, the first stage in the resumption of social life, followed by the other, more crucial, stage of 1 September.

Was I, in the end, as unhappy as all that? If, unusually, one of the humans with whom I came into contact (the receptionist at the Hôtel Mercure, the waiters at the café O'Jules, the girl on the till at Carrefour City) had asked about my mood, I would have been inclined to call it 'sad', but it was a peaceful, stable sadness, not susceptible to increase or decrease; a sadness, in short, that to all intents and purposes appeared definitive. But I wasn't falling into that trap; I knew that life might still have plenty of surprises, either atrocious or delightful, in store for me.

That said, for now I felt no desire, something which many philosophers had judged to be an enviable state, or at least that was my impression; the Buddhists, by and large, were on the same wavelength. But other philosophers, as well as all psychologists, considered an absence of desire to be pathological and unhealthy. After a month's stay at the Hôtel Mercure, I still felt unable to engage in that classic debate. I renewed my stay weekly, so that I could remain in a state of freedom (a state which is looked upon favourably by all existing philosophies). In my view I wasn't doing too badly. In fact, my mental state caused me considerable concern on one point only, and that was bodily care, even simple hygiene. I could just about manage to brush my teeth, that was still possible, but I was frankly repelled by the prospect of taking a shower or a bath; in fact, I would have liked to no longer have a body; I was finding the prospect of having a body, of having to devote care and attention to it, more and more intolerable, and although the impressive increase in homelessness had gradually made Western society relax its criteria in this field, I knew that too pronounced a stench would eventually make me stand out in an inappropriate fashion.

I had never consulted a psychiatrist, and basically I didn't much believe in the effectiveness of that profession, so I looked on Doctolib for a GP in the thirteenth arrondissement, to minimise travelling time.

Leaving Rue Bobillot and turning into Rue de la Butte-aux-Cailles (they join up again at Place Verlaine) meant leaving the universe of ordinary consumers and entering a world of militant *creperies* and alternative bars (the 'Temps des cerises' and the 'Merle moqueur' were practically opposite one another), with a scattering of fair-trade organic shops and boutiques offering piercings or afro cuts; I had always had a sense that the 1970s hadn't disappeared in France, they had just made a temporary retreat. Some of the graffiti wasn't too bad, and I followed the street to the end, missing the turn-off into Rue des Cinq Diamants, where Dr Lelièvre had his practice.

He had something of the tree-hugger about him, I said to myself at first glance, with his shoulder-length curly hair starting to be invaded by threads of white; but his bow-tie didn't fit with that initial impression, and neither did the luxurious furniture in his office, so I reconsidered my point of view: he was a sympathiser at most.

When I had finished summing up my recent life to him, he agreed, in fact, that I genuinely needed a course of treatment, and asked me if I had had thoughts of suicide. No, I replied, death doesn't interest me. He suppressed a grimace of discontent and replied in a cutting voice – he clearly didn't find me sympathetic – that there was a new-generation antidepressant (it was the first time I had heard the name

Captorix, which would later play such an important part in my life), which might prove useful in my case; you had to allow one or two weeks for the effects to kick in, but it was a medication that required rigorous medical surveillance, so it was imperative that we meet up again in a month.

I hurriedly agreed, struggling not to grab the prescription too avidly; I had decided never to see this idiot again.

Back at home, or rather in my hotel room, I carefully studied the instructions, which informed me that I would probably become impotent, and that my libido would disappear. Captorix worked by increasing the secretion of serotonin, but the information I was able to find on the Internet about the effect of hormones on the workings of the psyche left an impression of confusion and incoherence. There were certain common-sense observations, along the lines of: 'A mammal doesn't decide, when it wakes up every morning, whether it is going to stay with the group or move away to live its life,' or again: 'A reptile has no sense of attachment to other reptiles; lizards don't trust lizards.' More specifically, serotonin was linked to self-esteem, to the sense of recognition obtained from the group. But in any case, it was essentially produced within the intestine, and it had been found to exist in a great variety of living creatures, including amoebas. What feeling of self-esteem could exist among amoebas? What sense of recognition from the group? I gradually reached the conclusion that medical art remained confused and imprecise about these matters, and that antidepressants were among the many medications that work (or don't) without anyone knowing exactly why.

In my case it seemed to work – the shower was still a bit too violent but I gradually managed to take a tepid bath and to vaguely soap myself. And my libido didn't change much; in any case I hadn't felt anything resembling sexual desire since seeing the chestnut-haired girl in El Alquián, that unforgettable chestnut-haired girl.

So it certainly wasn't a lustful impulse that drove me, a few days later, in the middle of the afternoon, to call Claire. What was it that drove me, then? I had absolutely no idea. It had been over ten years since we'd been in touch; to tell the truth I expected her to have changed her telephone number. But no, she hadn't. She hadn't changed her address either, but that I suppose is normal. She seemed a bit surprised to hear from me – but basically nothing more than that, and she suggested that we have dinner together that very evening in a restaurant near where she lived.

I was twenty-seven when I first met Claire, my years as a student were behind me and there had already been a fair number of girls – foreigners, essentially. You have to realise that Erasmus scholarships, which would later facilitate sexual exchanges between European students, didn't exist at the time, and one of the only places to pick up foreign students was the International University City on Boulevard Jourdan, where by some miracle Agro had a building which held concerts and parties. So I had carnal knowledge of girls from different countries, and had come to the conclusion that love can only develop on the basis of a certain level of difference, that like never falls in love with like, and in practice many differences may come into play: an extreme difference in age, as we know, can give rise to unimaginably violent passions; racial difference remains effective; and even mere national and linguistic difference should not be scorned. It is bad for those who love each other to speak the same language, it is bad for them to truly understand one another, to be able to communicate through words, because the vocation of the word is not to create love but to engender division and hatred, the word separates as it produces, while a formless, semi-linguistic babble – talking to your lover as you might talk to your dog – creates the basis for unconditional and enduring love. If we could also restrict ourselves to immediate and con-crete topics – where are the keys to the garage? What time is the electrician coming? – everything might still be fine, but beyond that begins the realm of disunity, division and divorce.

So there were different women, mainly Spanish and German, a few South Americans, and a Dutch one too, plump and appetising, who really looked like an advertise-ment for Gouda. Then there was Kate, the last of my youthful loves, the last and the most serious; after her you could say that my youth ended, never again did I know those mental states habitually associated with the word 'youth' – that charming insouciance (or, if you prefer, that disgusting irre-sponsibility), that sense of an undefined and open world – after her reality closed over me once and for all.

Kate was Danish, and she was probably the most intelligent person I have ever met; well, not that it has any real impor-tance, intelligence barely has any importance in a friendship let alone in a romantic relationship, it has less weight than a good heart; I mention it particularly because her incredible intellectual agility and her unusual capacity for assimilation were truly a curiosity, a phenomenon. She was twenty-seven when we met – so five years older than me – and she had a much greater experience of life, I felt like a little boy beside her. After completing her legal studies in record time, she had become a corporate lawyer in a London office. '*So, you must have met some kind of yuppies . . .*' I remember saying to her on the morning after our first night of love. 'Florent, I was a yuppie,' she replied gently; I remember that answer, and I remember her firm little breasts in the morning light – every time I think about it I have a very powerful desire to die, but let's move on. After two years, it had become clear to her: yuppiedom did not correspond in any respect to her aspirations, her tastes, her general way of imagining life. So she had decided to resume her studies, this time in medicine. I don't remember very clearly what she was doing in Paris, I think she was at a Paris hospital that enjoyed a great international reputation in some tropical illness, I can't remember which. To give you an idea of her abilities: on the evening that we met – she had happened on me, or rather I had offered to help her carry her luggage to her room on the third floor of the Danish building, where we had one beer, then two, etc. – she had arrived in Paris that morning and didn't speak a word of French; two weeks later she had almost perfectly mastered the language.

The last photograph I have of Kate must be somewhere on my computer, but I don't need to turn it on to remember it,

I only need to close my eyes. We had spent Christmas at her place – or rather at her parents' house, which wasn't in Copenhagen, the name of the town escapes me – either way I wanted to come back to France slowly, by train; the journey started strangely, the train sped along the surface of the Baltic Sea, with only two metres separating us from the grey surface of the water and sometimes a wave stronger than the others struck the window of our carriage; we were alone in our compartment between two vast abstractions, the sky and the sea, and I had never been so happy in my life – my life should probably have stopped there, a groundswell, the Baltic Sea, our bodies merged once and for all; but that didn't happen and the train reached its destination (was it Rostock or Stralsund?) where Kate had decided to come with me for a few days, her university course began again the following day, but she could look after herself.

The last photograph I took of Kate was in the gardens of the castle in Schwerin, a small German town, capital of the region of Mecklenburg-West Pomerania, and the gardens' avenues are covered with thick snow, and you can see the turrets of the castle in the distance. Kate is turning towards me and smiling, I must have called to her to turn round so that I could take a picture; she is looking at me and her face is full of love, but also of indulgence and sadness because she has probably already realised that I'm going to betray her, and that our affair will come to an end.

That same evening, we had dinner in a pub in Schwerin, and I remember the waiter: a thin man in his forties, nervous and unhappy, probably touched by our youth and by the love emanating from us and, to tell the truth, especially from her;

he even paused, once the plates had been set down, and turned towards me (or in fact towards both of us, but particularly towards me as he must have sensed I was the weak link), to tell me, in French (he must have been French, but how could a Frenchman have ended up serving in a pub in Schwerin? People's lives are a mystery), and say to me with unfamiliar, sacred gravity: 'Stay like this, both of you. Please stay like this.'

We could have saved the world, and we would have saved the world in the blink of an eye, *in einem Augenblick*, but we didn't, or I didn't, and love didn't triumph; I betrayed love, and often when I can't sleep, which is to say almost every night, I hear in my head the message on her answering machine, 'Hello, this is Kate, leave me a message,' and her voice was so fresh, like diving into a waterfall at the end of a dusty summer afternoon: you immediately felt washed of all dirt, all discomfort and all evil.

Our last seconds together took place in Frankfurt, in the central station, Frankfurter Hauptbahnhof, this time she really had to go back to Copenhagen even though she had played down her obligations at university – well, at any rate she couldn't come back to Paris with me – and I see myself standing by the door of the train, she was on the platform; we had fucked all night until eleven o'clock in the morning when it was really time to go to the station – she had fucked and sucked me with all her might and her might was great at the time and I too got hard quickly – well, in fact that's not the question, it isn't *essentially* that, it's mostly that Kate, standing on the platform, started crying, not really crying, some tears ran down her face; she was looking at me, she looked at me for over a minute until the train departed, her eyes didn't leave mine for a second and at a particular moment, in spite of herself, tears started flowing, and I didn't move, didn't jump on to the platform, I waited for the doors to close again.

For that I deserve death, and even more serious punishments; I can't hide the truth: I will end my life unhappy, cantankerous and alone, and I will have deserved it. How could a man who had known Kate turn away from her? It's incomprehensible. In the end I called her after leaving I don't know how many of her messages unanswered – all for an awful Brazilian girl who would forget me the day after she got back to São Paulo – I called Kate and I called her just *too late*; she was leaving for Uganda the next day where she had joined a humanitarian mission, and she was disappointed in Westerners, but most of all in me.

It always boils down to paying service charges. Claire had had her share of melodrama, she had had her troubled years, without really getting anywhere close to happiness – but who can? she thought. No one in the West will ever be happy again, she also thought, never again; happiness today is nothing but an old dream, the past conditions for its existence are simply no longer being fulfilled.

Dissatisfied and with her personal life in a state of despair, Claire had none the less known intense joys when it came to property. When her mother had yielded her little soul to God – or more probably to the void – the third millennium had just begun, and for the West, which had previously been known as Judaeo-Christian, it was one millennium too many in the way that boxers have one fight too many; at any rate the idea was quite widespread in the West previously known as Judaeo-Christian – well, I'm just calling it that to provide a context – but none of that concerned Claire in the slightest, she had other things on her mind, most of all her career as an actress; and then, gradually, paying the service charges had assumed a prominent place in her life, but let's not jump ahead.

I first met her on New Year's Eve in 1999, which I spent with a specialist in crisis management whom I had met at work – I was employed by Monsanto at the time, and Monsanto was more or less permanently in a state of crisis management. I don't know how the specialist knew Claire, in fact I think he didn't know her at all but was sleeping with one of her friends – well, maybe 'friend' isn't the right word, let's say another actress who had a part in the same play.

At the time, Claire was just starting her first great theatrical success – which would also be her last. Until then she had had to settle for small parts in low- or medium-budget French films and a few radio dramas on France Culture. But this time she had the main female role in a play by Georges Bataille – although it wasn't exactly or indeed at all a play by Georges Bataille, the director had *adapted* different texts by Georges Bataille, some fictional, others theoretical. From what he said in several interviews, his plan was to re-envision Bataille in the light of new virtual sexualities. He declared himself particularly concerned with masturbation, and he wasn't trying to conceal the difference, indeed the opposition, between the positions of Bataille and Genet. The whole affair was put on in a subsidised theatre in the east of Paris. In short, major media attention was on the cards this time.

I went to the premiere. I had been sleeping with Claire for just over two months, but she had already moved in with me,

I would have to admit that the room where she had lived was frankly pathetic; the shower on the landing, which she shared with about twenty other tenants, was so filthy that she had ended up joining the Club Med Gym just to wash. I wasn't all that impressed by the play – but I was impressed by Claire, who emanated a kind of icy eroticism throughout the whole performance; the costume and lighting designers had done a good job; it wasn't so much that you wanted to fuck her but you wanted to be fucked by her, you had a sense that she was a woman who could, from one moment to the next, be gripped by an irresistible impulse to fuck you, and besides, that was what happened in our daily life; her face was expressionless one minute and then suddenly she would put her hand on my cock, open the fly in a few seconds and kneel down to suck me off; or she would take off her panties and start frigging herself, and I remember that happening pretty much anywhere, including once in the waiting room at the tax office, where a black woman with two children had seemed a bit shocked; in short, she was in a state of permanent sexual arousal. The critics were unanimously complimentary, and the play was given a whole page in the cultural section of *Le Monde* and two in *Libération*. Claire received more than her share of this chorus of praise; *Libération* in particular compared her to those Hitchcock heroines: blonde and cold but really boiling inside, well, those Norwegian-omelette-style comparisons that I had already read dozens of times, so much so that I knew immediately what they were talking about even though I'd never seen a Hitchcock film – I was more of the *Mad Max* generation – but either way in the end it was quite accurate when it came to Claire.

In the second-last scene of the play, which the director clearly saw as key, Claire pulled up her skirt and, legs spread facing the audience, masturbated while another actress read a long piece by Georges Bataille primarily concerned, it seemed to me, with the anus. The reviewer in *Le Monde* particularly relished that scene, and praised the 'hieratic character' of her interpretation. 'Hieratic' struck me as a bit strong, but let's say that she was calm and didn't seem at all aroused – and hadn't been at all, as she confirmed to me on the evening of the premiere.

All in all her career had been launched, and that first joy was complemented by a second one when Air France flight AF232 for Rio de Janeiro crashed into the middle of the South Atlantic one Sunday in March. There were no survivors, and Claire's mother was among the passengers. A psychological support group was immediately set up for the families of the victims. 'That was where I discovered that I was a good actress . . .' Claire told me on the evening of her first encounter with the psychologists. 'I played the crushed and devastated daughter, I think I really managed to conceal my joy.'

In fact, in spite of the hatred they felt for one another, her mother, she sensed, was too egocentric to have gone to the trouble of writing a will, to devote a single minute to reflecting about what might happen after her death, and in any case it is difficult to disinherit your own children, so as an only daughter Claire had a legal and inalienable right to 50 per cent of the inheritance; in short, she didn't have much to fear, and a month after that miraculous plane crash she found herself in possession of her inheritance, which essentially consisted of a magnificent apartment on Passage du Ruisseau-de-Ménilmontant, in the twentieth arrondissement. We moved in two weeks later, giving us enough time to get rid of the old woman's things – though she wasn't as old as all that, she was forty-nine, when the plane crash that cost her her life happened while she was setting off on holiday in Brazil with a twenty-six-year-old, exactly my age then too.

The apartment was in an old thread factory that had closed its doors in the early 1970s, and had remained unoccupied for a few years before Claire's father bought it – an enterprising architect who was quick to spot a juicy deal, and who had turned it into a set of lofts. The entrance was a big porch secured by a metal gate with enormous bars, the digicode had just been replaced by a biometrical system of iris recognition; there was an intercom connected to a video camera for visitors.

Once you passed through the gate, you entered a vast paved courtyard surrounded by old industrial buildings – there were about twenty co-owners. The loft that Claire's mother owned, one of the largest, consisted of a large open space of 100 square metres – with a six-metre-high ceiling – leading to an open-plan kitchen with a central island, a big bathroom with an Italian-style shower and a jacuzzi, two bedrooms including one on a mezzanine and the other one complemented by a dressing room, and an office opening on to a small bit of garden. The whole thing was a little over 200 square metres.

Even if the term was not very widespread at the time, the other co-owners were exactly what would come to be known as *bobos* – bourgeois bohemians – and they could only have been delighted to have a theatre actress as a neighbour; what would the theatre be without *bobos*? At the time the newspaper *Libération* was not yet read only by casual theatre workers but also by a part (albeit a decreasing one) of their audience, and *Le Monde* was still more or less keeping up its sales and its prestige; in short, Claire was given an enthusiastic welcome in the building. My own situation, as I was well aware, was more delicate; Monsanto must have seemed to them like a company that was about as honourable as the CIA. A good lie always borrows certain elements from reality, so I immediately told them that I worked in genetic research for rare diseases – rare diseases are unimpeachable, you immediately think of autism or one of those poor little child victims of progeria who already looks like an old person at the age of twelve – and though I would have been incapable of working in that field, I knew enough about genetics to hold my own against any *bobo*, even an educated one.

To tell the truth, I felt increasingly uneasy in my job. There was no clear proof of the dangers of GMOs, and most radical ecologists were ignorant idiots anyway, but there was no proof of their harmlessness either, and my superiors within the company were quite simply pathological liars. The truth is that we knew nothing, or practically nothing, about the long-term consequences of genetic plant manipulations, but in my eyes the problem didn't even lie there; it was that seed-producers and manufacturers of fertilisers and pesticides, on an agricultural level, were destructive and lethal; it was that this intensive agriculture, based on massive exploitation and the maximisation of yields per hectare, this agricultural industry based entirely on export and on the separation of agriculture and animal-rearing, was in my eyes the precise opposite of what needed to be done if we were to achieve acceptable development; we had to prioritise quality, we had to consume and produce locally, protect the soil and the water tables, by going back to complex crop rotations and the use of animal fertilisers. I must have surprised the odd person, at one of the *neighbourly drinks* that followed our first few months of moving in, with the vehemence and the extremely well-documented nature of my interventions on these subjects; of course they thought the same as I did but without knowing anything about it, simply out of pure left-wing conformity to tell the truth, and the fact remained that I had had ideas, perhaps I had even had ideals – it was no coincidence that I had gone to Agro rather than attending a general school like the Polytechnique or the HEC – in short, I had ideals and I was busy betraying them.

But resigning was out of the question; my salary was indispensable to our survival because Claire's career, in spite of the critical success of that play adapted from Georges Bataille, remained stubbornly stalled. Her past trapped her in the cultural field, which was a misunderstanding because her dream was to work in commercial cinema; she only ever went to see films immediately accessible to everybody; she had loved *The Big Blue*, and even more than that *The Visitors*, while she found Bataille's play 'completely idiotic', and it was the same with a play by Leiris that she got involved with a little later, but the worst was probably a one-hour reading of Blanchot for France Culture – she would never have suspected, she told me, that such crap existed, it was baffling she said for them to offer such nonsense up to the public. For my part, I had no opinion about Blanchot, I just remembered an amusing phrase by Cioran in which he explained that Blanchot is the ideal author for learning to type, because one is not 'troubled by meaning'.

Unfortunately for Claire her physique went in the same direction as her CV: her beauty, blonde, elegant and cold, seemed to predispose her towards texts read out in a blank voice in a subsidised theatre; at the time, the entertainment industry was keen on Latina or hot mixed-race girls – in short Claire absolutely wasn't on trend, and over the next year she didn't manage to land a single part except in the off-off productions I've mentioned, despite regularly reading *Film français*, despite a determination, which she never denied, to turn up to pretty much every casting. Even in deodorant ads there was clearly no room for Norwegian omelettes. She might, paradoxically, have had more of a chance in porn: obviously not to undermine the hot black or Latina babies, this sector tried to maintain a great diversity of physiques and ethnicities among its actresses. She might have bitten the bullet in my absence, even though she knew very well that a career in porn would never lead to a career as an actress in mainstream cinema, but I think that had they been more or less identical salary levels, she would still have preferred porn to reading Blanchot on France Culture. In any case it wouldn't have lasted very long, professional porn was going through its last few months before amateur porn on the Internet destroyed it. YouPorn would destroy the porn industry even faster than YouTube had destroyed the music industry – porn has always been at the forefront of technological innovation, as numerous essayists have observed, even though none of them is alert to the paradoxical nature of this observation, where pornography remains the sector of human activity in which there is least room for innovation, and absolutely nothing new happens; everything imaginable, broadly speaking, existed in the pornography of Greek or Roman antiquity.

As for me, Monsanto was really starting to get on my nerves, and I was beginning to look at other job listings, more or less via all the means offered to an Agro graduate and particularly through the alumni association, but it wasn't until early November that I happened upon a truly interesting offer from the Regional Directorate of Agriculture and Forestry for Lower Normandy. It involved setting up a new structure dedicated to the export of French cheeses. I sent off my CV and quickly got an interview, and went to and from Caen in a day. The director of DRAF was another Agro old boy, a young old boy: I knew him by sight, he had been in his second year when I was in my first. I don't know where he did his final-year training course, but he had retained the habit (not widespread in French administrative circles at the time) of using Anglo-Saxon terms to no good effect. His initial observation was that French cheese was still exported almost exclusively within Europe, that its position remained insignificant in the United States and above all that, unlike wine (at this point he launched into a long and sustained tribute to inter-branch organisations with regard to the wines of Bordeaux), the cheese sector had not been able to anticipate the arrival of emerging markets: essentially Russia, but soon China, probably followed by India a little later.

That applied to all French cheeses; but we were in Normandy, he pertinently stressed, and the first aim of the task force he planned to put in place would be to promote the 'lords of the Normandy trilogy': Camembert, Pont-l'Évêque, Livarot. Only Camembert, until now, had really enjoyed international fame, for historical reasons that were exciting but which he didn't have time to expand upon; Livarot and even Pont-l'Évêque remained completely unknown in Russia and China; he didn't have limitless funds, but he had still managed to assemble the budget required to recruit five people, and what he was looking for first and foremost was the head of this *task force*, and was I interested in the *job*?

I was, and confirmed as much with an appropriate combination of professionalism and enthusiasm. One initial idea had come to me, and I thought it might be a good idea to share it with him: many Americans – well, maybe not many, let's just say Americans – came every year to visit the Landing Beaches where members of their families, and sometimes even their own parents, had made the supreme sacrifice. Of course, they all needed time for contemplation, we weren't thinking of organising cheese tastings by the gates of military cemeteries; but everybody ultimately has to eat, and were we sure that Normandy cheeses were taking sufficient advantage of this memorial tourism? He reacted enthusiastically: that was precisely the kind of thing, in fact, that needed to be set in motion, and imagination more generally needed to be part of the mix; the synergies that champagne-makers had developed with the French luxury goods industry were unlikely to be reproduced straight away: was it possible to imagine Gisele Bündchen tasting a piece of Livarot (whereas her sipping from a *coupe* of champagne was indeed possible)? In short, I would more or less have *carte blanche* and he would not attempt to rein in my creativity, and besides, my work at Monsanto couldn't have been easy either (in truth I hadn't had to make much of an effort as the arguments put forward by the seed manufacturer were brutally simple: without GMOs we wouldn't be able to feed a constantly growing human population, by and large it was Monsanto or famine). In short, when I left his office I already knew, particularly from the way he had talked about my work at Monsanto in the past tense, that my application had been successful.

My contract started on 1 January 2001. After a few weeks in the hotel I found a pretty house to rent, isolated in the middle of a rolling landscape of groves and pastures, two kilometres from the village of Clécy, which prided itself on holding the slightly overstated title of 'capital of *Suisse normande*'. It really was a ravishing house, with dovecotes; there was a large sitting room on the ground floor covered in terracotta tiles, three bedrooms with parquet floors, and a study. In the annexe, there was an old converted wine press that could be used as a spare room; central heating had been installed.

It was a ravishing house, and while being shown around I felt that its owner had loved it immensely and had maintained it with meticulous care; he was a little withered old man somewhere between the ages of seventy-five and eighty and he had lived well here, he told me straight away, but it had become impossible now as he needed frequent medical assistance, a nurse at home at least three times a week and every day in times of crisis, so an apartment in Caen was more sensible; he was lucky that his children looked after him well, his daughter had chosen to train as a nurse herself, he was lucky considering what you saw these days, and I agreed with him, he was lucky; only it hadn't been the same since his wife died, and it would never be the same again. He was clearly a believer and suicide was something that he would never have imagined, but sometimes he thought that it was taking God a long time to remember him, at his age it might have been useful; I had tears in my eyes almost throughout the whole visit.

It was a ravishing house, but I would be living alone there. Claire had clearly and frankly rejected the idea of moving to a village in Lower Normandy. For a moment I imagined suggesting to her that she could 'come back to Paris for castings' before realising the absurdity of the idea: she went to about ten castings a week and it made no sense, moving to the country would be career suicide; though is it really a serious matter for something to commit suicide when it is already dead? That was what I thought deep down, but obviously I couldn't say that to her, not as directly as that, and how could you say it indirectly? No solution came to mind.

So we agreed, apparently reasonably, that I was the one who would come to Paris for the weekend; we probably shared the illusion that this separation and weekly reunions would give our relationship energy and the chance to breathe, that each weekend would become a celebration of our love, etc.

*

There was no break between us, no clean and definitive break. It isn't difficult to take the Caen–Paris train, it's direct and it takes just over two hours; it just happened that I started taking it less and less often, at first using the excuse of having too much work, then not using any excuse at all, and after a few months it was all over. Deep down, I had never given up on the idea that Claire would come and join me in this house, that she would give up on her improbable career as an actress, and she would agree to be just my wife. Several times I had even sent her pictures of the house taken in fine weather, with the windows wide open on to the groves and pastures; I am a little ashamed to think about it now.

In retrospect the most remarkable thing is that, as with Yuzu twenty years later, all of my earthly possessions could be contained in a suitcase. I had decidedly little appetite for material things; which, in the eyes of certain Greek philosophers (Epicurians? Stoics? Cynics? More or less all of them?) is a very favourable mental disposition; the opposite stance, it seemed to me, had rarely been taken; so there was, on this precise point, a *consensus* among philosophers – which is rare enough to be stressed.

It was just after five o'clock when I hooked up with Claire again, and I had three hours to kill before dinner. Quite quickly, within just a few minutes, I began to wonder if this meeting was really a good idea. It clearly wasn't going to lead to anything positive; its only result would be to awaken feelings of disappointment and bitterness that we had, after about twenty years, more or less managed to escape. We were both well aware that life is bitter and disappointing, so was there any point in getting a taxi or paying a restaurant bill to receive additional confirmation? And did I really want to know what *had become* of Claire? Probably nothing very brilliant, nothing in line with her hopes at any rate, but I might have realised that just by looking at film posters in the street. My own professional aspirations were less clearly defined, and that meant failure was less visible, but I still had a quite distinct feeling that I was a failure by now. The meeting of two forty-year-old losers and former lovers could have been a magnificent scene in a French film, with the appropriate actors – let's suggest Benoît Poelvoorde and Isabelle Huppert for the sake of argument; in real life, was that what I wanted?

In certain critical moments of my life, I resorted to a form of *telemancy*, which to my knowledge I had invented. When they had a difficult decision to make, the knights of the Middle Ages, and later the Puritans of New England, opened their Bibles at random, rested their fingers also at random on the page and gave an interpretation of the verse they were pointing to, then took the direction indicated to them by God. Similarly, I sometimes turned on the television at random (without choosing the channel, just by pressing the On button) and tried to interpret the pictures transmitted to me.

At precisely 6.30 p.m., I pressed the On button of the television in my room in the Hôtel Mercure. The result seemed disconcerting at first, and difficult to decode (but that sometimes happened to the medieval knights too, and even to the Puritans of New England): I happened upon a tribute to Laurent Baffie, which in itself was surprising (was he dead? he was still young, but some television presenters are struck down at the peak of their glory and violently torn from the love of their fans, that's life). At any rate the tone of the programme was one of tribute, and all the participants stressed Laurent's 'deep humanity'; for some he was a 'terrific pal, a master prankster, a total loon', others who hadn't known him as closely stressed his 'impeccable professionalism'; that polyphony, well orchestrated by the way the programme had been edited, led to an actual rereading of Laurent Baffie's work, and finished symphonically with the almost choral repetition of an expression which all of the participants agreed on: Laurent was, however you looked at it, a 'beautiful person'. At twenty past seven I called a taxi.

I arrived at the Bistrot du Parisien on rue Pelleport at precisely 8.00 p.m. Claire had in fact booked a table, that was one positive thing, but from the first few seconds, as I crossed the restaurant that wasn't busy – but it was a Sunday evening after all – I could tell it would be the only one that evening.

After ten minutes, a waiter came to ask me if I wanted an aperitif while I was waiting. He seemed benevolent and devoted by nature, and I sensed that he anticipated a problematic encounter (how could a waiter in the twentieth arrondissement not be a bit of a shaman, or indeed a bit of a psychopomp?), and I also noticed that he would tend to side with me that evening (had he already spotted my mounting anxiety? It's true that I had already eaten a large number of breadsticks), so much so that I ordered a triple Jack Daniel's.

Claire arrived at about 8.30 p.m., walking carefully, supporting herself on two tables before reaching ours, and already visibly quite drunk; was the idea of seeing me again so distressing, the reminder of the promise of happiness that life had dashed for her so painful? I hoped so for a few seconds, no more than two or three, and then a more realistic thought occurred to me: Claire was probably in this same state at the same time every day, plastered more or less to the same degree.

I spread my arms enthusiastically to exclaim that she looked fantastic and she hadn't changed at all; I don't know where I got this aptitude for lying, not from my parents in any case, perhaps from my first years at *lycée*, but the truth is that she had swollen up horribly, there was fat poking out more or less everywhere and her face was frankly covered with blotches; her expression was a little doubtful at first, her initial thought was probably that I was making fun of her, but that didn't last more than ten seconds and she quickly lowered her head then raised it again straight away with a changed expression: the girl in her reappeared, and she gave me an almost flirtatious wink.

I let a considerable amount of time pass by consulting the pleasantly bistro-like menu. In the end I opted for a small pot of Burgundy snails (six) with garlic butter, followed by pan-fried scallops in olive oil with tagliatelle. I hoped to sidestep the traditional surf-and-turf dilemma (red wine vs white wine) by choosing courses that would allow us to have a bottle of each. Claire seemed to be thinking along similar lines, declaring her desire for bone marrow and toast with *sel de Guérande* followed by a monkfish *bourride à la Provençale* with *aioli*.

I was worried that I would have to express myself in personal terms and tell her my life story, but that didn't happen because as soon as she had given her order, Claire launched on a lengthy narrative designed to summarise the twenty or so years that had passed since our last meeting. She drank quickly and thirstily, and it swiftly became apparent that we would need two bottles of red (and also, a little later, two bottles of white). Nothing had worked out for her after I had gone, she had looked for roles in vain, and the situation had finally become a little strange when property prices in Paris doubled between 2002 and 2007, and the increase had happened even faster in her district: Rue de Ménilmontant was becoming more and more *hip* and a stubborn rumour had circulated that Vincent Cassel had just moved there, soon to be followed by Kad Merad and Béatrice Dalle; having coffee in the same establishment as Vincent Cassel was a considerable privilege and that rumour, which no one denied, prompted another leap in prices, so in around 2003–2004 she realised that her apartment was earning much more than she did every month and she absolutely had to keep it as selling it now would have meant property suicide, so she came up with desperate solutions such as getting involved in the recording of a series of CDs by Maurice Blanchot for France Culture; her trembling intensified, she looked at me with crazy eyes and literally gnawed on her marrow bone, and I gestured to the waiter to speed things up.

The monkfish *bourride* calmed her down a little, and coincided with a more tranquil moment in her story. Early in 2008 she replied to an offer from the Job Centre: the organisation suggested setting up theatre workshops for the unemployed, the idea being to restore their self-confidence, and while the salary wasn't huge, it came in regularly every month, and that was how she had been making her living for over ten years now; she was part of the furniture at the Job Centre and the idea, she could now say with hindsight, was far from ridiculous; at any rate it worked better than psychotherapy, and it was true that a long-term unemployed person inevitably turned into a little mute and huddled being, and that theatre, and especially the vaudeville repertoire for some obscure reason, gave these unhappy creatures the minimum social ease required for a job interview. In any case she could have got by on that modest but regular salary, had it not been for the problem of service charges, because some of the co-owners – drunk on the dazzling gentrification of the area around Ménilmontant – had got it into their heads to make truly crazy investments: replacing the digicode with a biometric system of iris recognition had been only the prelude to a sequence of insane projects, such as replacing the paved courtyard with a zen garden with little waterfalls and granite blocks imported directly from the Côtes d'Armor, all under the watchful gaze of an internationally famous Japanese master. Now she had made her decision, reinforced by the fact that after a second, shorter burst in around 2015–2017, the Paris property market had finally settled down for a lengthy period; she was going to sell up, and she had in fact just contacted her first estate agent.

She had less to say about her love life: there had been a few relationships, and even two attempts at cohabitation. She managed to muster enough emotion to talk about it, but she still couldn't hide it: the two men (both actors, more or less as successful as she was) who had imagined sharing her life had been less in love with her than they had been with her apartment. In the end I was perhaps the only man who had really loved her, she concluded with a kind of surprise. I stopped myself from disillusioning her.

In spite of the disenchanted and frankly sad nature of this story, I had enjoyed my scallops, and bent with interest over the dessert menu. The frozen Vacherin with raspberry coulis immediately grabbed my attention; Claire opted for profiteroles with hot chocolate, a classic; I ordered a third bottle of white wine. I was really starting to wonder whether, at some point, she was going to say to me, 'What about you?'; you know, the things you say in those situations, at least in films and even, it seemed to me, in real life.

Given the way the evening had gone, I would normally have had to refuse to 'have one more glass' at hers, and even now I wonder what led me to accept. Perhaps it was partly the curiosity of having another chance to see that apartment where I had, after all, spent a year of my life; but I must also have started wondering what I had seen in her. There must have been something to her besides sex; or perhaps not – it was frightening to think that maybe there had in fact been only sex.

Her own intentions, in any case, were unambiguous, and after offering me a glass of cognac she tackled me in that direct way that she had. Filled with goodwill, I took off my trousers and my pants to make it easier for her to take me in her mouth, but in truth I had already had a disturbing pre-monition, and when she had chewed away on my inert organ for three minutes with no result, I felt that the situation risked degenerating, and I confessed to her that I was taking antidepressants ('massive doses' of antidepressants, I added for good measure), which had the inconvenient effect of entirely suppressing my libido.

The effect of those few words was magical: I immediately felt that she was reassured, clearly everyone always prefers blaming the other person's antidepressants rather than their own rolls of fat, but a flicker of sincere compassion passed over her face, and for the first time that evening she seemed to be interested in me when she asked me if I was going through a period of depression, why and since when.

I then produced a simplified story of my last marital mis-adventures, telling her more or less the truth about everything (apart from Yuzu's canine adventures, which I thought contributed little to the overall tale); the only notable difference was that, in my story, it was Yuzu who had finally decided to go back to Japan, ultimately yielding to the demands of her family, and presented in that way the whole story became quite lovely: a classic conflict between love and family and/ or social duty (as a 1970s liberal would have said), a bit like a novel by Theodor Fontane, I explained to Claire, even though she probably didn't know who he was.

The Japanese girl gave the adventure a certain exotic pres-tige in the style of Loti – or maybe Segalen, I get them mixed up – either way, she was plainly very pleased with the story. Taking advantage of the fact that I could see her sinking into womanly meditations which a second glass of cognac had aggravated, I discreetly got myself dressed again, and just as I was fastening my fly I found myself thinking that it was the first of October; the last day of my lease on the apartment in the Totem Tower. Yuzu would probably have waited for the final day, and at that moment she was probably on the flight taking her back to Tokyo; perhaps the plane was already beginning its descent to Narita airport and her parents were standing behind the barriers in the arrivals hall, with her fiancé probably waiting near the car in the car park; everything was written and now everything was coming to be, and perhaps it was for that very reason that I had called Claire. Until a few minutes ago I had forgotten that it was the first of October, but something in me, probably my unconscious, had not forgotten – we were living in the grip of uncertain divinities, 'the path that those girls made us take was entirely fallacious, I should add that it was raining', as Nerval probably wrote somewhere; I hadn't often thought about Nerval lately, but he had hanged himself at the age of forty-six, and Baudelaire too had died at that age; it isn't an easy one.

Claire's chin was now resting on her chest and snores rose from her throat; she had clearly blacked out and in principle I should have left right then, but I was comfortable on the enormous sofa in her open-plan space, and I was filled with an extreme weariness at the thought of crossing Paris again, so I lay down and turned on my side to avoid seeing her and a minute later I fell asleep.

There was only instant coffee in this prison, which was already a scandal in itself – if there wasn't a Nespresso machine in an apartment like this, then where could there be one – well, I made myself an instant coffee, the day shone faintly through the shutters and in spite of all my precautions I bumped into a few items of furniture; Claire immediately appeared in the kitchen doorway, her short and semi-transparent nightgown barely concealing her charms. Luckily she seemed to be thinking about something else and accepted the glass of instant coffee that I held out to her – fucking hell, she didn't even have any cups – and a single sip was enough for her to start talking immediately; it was funny that I lived in the Totem Tower, she said (I hadn't mentioned the fact that I had recently moved into the Hôtel Mercure), because her father had begun the project, as the assistant to one of the two architects; she hadn't known her father very well and he had died when she was six, but she remembered that her mother had kept a press cutting in which he justified himself in response to the controversies that the construction had generated: the Totem Tower had been listed several times among the ugliest buildings in Paris, though never rising to the heights of the Montparnasse Tower, which regularly featured in surveys as the ugliest building in France and, in a recent survey in *Touristworld*, as one of the ugliest in the world, just behind Boston City Hall.

She moved over to the open space, and to my slight alarm returned two minutes later with a photo album that threatened to form the basis of a lengthy life story. During the far-off 1960s, her father had clearly been a flashy kind of man-about-town and photographs of him in a Renoma suit, leaving the Bus Palladium nightclub, left no doubt about that; in short, he had led the life of an affluent young man in the sixties; he looked a bit like Jacques Dutron and had gone on to become an enterprising (and probably a bit corporate-minded) architect throughout the Pompidou and Giscard years, before dying at the wheel of his Ferrari 308 GTB on his way back from a weekend in Deauville spent with his Swedish mistress, on the day of François Mitterrand's election as president of the Republic. His already quite decent career could have taken a new leap – he had many friends in the Socialist Party, François Mitterrand was a president with plenty of building projects and there was little to keep him from reaching the highest level of his profession, but a thirty-five-tonne truck swinging into the middle of the lane had decided otherwise.

Claire's mother missed her husband, who had been flighty but generous, who had also given her quite a lot of freedom, but most importantly she couldn't bear the idea of being alone with her daughter; her husband might have been a swordsmith, but he was also an affectionate father who played quite a large part in looking after their child, and she didn't have a single maternal fibre, not a single one, and for mothers it's either you dedicate yourself to them entirely and forget your own happiness in devoting yourself to theirs, or else the opposite happens, and they become only an embarrassing and soon hostile presence in your life.

At the age of seven, Claire was placed in an all-girls' boarding-school in Ribeauvillé, run by the Congregation of the Sisters of Divine Providence – I already knew that part of the story and there weren't even any croissants, not even a *pain au chocolat*, not a thing; Claire poured herself a glass of vodka, there you had it, she started straight off at seven in the morning. 'You ran away at the age of eleven . . .' I cut in to shorten her narrative. I remembered her escape, it was a powerful moment in her heroic gesture, her conquest of her independence; she had hitch-hiked her way back to Paris, it was risky and anything could have happened to her, and more so in that she was seriously starting to, as she put it, 'develop an interest in cock', but nothing at all did happen to her, and she took this as a sign. I sensed in that moment the coming of the dark turn in her relations with her mother, and had the courage to demand that we go out to a café for a normal breakfast: a double espresso with some bread and jam, and perhaps even a ham omelette. I was hungry, I said plaintively, I was really hungry.

She put a coat over her nightgown; they were bound to have anything we needed on Rue de Ménilmontant and perhaps we would get to see Vincent Cassel sitting at a table over a hazelnut latte, but in any case we had got out of the apartment and that was a start – it was already an autumn morning outside, windy and crisp, and just in case this all dragged on I had taken the precaution of inventing a doctor's appointment mid-morning.

To my great surprise, as soon as we sat down Claire returned to the story of 'my Japanese girl'; she wanted to know about her and she had been struck by the coincidence of the Totem Tower. 'Coincidences are winks by God' – was that Vauvenargues or Chamfort? I had forgotten, or maybe it was La Rochefoucauld or nobody at all – either way I could expatiate at length on the subject of Japan, I had already tried. I started by saying subtly: 'Japan is a more traditional society than we sometimes think,' and then I could go on for two hours without risk of being contradicted, and in any case nobody knew anything about Japan or the Japanese. After two minutes, I realised that talking was more tiring than listening – human relationships in general caused me problems, and more particularly, I had to agree, relationships with Claire – so I passed the baton of the conversation to her. The decor of this café was pleasant but the service was a bit slow, and we dived back into Claire at age eleven while customers gradually invaded the café, all of whom looked like casual theatre workers.

Straight away Claire found herself struggling with her mother, a struggle that lasted almost seven years, a fierce struggle based above all on perpetual sexual competition. I already knew some of the highlights, like when Claire, having discovered some condoms when rummaging in her mother's handbag, had called her an 'old slag'. I was less aware (though I soon discovered it) that Claire, putting her money where her mouth was in a way, had set about seducing most of her mother's lovers, using the simple but effective technique that I had seen her use with me. I was even less aware that Claire's mother, counter-attacking with the more sophisticated means that a mature woman gradually learns from reading women's magazines, had for her part set about getting off with Claire's boyfriends.

If this were a YouPorn film it would have had a sequence along the lines of '*Mom teaches daughter*', but the reality was less funny, as it so often is. The croissants arrived quite quickly but the ham omelette took longer and arrived just as Claire was reaching the age of fourteen, and I finished it before she celebrated her sixteenth birthday; I was wide awake now, and feeling quite well and suddenly I felt as if it would be possible to bring our meeting to a quick end by summing up in an intense and happy voice: 'And then on your eighteenth birthday you left and found a job in a bar near Bastille and a room of your own, and then we met, my love – I forgot to tell you but I have an appointment with my cardiologist at ten o'clock so big kisses and let's speak very soon'; I had already put a twenty-euro note on the table, I hadn't given her a chance. She looked at me strangely, a little beaten, when I left the café with a big wave of my hand; I fought down one final compassionate impulse for a couple of seconds, then swiftly headed down Rue de Ménilmontant. Purely automatically, I turned off down Rue des Pyrénées, maintained a steady trot and in less than five minutes I was at Gambetta Métro station. Claire was clearly fucked, her alcohol consumption wasn't going to stop rising, and very soon it wouldn't be enough any more and she would add drugs, in the end her heart would give out and she would be found, having choked on her own vomit, in the middle of her little two-bedroom flat with a courtyard on Boulevard Vincent-Lindon. Not only was I unable to save Claire, but nobody could save Claire now, apart from certain members of Christian sects perhaps (the ones who give, or pretend to give, a warm welcome, as brothers in Christ, to the elderly, the disabled and the poor) whom Claire wouldn't have been able to bear, she would fire their brotherly compassion right back at them with her eyes; what she needed was ordinary conjugal affection and more immediately a cock in her cunt, but that was precisely what was no longer possible for her; ordinary conjugal affection could only come now together with sexual satisfaction, it would imperatively have to fall under the heading of 'sex' which was closed off to her now and for ever.

It was certainly sad; however for a few years, before sinking once and for all into alcoholism, Claire must have been a relatively flamboyant forty-something, perhaps even comparable to a cougar or a MILF, a childless MILF, admittedly – either way I was sure that her pussy had remained wettable for a long time, so come on, she hadn't had that bad a life. By contrast I remembered three years ago, when immediately before falling into the clutches of Yuzu, I had the unfortunate idea of meeting up with Marie-Hélène again. I was going through one of my many periods of sexual apathy and I probably planned just to make contact, not to get laid, or circumstances would have had to be truly propitious, and that seemed very unlikely with poor Marie-Hélène. I was expecting the worst when I rang her doorbell, but the reality was somehow even worse than I had imagined; she had fallen victim to some kind of psychiatric crisis – bipolar or schizophrenia, I can't remember which – and she had been horribly diminished by it. She was living in a high-security residence on Avenue René-Cory, her hands trembled constantly and she was literally afraid of everything: of genetically modified soya, of the *Front national* coming to power, of small-particle pollution . . . She fed herself on green tea and flax seeds, during my half-hour visit she spoke only about her disability benefits. I left again with a desire for large draught beers and *rillette* sandwiches, aware that she was going to remain like that for a very long time, at least until the age of ninety, and would probably outlive me by a long way, getting more and more shaky, more and more dried up and fearful, ceaselessly creating problems with the neighbours when in fact she was already dead; I had been led to *stick my nose into a dead woman's cunt*, to repeat the telling expression that I had read I can't remember where, probably in a novel by Thomas Disch, a science-fiction author and poet who had had his moment of glory and was now unfairly forgotten, who hid killed himself one 4th of July, partly it's true because his partner had just died of AIDS, but also because his income as an author simply no longer gave him enough to live on and he wanted to bear witness, with the symbolic choice of that date, to the fate that America kept in store for its authors.

In comparison Claire was almost well – after all, she could still join Alcoholics Anonymous, apparently they sometimes have surprising results – and also, I realised when I got back to the Hôtel Mercure, Claire was bound to die alone, and unhappy, but at least she wouldn't die poor. After selling her loft, and taking into account the market price, she would end up with three times as much money as me. A single property purchase enabled her father to earn so much more than mine had in forty years of struggle, writing authenticated deeds and recording mortgages, where the money had never been an adequate recompense for the work, strictly speaking there was no connection between the two, no human society had ever been based on the fair remuneration of work, and even a future communist society was not supposed to be based on it; for Marx, the principle of wealth distribution was reduced to this entirely hollow formula: 'To each according to his needs', an endless source of carping and quibbling if by some misfortune someone tried to put it into practice, but luckily that had never happened, no more in the communist countries than anywhere else; money went to money and kept company with power, that was the final word in social organisation.

By the time I separated from Claire, my fate had been notably sweetened by my acquaintance with Normande cows; they were a consolation to me, a revelation almost. I was, however, no stranger to cows; as a child I had spent a summer month every year in Méribel, where my father had a time-share in a chalet. While my parents spent their days hiking like a pair of lovers along the mountain paths, I watched television, especially the Tour de France, to which I would develop a lasting addiction. From time to time, though, I used to go out; adult interests were a mystery to me, and there must certainly have been something interesting, I said to myself, in climbing those high mountains, because so many adults did so, starting with my own parents.

I failed to develop any real aesthetic emotion at the sight of the Alpine landscapes; but I did feel affection for the cows, often coming across a herd of them walking from one summer pasture to another. They were Tarentaises, lively little cows with tawny coats, excellent walkers with an impulsive nature; they often gambolled along the mountain paths, and the bells around their necks produced a pretty sound even before one had seen them.

On the other hand nobody imagined a Normande cow beginning to *gambol*, there was something so irreverent about the very idea that in my opinion a simple acceleration of their gait could only have occurred under extreme threat to life. Normande cows *were* ample and majestic, and broadly speaking that seemed to be enough for them; it was only by discovering Normande cows that I understood why the Hindus held the animal to be sacred. During the solitary weekends that I spent in Clécy, ten minutes contemplating a herd of cows grazing in the surrounding fields was enough to make me forget Rue de Ménilmontant, the castings, Vincent Cassel, Claire's desperate efforts to be accepted by a circle that wanted nothing of her, and finally to forget Claire herself.

I wasn't yet thirty, but I was gradually entering a wintry zone unlit by any memory of my loved one or any hope of repeating the miracle, and weakness of the senses was reinforced by a growing professional disinvestment; the task force was slowly falling apart; there were still a few sparks, a few principled declarations notably during work drinks (there was at least one of these a week at DRAF), but we had to agree that the Normans didn't know how to sell their products; calvados for instance had all the qualities of a great spirit – a good calvados was comparable to a bas-Armagnac or even a cognac – but it was a hundred times less visible in airport duty-free shops, pretty much everywhere in the world; and its place was generally symbolic even in French supermarkets. As for cider, let's not even mention it; cider was virtually absent from large-scale distribution and was barely even served in bars. Positions were still vehemently adopted during those work drinks, promises were made to act without delay, and then everything subsided gently over the subsequent identical, and not entirely disagreeable, weeks, and the idea that there isn't much that you can do about anything anyway gradually imposed itself; even the director, so aggressive and dashing when I had started, gradually lost his edge, he had just got married and talked mostly about planning for the farmhouse that he had just bought as a home for his future family. There had been a bit more excitement for several months during the brief tenancy of an exuberant Lebanese intern, who notably took down a photograph of George W. Bush paying homage to a hearty plate of cheeses, a photograph that prompted a mini-scandal in some American media – apparently that idiot Bush had been unaware that the importation of unpasteurised cheeses had just been forbidden in his country – so there was a slight media impact, but sales still didn't take off, and repeated dispatches of Livarot and Pont-l'Évêque to Vladimir Putin proved no more effective.

I wasn't very useful but I wasn't harmful either, and there had in fact been some progress with Monsanto, and in the morning when I went to work, passing through the banks of fog that floated over the countryside at the wheel of my G 350, I was still able to tell myself that my life wasn't a definitive failure. Each time I passed through the village of Thury-Harcourt I wondered if there was a connection there with Aymeric, and in the end I looked for the answer on the Internet – which was much more laborious in those days and the network less fully developed – but in the end I found the answer on the still embryonic website of *Patrimoine Normand*, 'the magazine of Norman history and the Norman way of life'. Yes, there was a connection, and a direct one at that. The village had originally been called Thury, then Harcourt, with reference to the family; it had become Thury again during the Revolution before assuming its present name of Thury-Harcourt in an attempted reconciliation between *les deux France*. In the days of Louis XIII an enormous château had gone up, sometimes referred to as a 'Norman Versailles', which had been first the residence of the Dukes of Harcourt, then of the governors of the province. Left almost entirely intact by the Revolution, it had been burned down in August 1944 during the retreat of the 'das Reich' division which the 59th Staffordshire Regiment caught in a pincer movement.

During my three years of study at Agro, Aymeric

d'Harcourt-Olonde had been my only true friend, and I had spent most of my evenings in his room – first at Grignon, then in the Agro building in the Cité Internationale – downing cans of strong lager and smoking weed (well, he did most of the smoking, I preferred beer, but he must have been on about thirty joints a day, he must have been high pretty much all the time during his first two years as a student), and most importantly listening to records. With his long blond curly hair and his Canadian lumberjack shirt, Aymeric had quite a typical grunge look, but he took it much further than Nirvana and Pearl Jam, he had really gone back to the sources, and in his room all the shelves were occupied by hundreds of vinyl records from the sixties and seventies: Deep Purple, Led Zeppelin, Pink Floyd, the Who, he even had the Doors, Procol Harum, Jimi Hendrix, Van der Graaf Generator . . . YouTube didn't exist yet and hardly anybody at the time remembered those groups, but anyway for me it had been a total discovery, an absolute wonder.

We often spent the evening together, sometimes with one or two other guys from the course – not very remarkable, I can hardly remember their faces and I've completely forgotten their names – but on the other hand there were never any girls, which is a strange thing when I think about it: I don't remember knowing Aymeric ever having a sexual relationship. He wasn't a virgin, or at least I don't think so, and he didn't give the impression of being afraid of girls, but rather he seemed to be thinking about something else, perhaps his career; he had a seriousness that probably escaped me at the time because I didn't give a damn about my career – I don't think I thought about it for more than thirty seconds, it seemed so unlikely that anyone could seriously be interested in anything but girls – and the worst thing is that now, at forty-six, I realise that I was right at the time: girls are whores if you want to see them that way, but a career is a more considerable whore and one that doesn't give you any pleasure.

At the end of my second year I expected Aymeric to choose, like me, a fake specialisation like rural sociology or ecology, but instead he signed up for animal husbandry, a field for hard workers. At the end of the holidays in September, he turned up with short hair and a completely new wardrobe, and when he went off for his end-of-year internship at Danone he was even wearing a suit and tie. We saw each other a bit less that year, which I remember as a year of holidays: I had chosen to specialise in ecology and we spent our time travelling all over France to study a particular plant formation in its habitat. By the end of the year I had learned how to recognise the different plant formations that existed in France and I could predict their occurrence using a geological map and local meteorological data, and that was more or less it, and it would later help me shut up Green activists when the conversation turned to the real consequences of climate change. Aymeric, on the other hand, spent most of his internship in the marketing department of Danone, and one might reasonably have expected him to devote his career to the creation of new drinking yoghurts or smoothies. He surprised me once again on the evening of our graduation ceremony, when he told me that he planned to take over a farming business in Manche. Agronomic engineers were present in almost every area of agribusiness, sometimes in technical posts and most often directorial, but hardly ever became farmers themselves; consulting the directory of Agro alumni in search of his address, I noticed that Aymeric was the only one from our year who had made that choice.

He lived in Canville-la-Rocque, and told me on the phone that I would have trouble finding it, and that I would have to ask the locals for the Château d'Olonde. Yes, that belonged to his family too, but it was from before the days of Thury-Harcourt: the château had been destroyed for a first time in 1204, then rebuilt in the middle of the thirteenth century. Apart from that he had got married the previous year, and had a herd of three hundred dairy cows on his farm; he hadn't invested badly and, well, he would talk to me about it. No, he hadn't seen anyone from the Agro since moving there.

I arrived outside the Château d'Olonde at dusk. It was less of a castle than an incoherent collection of buildings in various states of conservation, but it was hard to reconstruct the initial plan; in the centre, a main residential building, massive and rectangular, seemed to be standing more or less, and although grass and moss had begun to nibble at the stones, they were thick blocks of granite, probably Flamanville granite, and it would take another few centuries to erode them seriously. Further towards the rear, a tall, thin cylindrical keep seemed to be almost fully intact; but closer to the entrance of the main keep – which must have been square originally and have constituted the military core of the fortress, but had now lost its windows and roof – erosion had softened and rounded the remaining scraps of walls; they were gently approaching their geological fate. About a hundred metres away, the metal gleam of a big shed and a silo clashed with the landscape; I think this was the first modern building that I had seen for about fifty kilometres.

Aymeric had grown his hair again, and had started wearing big checked shirts like before, but now they had returned to their original purpose as work clothes. 'This place was the setting for the last novel by Barbey d'Aurevilly, *A Nameless Story*,' he informed me. 'In 1882, Barey called it an "old and almost dilapidated" castle; as you can see, it hasn't got much better since then.'

'Didn't you get any help from Historical Monuments?'

'Vaguely . . . We signed up for listed status anyway, but you hardly ever get any help. Cécile, my wife, would like to do some large-scale renovation work and turn it into a hotel, a *hôtel de charme*, that kind of thing. Basically there are about fourteen unoccupied buildings, and we heat five rooms in all. What can I get you to drink?'

I accepted a glass of Chablis. I didn't know if there was any point to the planned *hôtel de charme*, but in any case the dining room was warm and pleasant, with a big fireplace, deep bottle-green leather armchairs, and that arrangement couldn't have had anything to do with Aymeric: he was entirely indifferent to decoration, his bedroom in the Agro was one of the most anonymous I've ever seen and had looked like a soldier's bivouac – apart from the records.

Here they occupied a whole chunk of wall, it was impressive. 'I counted them last winter, I've got just over five thousand . . .' Aymeric said. He still had the same player, a Technics MK2, but I'd never seen the speakers – two enormous parallelepipeds of raw walnut, over a metre tall. 'They're Klipschorns,' Aymeric said, 'the first speakers manufactured by Klipsch, and perhaps the best; my grandfather bought them in 1949, he was crazy about opera. When he died, my father gave them to me – he's never been interested in music.'

I had a sense that this equipment wasn't used very often, and a light layer of dust had settled on the lid of the MK2. 'Yes, it's true . . .' Aymeric confirmed my suspicion; he must have caught something in my expression, 'I'm never really in the right state of mind to listen to music. It's hard, you know, I've never managed to achieve financial equilibrium, and then in the evening I ruminate and do the accounts again, but hey, since you're here let's put something on – top yourself up while we're waiting.'

After rummaging through his shelves for a minute or two he took out *Ummagumma*. 'The one with the cow seems appropriate . . .' he observed before setting the needle down at the beginning of 'Grantchester Meadows'. It was extraordinary; I'd never heard, or even suspected, the existence of such a sound; every birdsong, every splash of the river was perfectly defined, the bass notes were tense and powerful, the high notes incredibly pure.

'Cécile will be back shortly,' he went on, 'she had a meeting at the bank for her hotel project.'

'I get the sense you don't really believe in it.'

'I don't know, do you get the sense of lots of tourists in the region?'

'Hardly any.'

'Well, there you are . . . However, I do agree with her on one point: we have to do something. We can't just go on losing money like that every year. If we can manage financially it's only thanks to leasing and selling land.'

'Do you have lots of land?'

'Thousands of hectares; we used to own almost the whole region between Carentan and Carteret. Well, I say "we", it still belongs to my father, but since I set up the farm he decided to leave me the product of the land leases, and even with that I'm often forced to put up a plot for sale. The worst thing is that I'm not even selling to local farmers, but to foreign investors.'

'From which countries?'

'Mostly Belgians and Dutch, and more and more often Chinese. Last year I sold fifty hectares to a Chinese conglomerate. They were willing to buy ten times more and pay twice the market rate. The local farmers can't match that: they already have trouble paying back their loans and paying their leases, you always have the ones who give up and put the key under the door, and when they're in difficulty I have trouble putting too much pressure on them, I understand them all too well, I'm now in the same situation as they are. It was easier for my father, he lived in Paris for a long time before coming back to Bayeux, and after all he was the lord of the manor . . . So you're right, I'm not sure about this hotel, but there may be a way . . .'

On the journey there I'd been trying to think about what I was going to tell Aymeric about my precise role at DRAF. I couldn't see myself admitting to him that I was directly implicated in this project promoting the export of Normandy cheeses. I stressed the more administrative tasks, connected with the transformation of the French AOCs into European AOPs; and that wasn't untrue, those questions of exasperating legal formalism occupied a growing part of my working time, you constantly had to be 'on top of things' – on top of what I never really knew – and there can't be an area of human activity as utterly boring as the law. But in the end I had enjoyed a certain amount of success in my new tasks; for example it was one of my recommendations, formulated in a briefing note, which would lead – a few years later and with the adoption of the decree that defined AOP Livarot – to the decision that this cheese must be made of milk from Normande cows. At that moment I was involved in a procedural conflict that I was about to win with the Lactalis group and the cooperative of Isigny Sainte-Mère, who wanted to free themselves from the obligation to use unpasteurised milk in the manufacturing of Camembert.

I was in the middle of my explanations when Cécile arrived. She was a pretty brunette, thin and elegant, but her face was marked by tension that was almost like suffering; she had plainly had a hard day. She was nice to me, and did her best to prepare a meal, but I had the sense that she had taken on a huge amount, that her first reaction on her return, if I hadn't been there, would have been to go to bed with some painkillers. She was happy, she told me, that Aymeric had received a visit; they were working too hard and they didn't see anyone any more, they buried themselves away even though they weren't yet thirty. To tell the truth I was in the same situation, apart from the fact that my workload wasn't excessive, and basically everyone was in the same situation; our student years are the only happy ones, when the future seems open, when everything seems possible, and after that adulthood and a career are only a slow and progressive process of ending up in a rut. That's probably also why the friendships of our youth, the ones we make during our time as students and which are our only true friendships, never survive into adulthood: we avoid seeing them so as not to be confronted by witnesses to our crushed hopes, the evidence of our defeat.

That visit to Aymeric was, in short, a mistake, but not too severe a mistake; for two days we would put on a good performance, and after dinner he played the record of Jimi Hendrix live at the Isle of Wight – it certainly wasn't his best concert, but it was the last one, less than two weeks before he died. I felt that Cécile was slightly appalled by this return to Aymeric's past, she herself certainly hadn't been a grunge girl – I saw her more as a *Versaillaise*, well, moderately *Versaillaise*, a bit traditional without being fundamentalist – Aymeric had married within his circle, that's what happens most often in the end, and it's what gives the best results in principle, well, that's what I'd heard anyway, but my problem is that I had no circle, no precise circle.

The next morning I got up at about nine o'clock and found him sitting at the table in front of a hearty breakfast of fried eggs, grilled black sausage and bacon, accompanied by coffee and then calvados. His day had started a long time ago, he explained: he got up at five every morning for milking, he hadn't bought a milking machine – it was a disproportionate investment for him, most of his colleagues who had got into that way of doing things had gone under shortly afterwards, and the cows liked being milked by human hands, or that was what he thought; there was a sentimental side to it too. He suggested that we go and see the herd.

The brand-new metal shed that I had seen when I turned up the previous day was basically a byre, with the stalls arranged in four rows almost all occupied, by Normande cows only, I noticed immediately. 'Yes, it's a choice,' Aymeric confirmed to me, 'their yield isn't quite as good as that of the Prim'Holstein, but I find their milk really superior. So obviously I was interested by what you were saying yesterday about the Livarot AOP – even though at the moment I tend to sell more to the producers of Pont-l'Évêque.'

At the end of the building, plywood partitions isolated a little office with a computer, printer and metal filing cabinets. 'Do you use the computer to order their food?' I asked him.

'Possibly, the computer regulates the maize silage food supply; I can also programme the addition of vitamin supplements because the chambers are connected. Well, yeah, it's a bit gadgety – in fact I use it mostly to do the accounts.' The word 'accounts' had been enough to darken his mood. We went out under the peaceful, bright blue sky. 'Before DRAF I worked at Monsanto,' I admitted, 'but I don't suppose you use GM maize.'

'No, I respect organic specifications, and I try to limit my use of maize; in principle a cow eats grass and this isn't industrial animal rearing here – you've seen the cows have plenty of room and they go out a little every day, even in winter. But the more I try to do things correctly, the harder it gets to make ends meet.'

*

What could I possibly say to that? I could easily have spent three hours in a debate devoted to these questions on some news channel or other. But it was Aymeric, and in his situation, I couldn't tell him much; he knew all the elements as well as I did. The sky was so clear that morning that you could see the ocean in the distance. 'Danone suggested that I stay with them at the end of my internship . . .' he said thoughtfully.

I devoted the rest of my day to seeing the château. There was a chapel where the lords of Harcourt must have worshipped, but the most impressive thing was a gigantic dining room: its walls were entirely covered with portraits of ancestors and with a seven-metre-wide fireplace that you could easily imagine being used to roast boar or deer during interminable medieval feasts; the idea of a *hôtel de charme* started to make a bit more sense. I hadn't dared say so to Aymeric but it seemed unlikely to me that the situation for stockbreeders was getting any better, and I had heard rumours that they were starting to discuss the idea of getting rid of milk quotas in Brussels – that decision that would plunge millions of French stockbreeders into penury, and reduce them to bankruptcy, was only definitively adopted in 2015 under the presidency of François Hollande, but the arrival of ten new countries into the European space in 2002, following the Athens Treaty, put France in a clearly minority position, making it more or less inevitable. More generally, it was becoming increasingly difficult for me to speak to Aymeric; even though all my sympathy went out to the farmers, and I found myself prepared to argue their cause under any circumstance, I was forced to accept that I was now on the side of the French government, and so we were no longer entirely on the same side.

I left after breakfast the next day, under a brilliant Sunday sun, which contrasted with my growing sadness. It seems surprising to me today to think back to my sadness, while I drove at low speed along the deserted by-roads of Manche. We like there to be premonitions or signs, but as a rule there aren't any, and nothing on that sunny and dead afternoon indicated to me that I would meet Camille the following morning, and that that Monday morning would be the start of the loveliest years of my life.

Before we come to my first meeting with Camille, let's go back almost twenty years to a very different November, a much sadder November in that the *vital issues* (as we might speak of *vital functions*) had already been broadly determined. Towards the end of the month, the first Christmas decorations started filling the Italie II shopping centre and I began to wonder if I would stay at the Hôtel Mercure during the holiday period. I had no real reason to leave other than shame, and that in itself is already a serious reason – confessing to absolute loneliness isn't that easy, even today – and I started thinking of different destinations. The most obvious one was a monastery; during those long days commemorating the birth of the Saviour, many people want to reflect – at least that was what I read in a special edition of *Pilgrim* magazine – and in that case solitude isn't just normal, it's even recommended; yes, it was the best solution, I would find out immediately about a few potential monasteries, but it wasn't just time, it was more than time (as an initial Internet search told me – and as that issue of

Pilgrim magazine had already led me to suspect) and all the monasteries I contacted were fully booked.

One other even more immediate problem was renewing my Captorix prescription; the usefulness of that drug was undeniable – thanks to it my social life was shock free, I was able to perform minimal but adequate ablutions each morning, and I greeted the waiters of the O'Jules with warmth and familiarity – but I had no desire to see a psychiatrist again, obviously not the psychiatrist on Rue des Cinq-Diamants, that caricature, but not any other psychiatrist either, psychiatrists in general *made me want to spew*; and it was then that I remembered Dr Azote.

This GP with the strange name had a surgery on Rue d'Athènes, a stone's throw from Gare Saint-Lazare, and I had seen him once for a kind of bronchitis I'd contracted after one of my weekly trips between Caen and Paris. I remembered him as a man in his forties, with a significant bald patch, his remaining hair long, grey and quite dirty; in fact he looked more like a heavy-metal bass player than a doctor. I also remembered that in the middle of the consultation he had lit a Camel – 'excuse me, it's a bad habit and I'm the first to advise against it . . . ' – and that he had, without making any fuss, prescribed me a codeine syrup, which had in itself aroused some suspicion among my colleagues.

He was twenty years older now, but his baldness hadn't really advanced (or of course retreated), and his remaining hair was still just as long, grey and dirty as before. 'Yes, Captorix is valuable, I've had good results . . .' he observed soberly. 'Do you want six months' worth?'

'What are you doing over the holidays?' he asked me a bit

later. 'You have to watch out for the holiday period, it's often fatal for depressives. I've had lots of patients I thought were stable and bam! on the 31st they lose it, always on the evening of the 31st, once they're past midnight it's fine. You have to imagine it: Christmas has already dealt them a blow, they've had a whole week to ruminate on their shitty lives, maybe they had plans to get away on New Year's Eve and those have collapsed, and then the 31st arrives and they can't bear it, so they go over to their window and throw themselves out or shoot themselves, it depends. I go on about it, that's how it is, but my job is basically to stop people from killing themselves; well, for a while, for as long as possible.' I opened up to him about my monastery idea. 'Yeah, that's not too fucked as ideas go,' he said approvingly. 'I have other clients who do that, but in my view you've left it a bit late. Otherwise there are also prostitutes in Thailand – people always forget how important Christmas is in Asia – and you can get yourself over there pretty easily for the 31st; you should be able to buy yourself a ticket, it's less booked up than the monasteries. I've only ever had a good time there and sometimes it's almost therapeutic; I've had guys coming back completely rebooted, with their belief in their seductive masculine charms right back up there; OK, these guys were a bit lame, the kind of idiot it's easy to con and unfortunately you don't give me that feeling. The other problem you've got, I guess, is that with Captorix you won't be getting hard-ons. Even with two pretty little sixteen-year-old hookers I can't guarantee it – that's the boring thing about the product, but at the same time you can't just come off it all at once, I'd honestly advise against that, it wouldn't do you any good anyway, just give you two weeks of latency – but ultimately if it has to happen you'll know that it's the drug. Worst case you could sunbathe and eat prawn curries.'

I replied that I would consider his suggestion, which was in fact interesting if not entirely appropriate to my case: it wasn't just the ability to have an erection that had deserted me, but all desire; the idea of fucking now struck me as idiotic, inappropriate, and even two little sixteen-year-old Thai hookers – I felt that this was quite obvious – wouldn't have been able to do anything. Anyway, Azote was right, it was OK for slightly pathetic guys, often working-class Brits, to believe in a woman's manifestation of love or even just sexual arousal, as unlikely as it might seem, and they re-emerged regenerated by her hands, her pussy and her mouth; they certainly weren't the same, ruined by Western women – the most flagrant cases in fact being those of Anglo-Saxon women – and they came back completely regenerated. But I wasn't one of them, I had no complaints to make about women and in any case it had nothing to do with me, I would never get another hard-on ever again, and even sex had vanished from my mental horizon, something that oddly enough I wouldn't have dared to confess to Azote – I'd only talked about 'erectile difficulties'. But he was still an excellent doctor, and as I left his surgery some of my confidence in humanity, medicine and the world had been restored; I was almost light-footed as I turned into the Rue d'Amsterdam, and it was round about Gare Saint-Lazare that I made the mistake, but was it a mistake, I have no idea, and I'll only know at the end – it's true that the end is approaching but it's not here yet, not completely the end.

*

I had the strange sense of entering a kind of autofiction as I walked into the entrance hall of Gare Saint-Lazare, which had been turned into quite an ordinary shopping centre based around clothes shops, but which deserved its name, the 'hall of lost steps'; my steps really were lost, and I wandered blankly among incomprehensible signs. In fact the term 'autofiction' only suggested vague ideas to me, I had memorised it when reading a book by Christine Angot (well, OK, the first five pages) but as I approached the platforms it seemed to me more and more that the word suited my situation, that it had even been invented for me. My reality had become untenable, no human being could survive in such strict solitude; I was probably trying to create a kind of alternative reality, returning to the origin of a split in time as a way of acquiring additional life credits – perhaps they had remained hidden there during all those years, waiting for me between two platforms, my life credits concealed under the dust and grease of the engines. At that moment my heart started racing crazily, like that of a shrew spotted by a predator – pretty little things, shrews – I got to the end of platform 22 and it was there, exactly there, that Camille had waited for me, every Friday evening for almost a year, when I came back from Caen. As soon as she saw me, dragging my 'cabin bag' on its pathetic little wheels, she ran towards me, ran along the platform, ran as fast as she could, reaching the limit of her pulmonary capacities; then we were together and the idea of separation didn't exist, ceased to exist, there wouldn't even have been any point talking about it.

I have known happiness, I know what it is, I can speak about it competently, and I also know how it ends, as it usually does. You're missing a single person and everything is depopulated, as the poet said – in fact the term 'depopulated' is quite weak, it sounds a bit like that idiotic eighteenth century, where you haven't yet arrived at the healthy violence of early romanticism – but the truth is that you're missing a single person and everything is dead, the world is dead and you're dead, or else you're transformed into a ceramic figurine, and other people are ceramic figurines as well, perfect insulators from a thermal and electric point of view, and absolutely nothing can get to you but inner torment issuing from the collapse of your independent body; but I hadn't yet reached that point, and for now my body was behaving reasonably well, there was just the fact that I was alone, literally alone, and drew no pleasure from solitude or from the free working of my mind; I needed love, and love in a very precise form, I needed love in general but in particular I needed a pussy, there were so many pussies – billions on the surface of a moderate-sized planet, it's crazy how many pussies there are when you think about it, it makes you feel dizzy – and on the other hand pussies needed cocks, well, at least that's what we imagine (a lucky misunderstanding upon which man's pleasure and the perpetuation of the species, and perhaps even that of social democracy, is based), in principle the problem is solvable, but it no longer is in practice, it no longer is, and that's how a civilisation dies; without worries, without danger or drama and with very little carnage; a civilisation just dies of weariness, of self-disgust – what could social democracy offer me? Nothing of course, just the perpetuation of absence, a call to oblivion.

Being lost in thought on platform 22 at Gare Saint-Lazare cost me a few microseconds, I think, before it immediately occurred to me that our first meeting had actually taken place at the other end of the line – well, that depends on the trains, some go to Cherbourg and others stop in Caen; I don't know why I'm mentioning the useless scraps of information about the train timetables of Paris–Saint-Lazare that pass intermittently through my dysfunctional brain – either way, we met on platform C of Caen station, one sunny Monday morning in November, seventeen years ago now, or nineteen, I can't remember.

The circumstances were already strange; it was unusual for me to be asked to welcome a trainee in the veterinary service (Camille was a veterinary science student at the time, in her second year at the school in Maisons-Alfort), but I was now seen as something like a luxury intern to whom anyone could assign various tasks as long as they weren't too degrading; all the same I was an Agro alumnus but, well, there was an implicit admission that my 'Normandy cheeses' mission was being taken less and less seriously by my superiors. Having said that, we should not exaggerate the importance of chance in matters of love: if I had bumped into Camille a few days later in a corridor at DRAF, the same thing would have happened, more or less exactly; but it happened at Caen station, at the far end of platform C.

The keenness of my perceptions had clearly increased even a few minutes before the train arrived, which suggests a case of bizarre precognition; between the tracks I had noticed the existence not only of grass but also of plants with yellow flowers whose name I had forgotten – I had learned of their existence during the elective module on 'spontaneous vegetation in the urban setting' which I had taken during my second year of studies at the Agro, quite a fun EM that involved going and collecting specimens among the stones of the church of Saint-Sulpice or on the ring-road embankments ... Behind the station I had also noticed weird parallelepipeds with salmon, ochre and greyish-brown stripes, which made me think of a futuristic Babylonian city – in fact it was the Bords de l'Orne shopping centre, one of the prides of the new municipality; all the major trademarks of modern consumerism were represented there, from Desigual to The Kooples; thanks to this centre even the inhabitants of Lower Normandy were granted access to the modern world.

She came down the metal steps of her carriage and turned towards me, and I noted with strange satisfaction that she didn't have a suitcase on wheels – just a big duffel bag, the kind that you wear over your shoulder. When she said to me, after quite a long time during which there wasn't a hint of awkwardness (she looked at me, I looked at her, and that was absolutely all), but by the time she said to me, perhaps ten minutes later: 'I'm Camille,' the train had already left – for Bayeux, then Carentan and Valognes, and its final destination, Cherbourg station.

By this point a huge number of things had already been said, determined and, as my father would have put it in his lawyerly jargon, 'placed on file'. She had soft brown eyes, and she followed me along platform C then down the Rue d'Augue – I was parked about a hundred metres away – and when I had put her luggage in the boot she calmly sat down in the front seat as if she was going to do it dozens, hundreds, thousands of times again; there was absolutely nothing at stake and I felt so calm, a kind of calm that I had never known before, so much so that it took me, I think, a good half-hour before turning on the ignition. I may have moved my head back and forth like a happy idiot, but she showed no impatience, not even the slightest sign of surprise at my stillness; the weather was glorious, the sky a turquoise blue, almost unreal.

Driving along the Northern ring road, then past the UHC, I became aware that we were in a grim UDZ, consisting mostly of low grey corrugated-iron buildings; the environment wasn't even hostile, it was just frighteningly neutral; I'd driven through this setting every morning for a year without even noticing that it existed. Camille's hotel stood between a prosthetic limb factory and the offices of an accountancy firm. 'I couldn't decide between Appart'City and the Adagio Aparthotel,' I stammered. 'Obviously Appart'City isn't central at all but it's a quarter of an hour's walk from DRAF, and if you want to go out at night you're right next to the Claude-Bloch tram stop. It takes ten minutes to get to the centre of town and runs till midnight, and bear in mind that it's the same in the other direction too. You could get to work by tram, and from the Adagio you've got a view of the banks of the Orne, but on the other hand at Appart'City the premium studios have a terrace, and I thought that might be nice too; well, we can swap if you like, obviously DRAF's in charge of that . . .' She gave me a weird look, difficult to interpret, a mixture of incomprehension and compassion; later she explained that she'd been wondering why I was engaging in these laborious justifications, when it was obvious that we were going to live together.

In this hardcore peri-urban environment, the DRAF buildings created a strange impression of disuse, of neglect and abandonment, and it wasn't just an impression, I said to Camille, as soon as it rained most of the offices leaked, and it rained here most of the time. It looked less like a set of administrative buildings than a village of private houses scattered at random in what might have been a park but really looked more like a patch of waste ground, invaded by ineradicable vegetation, and the asphalt avenues between the buildings were starting to crack under pressure from the vegetation. Now, I went on, I would have to introduce her to her official traineeship supervisor, the director of veterinary services, who could only be described, I continued with resignation, as an old fool. Mean and belligerent by nature, he ruthlessly harassed all staff members who had the misfortune to be under his orders, especially the younger ones – he had a particular aversion to youth, and so it very much seemed as if he took personal offence at the obligation imposed on him of welcoming a young trainee. Not only did he hate young people, he didn't like animals that much either, apart from horses – for him, horses were the only animals that mattered and the other quadrupeds were merely a large animal sub-proletariat, destined in any case for slaughter very soon. He had spent most of his career at the National Stud in Le Pin-au-Haras, and even though his appointment to DRAF was a promotion – and, to tell the truth, the crowning glory of his career – he had taken it as an affront. Having said that, however, this encounter was just something she had to get through, I told her, and the director's aversion towards young people was such that he would do everything within his power to avoid all contact, so she could be more or less certain of never seeing him again in the three months of her traineeship.

Once that moment had passed ('He is actually an old fool . . .' she confirmed soberly), I entrusted her to one of the duty veterinarians – a nice woman of about thirty with whom I had always got on well. And for a week nothing happened. I had jotted Camille's number down in my diary, I knew it was up to me to call her, that was something that hadn't changed very much in relations between men and women – and besides, I was ten years older than her, that was a point to consider. I have a strange memory of that period; I can only compare it to those rare moments that come when one is extremely calm and happy, or about to topple into sleep, but holding back at the last minute, while at the same time being aware that the sleep about to come will be deep, delicious and restorative. I don't think I'm making a mistake comparing sleep to love; I don't think I'm mistaken comparing love to a kind of dream *à deux*, admittedly with some little moments of individual dreaming, little games of connection and encounter, but which enable us to transform our earthly existence into an endurable moment – the only way to do so, to tell the truth.

In fact, things didn't go as I had predicted; the outside world imposed itself, and did so brutally: Camille called me almost exactly a week later, early in the afternoon. She was in a panic, having taken refuge in a McDonald's in the industrial zone of Elbeuf; she had just spent the morning on a battery chicken farm, she had taken advantage of the lunch break to escape and I had to come, I needed to come and get her straight away and rescue her.

I hung up furiously: what idiot at DRAF sent her there? I knew that farm very well; it was a huge one, over three hundred thousand chickens, that exported eggs to Canada and Saudi Arabia, but most importantly had an appalling reputation, one of the worst in France, and the result of every inspection had been negative: thousands of chickens tried to survive in sheds lit from above by powerful halogens, crammed together so tightly that they touched; there were no cages which meant they were 'barn reared'; they were featherless and scrawny, their skin irritated and infested with red mites; they lived among the decomposing corpses of their fellows, and spent every second of their brief existence – a year at most – squawking with terror. That was true even in the best-kept poultry farms, and it was the first thing that struck you, that incessant squawking, and the permanent look of panic that the chickens gave you, that look of panic and incomprehension; they didn't ask for pity, they wouldn't have been capable of it, but they didn't understand, they didn't understand the conditions in which they had been called upon to live. Not to mention the male chicks, useless for egg-laying, who were thrown alive, by the handful, into crushers; I knew all of that, I had had the opportunity to visit several poultry farms of which Elbeuf was probably the worst, but the low moral standards which, like everyone else, I was capable of displaying had allowed me to forget it.

She ran towards me as soon as she saw me coming across the car park and she hugged me, she hugged me for a long time, unable to stop crying. How could men do that? How could they allow that to happen? I had nothing to say on the subject, only uninteresting generalisations about human nature.

Once we were in the car driving towards Caen, she addressed more embarrassing questions: how could vets, public health inspectors, let that happen? How could they visit places where animal torture was an everyday matter, and let them go on working, indeed collaborate with them when they were, in fact, vets? I confess that at that point I wondered: were they overpaid to keep silent? I don't think so. After all, I'm sure there were doctors with medical degrees in the Nazi camps. There too it was ultimately a source of banal and far from encouraging contemplations on humanity; I preferred to say nothing.

Still, when she told me that she was thinking of abandoning her veterinary studies, I intervened. It was a liberal profession, I reminded her; nothing forced her to work in an industrial animal-breeding facility, nothing could even force her to see one again, and I had to add that she had seen the worst, the worst of possible situations (well, the worst in France at least, there were chickens in worse conditions in other countries, but I refrained from saying so). Now she knew, that was all – it was a lot, but it was all. I also refrained from pointing out that it was no better for pigs, nor more and more frequently even for cows – she had already had enough for one day, it seemed to me.

Having reached her Appart'City, she told me she couldn't just go back to hers like that and absolutely needed a drink. There wasn't much in the area that lent itself to such a thing; in fact, there was only the Hôtel Mercure Côte de Nacre, whose clientele consisted exclusively of middle managers working for one or other of the companies in the industrial complex.

The bar proved to be strangely pleasant, scattered with sofas and deep armchairs covered with ochre fabric, and with the moderately discreet presence of a barman. Camille had really taken a moral knock; she was a very young girl and, after visiting an industrial chicken-breeding facility, it took her five Martinis to really be able to relax. I felt exhausted myself, extremely exhausted, as if a very long journey was coming to an end; I didn't even feel capable of taking to the road again to get back to Clécy, I didn't feel vigorous at all – in fact I was benign and happy. So we took a room for the night at the Hôtel Mercure Côte de Nacre and it was what you'd expect from a Hôtel Mercure; well, that's where we spent our first night, and in all likelihood I will remember it until my final days: images of that ludicrous decor will come back to haunt me until the very end, they already come back every evening and I know that isn't going to stop, that in fact it will only become more accentuated, more and more searing, until death delivers me.

I obviously expected that Camille would like the house in Clécy; I had a rudimentary aesthetic sense and, well, I could tell that it was a pretty house; on the other hand I hadn't anticipated that she would also make it *her* house, that from her first days there she would have ideas about how to decorate it and fit it out, that she would want to buy fabrics, move furniture, that in the end she would quite quickly come to act like a wife – in a decidedly un-feminist sense – even though she was only nineteen. Until now I had been living here as if I were in a hotel, a good hotel, a successful *hôtel de charme*, but it wasn't until Camille arrived that I had a sense that it was, truly, my house – and that was only because it was hers.

My daily life underwent other modifications; until now, quite prosaically, I had done my shopping at the Super U in Thury-Harcourt, which had the extra advantage of allowing me to fill up with diesel when I left the supermarket, and to check my tyre pressure every now and again: I hadn't even visited the little town of Clécy, although it no doubt had its charms, attested to by tourist guides of varying degrees of reliability, but being the capital of the Suisse Normande wasn't something to be scoffed at.

That all changed with Camille, and we became regular customers at the *boucherie–charcuterie* and the *boulangerie–patisserie*, both on Place du Tripot, with the town hall and the tourist office. Well, to be more precise, it was Camille who became a regular customer – in general, I just waited for her while drinking pints at the brasserie Le Vincennes, which also sold cigarettes and Loto-PMU tickets, on Place Charles-de-Gaulle, just opposite the church. Once we even went for dinner at Au Site Normand, the village restaurant, which prided itself on having hosted the Charlots for the shooting of a scene for the film *Rookies Run Amok* – there hadn't just been Pink Floyd and Deep Purple, the 1970s had had their shady side – but either way the restaurant was good, and had a sumptuous cheese board.

It was a new way of life for me, one I had never imagined as being possible with Claire, and which proved to be full of unsuspected charms; well, what I mean is that Camille had ideas about how to live; you put her in a pretty village in the middle of the Normandy countryside, and she immediately saw how to get to the best of that pretty Normandy village. Men in general don't know how to live: they have no true familiarity with life, and never feel entirely at ease in it, so they pursue different projects, more or less ambitious and more or less grandiose – generally speaking, of course, they fail and reach the conclusion that they would have been better off just living, but as a rule by that point it's too late.

I was happy, I'd never been so happy, and never would be

again; but at no point did I forget that the situation was transient. Camille was only an intern at DRAF and would inevitably leave in late January to resume her studies in Maisons-Alfort. Inevitably? I could have suggested that she give up her studies and become a housewife, my wife in fact, and in retrospect, when I think about it (and I think about it almost all the time), I think she would have said yes – particularly after the industrial chicken-rearing facility. But I didn't, and I probably couldn't have done; I hadn't been *formatted* for such a proposition, it wasn't part of my *software*; I was a modern man, and for me, like for all of my contemporaries, a woman's professional career was something that had to be respected above all else – it was the absolute criterion, it meant overtaking barbarism and leaving the Middle Ages. At the same time, I wasn't entirely a modern man because I had, even just for a few seconds, been able to imagine the imperative of her leaving it; but once again I didn't do anything, didn't say anything, and let events run their course, while I essentially placed no trust in this return to Paris: like all cities, Paris was made to generate loneliness, and we hadn't had enough time together, in that house, a man and a woman alone and facing one another; for a few months we had been the rest of each other's world, but would we be able to sustain such a thing? I don't know; I'm old now and can't really remember, but I think I was already afraid, and I'd understood, even then, that society was a machine for destroying love.

I only have two photographs from that time in Clécy; we had too much living to do to waste our time on selfies, I imagine, but perhaps that practice was less widespread at the time, social media was still in its infancy if it existed at all; yes, people lived more back then without a doubt. These photographs were probably taken on the same day, in a forest near Clécy; they're surprising, because they were probably taken in November, but everything in the picture – the fresh, vibrant light, the brilliance of the foliage – suggests early spring. Camille is wearing a short skirt and a matching denim jacket. Under the jacket is a white shirt knotted at the waist, decorated with printed red fruits. In the first photograph, her face is lit up by a radiant smile, really bursting with happiness – and it seems crazy today to tell myself that I was the source of her happiness. The second photograph is pornographic – it's the only pornographic picture of her that I've kept. Her handbag, bright pink, is set down on the grass beside her. Kneeling in front of me, she has taken my penis in her mouth, her lips are closed halfway down my glans. Her eyes are closed, and she is concentrating so hard on the act of fellatio that her face is blank, her features perfectly pure; I have never again had a chance to see such a representation of the gift.

I had been living with Camille for two months and had been based in Clécy for just over a year when my landlord died. It rained on the day of his funeral, as is often the case in Normandy in January, and just about the whole village was there, almost all of them old; his time had come, I heard as I followed the cortège, he had had a good life; I remember the priest came from Falaise, about thirty kilometres away, and with desertification, de-Christianisation and all those things beginning with 'de', the poor priest had his work cut out for him and was constantly on the road; but, well, this funeral was an easy one: the mortal being who had just passed on had never neglected the sacraments and his faith had remained intact; a genuine Christian had just yielded his soul to God and, the priest could assert with certainty, his place was now reserved by the side of the Father. His children, who were present, could certainly weep – the gift of tears had been granted to man and it was necessary – but they were to feel no fear as they would soon find themselves in a better world where death, suffering and tears would be abolished.

The two children in question were easy to recognise, they were thirty years younger than the population of Clécy, and I immediately sensed that the girl had something to say to me, something difficult, so I waited for her to come towards me, under a steady, cold rain, while the spadefuls of earth were slowly scattered into the grave, but she could only express herself in the café where the attendees had gathered at the end of the ceremony. So, she felt truly awkward having to tell me this, but I would have to move: her father's house was up for sale and the Dutch buyers wanted to get hold of it quickly; it's rare for life-annuity properties to be rented out, which happens in the case of an occupied life-annuity property sale where the seller has retained the usufruct. In that moment I worked out that they were really in the shit financially: renting out an occupied life-annuity property is a phrase that is hardly ever used, particularly because the tenant risks causing difficulties when returning the property. So

I immediately tried to reassure her that I wouldn't cause any difficulties, that I was fine and had a salary, but had they really come to this? Well, yes, they really had come to this: her husband had just lost his job at Graindorge, which was going through some real difficulties, and there they got to the heart of my work, the shameful heart of my incompetence. The Graindorge company, founded in 1910 in Livarot, had diversified into Camembert and Pont-l'Évêque, and had known an hour of glory (the uncontested leader in Livarot had hauled itself up to second place in the production of the two other cheeses in the Norman trilogy) before, in the early 2000s, entering a spiral of financial crisis that would become more and more acute, finally concluding in 2016 with its purchase by Lactalis, the global number one in milk production.

I was very well aware of the situation but I said nothing about it to the daughter of my former landlord because there are times when it's better to keep your trap shut – after all, there was nothing to boast about; I had failed to help her husband's company and in the end save his job, but I assured her in any case that she had nothing to fear, that I would free the house as soon as possible.

I had felt a real affection for her father, and I sensed that he liked me; every now and again he dropped by to bring a bottle – alcohol is very important for the elderly, it's almost all they've got left. I had immediately taken a liking to his daughter, and she had loved her father deeply, that was obvious; her filial love was open, whole, unconditional. However, we were not destined to see each other again, and we parted with the certainty that we would never see each other again, that the estate agents would take care of the details. Those kinds of thing happen constantly in human lives.

In fact I didn't have the slightest desire to live alone in that house where I had lived with Camille, and not the slightest desire to live anywhere else either, but I no longer had a chance – I had to act: her traineeship was really coming to an end, we had only a few weeks left, and soon only a few days. That's obviously the reason, the chief and almost sole reason, that I decided to come back to Paris, but I don't know what masculine modesty led me to mention other reasons when I talked to her, given that I talked about it to everybody and even to her; luckily she didn't fall for it, and when I talked to her about my professional ambitions and she gave me a hesitant and pained look; it was, in fact, regrettable that I didn't have the courage to just say to her: 'I want to return to Paris because I love you, and I want to live with you'; she must have told herself that men have their limitations – I was her first man, but I think she quickly and easily understood this.

Besides, this speech about my professional ambitions wasn't totally a lie; I had become aware of the severe constraints on my scope for action at DRAF and that the true power was in Brussels, or at least in the central administrative services in close relations with Brussels; that was where I had to go if I wanted to get my point of view across. Except jobs at that level were rare, much rarer than in DRAF, and it took me almost a year to achieve my goals – a year during which I didn't have the courage to look for a new apartment in Caen, so the Adagio Aparthotel offered a mediocre but acceptable solution for four nights a week, and it was there that I destroyed my first smoke detector.

There were work drinks at DRAF almost every Friday evening, and it was impossible for me to get out of them, so I don't think I ever managed to catch the 17.53 train. The 18.53 got me in to Gare Saint-Lazare at 20.46; as I have already said, I know happiness and the things which constitute it, and I know very well what it is about. All couples have their little rituals, their insignificant and even slightly ridiculous rituals, that they don't talk to anybody about. One of ours was to start our weekends by dining, every Friday evening, at Brasserie Mollard, just opposite the station. I think that I had whelks with mayonnaise and lobster Thermidor every time, and that every time I thought it was good; I never felt the need, or even the desire, to explore the rest of the menu.

In Paris, I had found a nice two-bedroom flat with a courtyard on Rue des Écoles, and found myself less than fifty metres from the studio flat where I had lived during my student years. But I can't say that life with Camille reminded me of my student years; it was no longer the same thing, aside from anything else I wasn't a student any more, and more importantly Camille was different; she didn't have that lightness, that recklessness that had been mine when I was studying at the Agro. It's a cliché to say that girls are more serious about their studies, and it's probably an accurate cliché, but there was something else too; I was only ten years older than Camille, but undeniably something had changed, the mood of that generation was not the same as ours; I realised that all her classmates, whatever their area of studies, were serious and hard-working, and placed a lot of importance on their scholarly success, as if they already knew that in the outside world nobody was going to be offering them anything on a plate, that the world awaiting them was inhospitable and harsh. Sometimes, they felt the need to decompress, and then they got drunk in a group, but their drinking sessions themselves were different from the ones that I had known: they got violently drunk, they gulped down huge quantities of alcohol at great speed, as if to reach a state of drunkenness as quickly as possible; they got drunk exactly as miners must have done in the time of *Germinal* – the resemblance was further enhanced by the return in force of absinthe, which reached startling levels of alcohol and in fact made it possible to get plastered in a minimum amount of time.

Camille manifested the same seriousness that she applied to her studies in her relationship with me. I don't mean to say that she was austere or prim – on the contrary, she was very cheerful, laughed over nothing, and in some respects she had even remained curiously childlike and sometimes had cravings for Kinder Bueno, that kind of thing. But we were a couple; it was a serious business, the most serious business of her life, and I was overwhelmed: my breath was literally taken away every time I read in her gaze the gravity, the depth of her commitment – a gravity, a depth which I would have been incapable of at the age of nineteen. Perhaps she also shared that trait with other young people of her generation – I know that her friends thought she 'was lucky to have found somebody', and the somewhat settled, bourgeois nature of our relationship satisfied a deep need in her – the fact that we went to an old-fashioned 1900-style brasserie every Friday evening, rather than a tapas bar in Oberkampf, struck me as symptomatic of the dream in which we were trying to live. The outside world was harsh, merciless towards the weak, and hardly ever kept its promises, and love remained the only thing in which one could still, perhaps, have faith.

But why drag myself to past scenes? as the poet said; I want to dream and not weep, he added as if one had the choice. I need only say that our relationship lasted a little over five years – five years of happiness is quite considerable and I certainly didn't deserve as much – and it came to an end in a horribly stupid way; things like that shouldn't happen, but they do happen, they happen every day. God is a mediocre scriptwriter, that's the conviction that almost fifty years of life have led me to form, and more generally God is mediocre: the whole of his creation bears the stamp of approximation and failure, when it isn't meanness pure and simple; of course, there are exceptions, there are definitely exceptions, the possibility of happiness had to exist *if only as bait* – well, I'm digressing, let's get back to my subject which is me, not that it's especially interesting but it's my subject.

In those years I enjoyed certain professional satisfactions; I even had during some brief moments – particularly when I was travelling to Brussels – the illusion of being an important man. And I probably was more important than when I had been involved in clownish promotional operations concerning Livarot; I played a certain part in the development of the French government's position on the European agricultural budget – but I soon came to realise that while that budget might have been the first European one, and France the first beneficiary country, the number of farmers was simply too high to reverse the trend towards decline; I gradually concluded that French farmers were condemned, so I detached myself from that job, as others did: I understood that the world wasn't one of the things I could change, and others were more ambitious, more motivated, probably more intelligent.

It was during one of my trips to Brussels that I had the wretched idea of sleeping with Tam. Pretty much anybody would have had that idea, I think, she was a ravishing little black girl, particularly her little arse, well, she had a pretty little black girl's arse and that says it all, and my method of seduction was directly inspired by it. It was a Thursday evening and we, a group of relatively young Eurocrats, were drinking beers at the Grand Central; maybe I made her laugh at some point – I was capable of doing that kind of thing in those days – although it was just as we were going out to continue the evening in a club on Place du Luxembourg that I put my hand on her arse; in principle simple methods don't work well, but it worked that time.

Tam belonged to the British delegation (Britain was still part of Europe at the time, or pretending to be) but she was originally from Jamaica I think, or maybe from Barbados – well, one of those islands that seem to be able to produce a limitless quantity of ganja, rum and pretty black girls with little arses; all things that help you to live but don't turn life into a destiny. I should add that she sucked dick 'like a queen', as they say strangely at least in certain circles, and certainly better than the Queen of England; well, I can't deny that I spent a pleasant night, a very pleasant one, but was it a good idea to start again?

Because I did start again during one of her stays in Paris; she came there from time to time – I have absolutely no idea why, certainly not to go shopping, Parisian women go shopping in London and never the other way around; well, tourists must have their reasons – in short I joined her at her hotel in the neighbourhood of Saint-Germain, and then I went out with her on Rue de Buci, holding her by the hand, probably with that slightly idiotic expression of a man who has just come, and I found myself face to face with Camille – I have no idea what she was doing in that part of town either; I said it was just a stupid affair. There was nothing but fear in the look she gave me, a look of pure terror; then she turned around and fled, literally fled. It took me a few minutes to catch up with the girl, but I'm pretty sure that I reached the apartment five minutes after her, not more. She didn't rebuke me, she showed no anger – it was more dreadful than that: she started to cry. She cried for hours, gently, tears flowed down her face and she didn't even think of wiping them away; it was the worst episode of my life, there is no doubt about that. My brain worked slowly, foggily, as I tried to find a phrase along the lines of: 'We're not going to throw everything away over some meaningless sex . . .' or: 'I don't feel anything for that girl, I'd been drinking . . .' (the former true, the latter obviously false). But nothing seemed adequate or appropriate. The next day she went on crying as she got her things together, while I racked my brain to find an appropriate phrase; to be honest, I spent the next two or three years searching for an appropriate phrase, and it's likely that I've never stopped searching.

My life carried on without any notable events – apart from Yuzu, who I've mentioned – and I found myself on my own again, more alone than I had ever been; well, I had hummus, which is suited to solitary pleasures, but as the Christmas period is more delicate I would have needed a seafood platter, but that is something that should be shared; having a seafood platter on your own is scraping the barrel – even Françoise Sagan couldn't have described that, it's too dreadful for words.

Which left me with Thailand, but I had a feeling I wouldn't get there; a few colleagues had talked about it: they were adorable girls but they did have a certain professional pride, and they weren't too keen on a client who couldn't get it up – they felt they were being called into question – and, well, I didn't want to cause a scene.

In December 2001, immediately after my meeting with Camille, I had found myself, for the first time in my life, facing a recurrent and inevitable drama: the Christmas period – my parents had died in June, what was there to celebrate? Camille had remained close to her parents, and often went for lunch with them on Sunday afternoon; they lived in

Bagnoles-de-l'Orne, about fifty kilometres away. I had sensed since the start that my silence on the matter of my parents intrigued Camille, but she refrained from talking to me about it and waited for me to broach the subject myself. I did so, at last, a week before Christmas, and told her the story of their suicide. It was a shock to her, I realised straight away, a deep shock; there are things you haven't really had the opportunity to think about at the age of nineteen, things that you really don't think about before life forces you to. It was then that she suggested spending New Year's Eve with her.

It's always a delicate and uncomfortable moment, being introduced to the parents, but I read something obvious in the look she gave me: under no circumstances would her parents call her choice into question, it wouldn't even occur to them; she had chosen me and I was part of the family, it was as simple as that.

What had led the Da Silvas to settle in Bagnoles-de-l'Orne would remain a mystery to me until the end, as would what had allowed Joaquim Da Silva – a simple construction worker at first – to become manager of the main, and only, newsagent's and tobacconist's in Bagnoles-de-l'Orne, which was in a remarkable location beside the lake. The stories of the lives of humans who belong to the generations immediately preceding our own often provide this kind of configuration in which we may observe the working of an arrangement that has become almost mythical, formerly known by the name of 'social climbing'. The fact remains that Joaquim Da Silva had lived there, with his wife who was also Portuguese, without ever looking back; he never dreamt of returning to the Portugal of his birth, and he fathered two children: Camille and then, much later, Kevin. Being as French as one can be, I had nothing to say about these subjects, but the conversation was easy and pleasant; my work interested Joaquim Da Silva, who came from farming origins like everybody – his parents had tried to grow I can't remember what in the Alentejo – and so he was not insensitive to the increasingly grievous distress of the farmers of his region; in fact, as the manager of a newsagent's and tobacconist's, he was sometimes not a long way from seeing himself as someone *privileged*. In fact, although he worked hard, he still worked less than the average farmer; in fact, although he didn't earn much he still earned more than they did. Conversations about the economy are a bit like conversations about cyclones or earthquakes; quite soon you end up not really understanding what you're talking about and feel as if you're discussing some dark divinity, so you top up the champagne, well, champagne particularly in the Christmas period; I ate remarkably well during that stay with Camille's parents, and I was made very welcome; more generally, they were adorable, but I think my parents would have come well out of that meeting too, in a slightly more bourgeois way but not that much; they knew how to put people at ease and I had had the opportunity to see them at work many times; the day before we left, I dreamt that Camille had been welcomed at my parents' house in Senlis and I nearly talked to her about it when I woke up, but then I remembered that they were dead – I've always had difficulties with death, it's a characteristic trait of mine.

*

I would still like to try, if only for an unusually attentive reader, to cast some light, however faint, on these subjects: why did I want to see Camille again? Why had I felt a need to see Claire again? And even to see the third girl – the anorexic one with the flax seeds whose name escapes me right now, but if the reader is as attentive as I imagine, he will be able to supply it – why had I wanted to see her again?

Most dying people (that is, apart from the ones who have themselves swiftly euthanised in a car park or a dedicated room) organise a kind of ceremony around their passing on; they want to see, one last time, the people who have played a part in the lives, and they want to talk to them, one last time, for a variable amount of time. This is very important to them, and I've seen it on many occasions: they're worried when you can't get the person on the telephone, and want to organise meetings as soon as possible, and of course that's understandable – they only have a few days at their disposal, but the exact number has not been communicated to them, though they are in any case not many, just a few. The palliative care units (at least the ones I've had the opportunity to see in operation, and there are inevitably quite a lot of those, at my age) address these requests with competence and humanity: they are admirable people, they belong to the small and courageous contingent of 'admirable little people' who allow society to carry on in an otherwise generally inhuman and shitty age.

Similarly, I probably tried – on a more limited scale but one that might be useful for training purposes – to organise a mini farewell ceremony for my libido or, in more concrete terms, for my cock at a time when it was announcing to me that it was preparing to bring its service to an end; I wanted to see, once again, all the women who had honoured it, who had loved it in their way. The two ceremonies in my case, the small and the large, were as it happens almost identical, since male friendship had counted for little in my life, basically there had only been Aymeric. It's strange, that wish to draw up a balance, to convince oneself at the last moment that one has lived; or perhaps it isn't strange at all, it's the opposite that is terrible and strange, it is terrible and strange to think about all the men and all the women who have nothing to tell, and who imagine no future fate other than to dissolve into a vague biological and technical continuum (because ashes are technical; even when they are only destined to become fertiliser you have to assess their potassium and nitrogen levels); all those people, in short, whose lives have played out without external incident, and who leave life without thinking about it, as one leaves a holiday home that was just fine, without, however, having an idea of a final destination, with just that vague intuition that it would have been preferable not to have been born – well, now I'm talking about the majority of men and women.

So it was with a clear sense of things being irremediable that I booked a room at the Hôtel Spa Béryl on the shores of the lake in Bagnoles-de-l'Orne for the night from the 24th to the 25th; then I set off on the morning of the 24th; the 24th was a Sunday and most people must have left on Friday evening, or first thing Saturday at the latest, as the motorway was deserted apart from the inevitable Latvian and Bulgarian HGVs. I devoted most of my journey to perfecting a mini narrative intended for the receptionist or the cleaning staff if there were any: the planned family party was so big that my uncle (it was happening at my uncle's house but all branches of the family would be there – I would be seeing cousins I hadn't seen for years, even decades) was unable to put them all up, so I had made the sacrifice of spending the night in a hotel. It was an excellent story, I think, and I gradually started to believe it; obviously I would be unable to call room service to make it really authentic, and so I bought regional products (Livarot, cider, apple juice, *andouille*) shortly before reaching my destination: the Pays d'Argentan service station.

I had made a mistake, a terrible mistake; moving through Gare Saint-Lazare had been painful enough, but mostly I had the image of Camille running along the platforms before breathlessly rushing into my arms, and this was worse, it was much worse; it all came back to me with hallucinatory clarity even before I reached Bagnoles-de-l'Orne, but as soon as I drove through the state forest of Andaines, where I had gone for a long hike with her, a long, interminable and in a sense eternal hike, one December afternoon; we had come back breathless and red-cheeked, so happy that I can no longer entirely imagine it, and had stopped off at an 'artisanal chocolatier' who had offered us a terribly creamy cake that he called 'Paris-Bagnoles', as well as some fake Camemberts made of chocolate.

It continued like that: I was spared nothing, and recognised the strange little tower with the white-and-red chequerboard pattern on top of the hotel–restaurant

La Potinerie du Lac (speciality *tartiflettes*) and the curious Belle-Époque house made of multicoloured bricks that stood almost next to it; I still remembered the curved little bridge that straddled the end of the lake, and the pressure of Camille's hand resting on my forearm to make me look at the swans gliding on the water; that was on 31st December, at sunset.

It would be untrue to say that it was in Bagnoles-de-l'Orne that I started loving Camille; as I said it started at the end of platform C in Caen station. But there is no doubt that something had deepened between us during those two weeks. I had always felt within myself that my parents' conjugal happiness was out of reach to me, first of all because my parents were strange people – uncomfortable on this planet, who could hardly serve as an example for a real life – but also because I felt that that marital model had somehow been destroyed; my generation had put an end to it, well, not my generation – my generation was incapable of destroying, even less of rebuilding, anything – let's say the previous generation, yes, the previous generation was certainly at fault; either way, Camille's parents, as an ordinary couple, represented an accessible example, an immediate, powerful and strong example.

As things stood, I walked the short hundred metres that separated me from the newsagent's and tobacconist's. On a Sunday afternoon, and on 24th December, it was obviously closed, but I remembered that her parents' flat was just above it. The flat was lit, brilliantly lit, and obviously I had a sense that it was *joyfully* lit; I stayed there for a length of time that is hard to gauge, probably brief in reality, but which seemed to me to stretch to infinity, and a thick mist was already rising from the lake. It was probably starting to get cold, but I only felt that for moments at a time and in a somehow superficial way; the light was on in Camille's room too, then it went out; my thoughts dissolved into a series of confused expectations, but I remained aware that there was no reason for Camille to open the window to breathe in the evening mist, absolutely none, and besides I didn't even want her to; I only became fully aware of the new configuration in my life, and also, with a certain unease, of the fact that the purpose of my journey had perhaps not been solely commemorative; that that journey was perhaps, in a way that I was going to be able to elucidate very soon, turned towards a possible future. I had a few years left to think about it; a few years or a few months, I didn't know exactly.

All in all, the Spa du Béryl made an execrable impression on me. I had made the worst of all the possible choices (and there was no shortage of them, in December, in Bagnoles-de-l'Orne); its architecture, among the ravishing Belle-Époque houses, was already the only one that shamed the otherwise harmonious shores of the lake, and I didn't have the courage to tell my story to the receptionist, who had responded to the sight of me with surprise and even open hostility – what the hell was I doing there one might actually wonder; having said that, solitary clients on Christmas Eve do exist, everything exists in the life of a receptionist, and I was only one particular form of unhappy existence; almost relieved by my status of anonymity, when she held out the key to my room I merely nodded. I had bought two whole *andouilles* and midnight mass would probably be shown on television, so I wasn't too badly off.

After a quarter of an hour I had, in reality, nothing left to do in Bagnoles-de-l'Orne; but having said that, going back to Paris the very next day struck me as imprudent. I had cleared the hedge of the 24th, but I still had to jump the one of the 31st – which was tougher, according to Dr Azote.

You plunge into the past, you begin to plunge into it and then it seems as if you're being engulfed by it, and nothing can put a limit on that engulfment. I had heard from Aymeric occasionally during the years following my visit, in essence news of births: first Anne-Marie, then three years later, Ségloène. He never spoke to me about the health of his farm, which led me to suppose that it was still poor or indeed that it had got worse; among people of a certain upbringing, no news necessarily means bad news. Perhaps I too belonged to that unfortunate category of well-mannered people; my first emails after meeting Camille were overflowing with enthusiasm; but I had refrained from talking about our break-up; then contact had ceased completely.

The website of Agro alumni was now accessible on the Internet, and nothing in Aymeric's life seemed to have changed: he still had the same job, the same address, the same email, the same telephone number. And yet as soon as I heard his voice – weary, slow, he had terrible trouble finishing his sentences – I understood *something* had changed. I could drop in whenever I liked, even tonight why not, and he could easily put me up, even if the nature of the accommodation had changed; well, he would explain.

It was a slow, very slow drive between Bagnoles-de-l'Orne and Canville-la-Rocque from the Orne to Manche, along deserted, foggy minor roads – it was, I should point out again, 25th December. I stopped quite often and tried to remember why I was there, but I couldn't quite do it; banks of fog floated over the pastures, and there were no cows to be seen. I imagine one could have called my journey *poetic*, but the word has come to give off an irritating impression of lightness and evanescence. I was aware, at the wheel of my Mercedes 4x4 that purred nicely along these easy roads while the air conditioning gave off a pleasant warmth: there is also tragic poetry.

The Château d'Olonde had not notably become more dilapidated since my last visit about fifteen years earlier; inside was a different matter, and the dining room, previously a pleasant room, had become a grim, dirty and foul-smelling cubby-hole, strewn here and there with ham wrappers and tins of cannelloni in tomato sauce. 'I have nothing to eat . . .' were the first words with which Aymeric welcomed me. 'I've still got an *andouille*,' I replied; that was how I spent my reunion with the man who had been, who still was in a sense (but rather by default), my best friend.

'What do you want to drink?' he went on; in terms of drink, by contrast, there seemed to be a plethora, and when I arrived he was busy necking down a bottle of Zubrowka, while I settled for a Chablis. He was also greasing and re-assembling the parts of a firearm that I identified as an assault rifle, having seen it on various television news programmes. 'It's a Schmeisser S4 .223 Remington,' he explained unnec-essarily. To lighten the mood I cut a few slices of *andouille*. He had changed physically, his features had grown thick and blotchy, but the most frightening thing was his gaze: a hol-low, dead gaze that he seemed unable to distract for more than a few seconds from contemplation of the void. There didn't seem to be any point in asking him a single question; I had already understood the essence of the situation, though I did have to try to talk, but our desire to be silent was pow-erful, and we regularly topped ourselves up, he with vodka and I with wine, rocking our heads back and forth: weary forty-year-olds. 'Let's speak tomorrow,' Aymeric said at last, putting an end to my embarrassment.

He drove ahead of me at the wheel of his Nissan Navara pick-up. I followed him for five kilometres along a narrow, bumpy road, barely wide enough for the car, with spiny hedges scratching our paintwork. Then he turned off the engine and got out, and I joined him: we were at the top of a huge semi-circular amphitheatre whose grassy slope ran gently down towards the sea. Far away on the surface of the ocean the full moon made the waves glitter, but one could just about make out the bungalows, arranged regularly on the slope a hundred or so metres apart. 'I have twenty-four bungalows in all,' Aymeric said. 'In the end we didn't get the grant to turn the castle into a hotel because they thought the Château de Bricquebec was already enough for Nord de la Manche, so we fell back on this bungalow project. It's not going too badly – well, it's the only thing that brings me in a bit of cash – and I'm starting to get customers over the May bank holidays; once the bungalows were even full in July. Obviously in winter it's completely empty – well, not completely; curiously enough at the moment there's one bungalow that's rented to a guy on his own, a German. I think he's interested in birdwatching; from time to time I see him in the meadows with his binoculars and telephoto lenses – he won't bother you, I don't think he's even addressed a word to me since he got here, he just nods in passing and that's it.'

From close by, the bungalows were rectangular blocks, almost cubical, covered with slats of varnished pine. The interior was in pale wood too, and the room was relatively huge: a double bed, a sofa, a table and four chairs – also in wood – a kitchenette and a refrigerator. Aymeric turned on the electricity meter. Above the bed was a little television on a wall bracket. 'I have a bungalow with a children's room as well, with a pair of bunk beds; and one with two children's rooms, so four extra rooms; given Western demographics, I thought that would be enough. Unfortunately I have no Wi-Fi . . .' he said with regret. I gave an indifferent grunt. 'It loses me a fair number of clients,' he stressed. 'For many people it's the first question they ask, and the high-speed plan is dragging a bit in Manche. But it's well heated,' he went on, pointing to the electric radiator. 'I've never had any complaints on that score. We paid attention to the insulation when we were building them – it's the main point.'

He fell silent all of a sudden. I sensed that he was about to talk about Cécile, so I fell silent too, waiting. 'Let's talk tomorrow,' he said again in a faint voice. 'I'll say goodnight.'

I lay down on the bed and turned on the television; the bed was cosy and comfortable and the room quickly warmed up – he was right that the heating worked well – it was just a bit of a shame to be alone, but life isn't simple. The window was very wide, almost like a picture window, probably put in with the intention of taking advantage of the view of the ocean; the full moon still lit the surface of the water, which it seemed to me had come notably closer since our arrival – it was probably a tidal phenomenon, but I don't know, I don't know anything about it. I lived in Senlis when I was young and had my holidays in the mountains, and later I went out with a girl whose parents had a villa in Juan-les-Pins, a little Vietnamese girl who could contract her pussy to an incredible degree; oh, no, I hadn't only had unhappiness in my life, but my experience of the tides remained more than limited. It was curious to be aware of that huge mass of liquid calmly rising to cover the earth; *On n'est pas couché* was on television, and the excitable talk-show contrasted oddly with the slow progression of the ocean; there were too many presenters and they talked too loudly, and the volume of the programme overall was excessively high so I turned off the television but immediately regretted it, as I now had a sense that I was missing something of the reality of the world, that I was withdrawing from history, and that the thing I was missing was probably essential; the casting of the guests was impeccable – these were *people who mattered*, I was sure of it. Looking through the window I noticed that the water seemed to have come closer still, and in a worrying way; were we going to be flooded in the next hour? In that case, we might as well have a bit of fun. In the end I drew the curtains, turned the television back on with the sound down and immediately realised that I had made the right choice; that was the way, the excitement of the programme was still vivid but the inaudibility of what was being said added to the joy; they were like little media figurines, slightly crazy but pleasing, and they were bound to help me get to sleep.

Sleep did in fact come, but it wasn't good, my night was disturbed by gloomy dreams, sometimes erotic but gloomy overall; I was afraid of my nights now, of letting my mind move without control because it was aware that my existence was now turned towards death, and never missed an opportunity to remind me of it. In my dream I lay half-reclining, half-buried in viscous, whitish soil; intellectually I knew we were in an area of medium-sized mountains even though there was nothing in the landscape to indicate as much; extending all around me as far as the eye could see was a cotton-wool atmosphere, also whitish. I called faintly, repeatedly, persistently, and my cries went unheard.

At around nine o'clock in the morning I knocked at the door of the château and got no reply. After a brief moment of hesitation, I headed towards the stable, but Aymeric wasn't there either. The cows watched curiously after me as I went back up the avenues; I ran my hand over the bars to touch their muzzles; they felt lukewarm, damp. Their eyes were bright, they seemed to be robust and in good health; whatever his difficulties, Aymeric was still managing to take care of his animals, so that was reassuring.

The office was open, and the computer turned on. On the task bar I recognised the Firefox icon. It wasn't as if I had all that many reasons to connect to the Internet; I had precisely one.

Like the directory of Agro alumni, the directory of Maisons-Alfort alumni was online now, and it took me about fifty seconds to find Camille's file. She had set up her own company and her offices were in Falaise. That was thirty kilometres from Bagnoles-de-l'Orne. So, after we split up, she had come back to live with her family; I should have suspected as much.

The file contained only the address and telephone number of her office – there was no personal information; I printed it out and folded it in four before putting it in a pocket of my reefer jacket, without knowing precisely what I planned to do with it, or more exactly without knowing if I would have the courage to do it, but fully aware that the rest of my life depended on it.

On the way back towards my bungalow I bumped into the German birdwatcher; well, I nearly bumped into him. Spotting me about thirty metres away, he froze abruptly and stood motionless for a few seconds before turning off down a path that climbed to the left. He had a rucksack and wore a camera with a huge telephoto lens on his chest. He was walking quickly, and I stopped to watch where he went: he practically climbed to the top of the slope, which was quite steep in that spot, and then he walked along it for almost a kilometre before coming back down at an angle towards his bungalow, which was about a hundred metres away from mine. That meant he had taken a detour which cost him a quarter of an hour just to avoid having to speak to me.

Spending time with birds must have had charms that had escaped me until then. It was 26th December, so the shops were bound to be open. In fact, in a gun shop in Coutances I bought a pair of powerful binoculars, Schmidt & Bender, which were, the shopkeeper assured me enthusiastically – he was pretty and homosexual, with a slight speech defect that made him speak a little like a Chinese person – 'leally the best on the malket, incompalable': their Schneider-Kreuznach lenses were exceptionally sharp, and they also had an efficient light amplifier: even at dawn, even at dusk, even in heavy fog, I'd definitely be able to achieve an enlargement of 50x.

I devoted the rest of my day to observing the jerky, mechanical walk of the birds on the beach (the sea had retreated by several kilometres, and it could just be seen in the distance, making way for a huge grey expanse and scattered with irregular pools whose water looked black – quite a grim landscape, to be honest). That afternoon spent as a naturalist was interesting, and it reminded me a little of my student years, apart from the fact that in the past I had been particularly interested in plants, but why not birds? There seemed to be three types: one completely white, another white and black, the third white with long legs and a matching beak. I didn't know their names, either their scientific or their common names; their activities, on the other hand, contained no mystery: frequently pecking the damp sand with their beaks, they devoted themselves to what is called *shore fishing* when a human does it. A tourist display panel a little way back told me that once the high tides had retreated one could easily find, in the sand or in the pools, an ample supply of whelks, winkles, razor shells, dog cockles and sometimes even oysters or crabs. Two humans (or more precisely, as the enlargement of my binoculars revealed, two humans in their fifties, with squat physiques) were also coming back up the beach, armed with buckets and spades, competing with the birds over their paltry fare.

I knocked on the door of the château again at about seven in the evening; this time Aymeric was there and he looked not only drunk but also a bit stoned. 'Been at the weed again?' I asked him. 'Yeah, I've got a dealer in Saint-Lô,' he confirmed, taking a bottle of vodka out of the freezer; for my part, I preferred to stick to Chablis. This time he wasn't stripping his assault rifle, but he had taken out a portrait of an ancestor, which was leaning against an armchair; it showed a squat man, with a square and perfectly hairless face, his eye malicious and beady, strapped into a suit of metal armour. In one hand he held a huge sword that almost came up to his chest, and in the other an axe; overall he emanated an impression of extraordinary physical power and brutality. 'Robert d'Harcourt, known as *the Strong* . . .' Aymeric observed, 'the sixth generation of Harcourts; so a good while after William the Conqueror. He went with Richard the Lionheart on the

Third Crusade.' I said to myself that it must actually be nice to have roots.

'Cécile left two years ago,' he went on without changing his tone. Here we go, we're getting to it, I said to myself; he was going to broach the topic at last. 'In a sense it's my fault: I made her work too hard; managing the farm was already a huge task but with the bungalows it got insane; I should have helped her, tried to pay her more attention. After moving here we didn't get a single day's holiday. Women need holidays . . .' He talked about her quite vaguely, as if discussing a species closely related to him but with which he was relatively unfamiliar. 'And then you saw where we'd got to: cultural distractions. Women need cultural distractions . . .' He waved a hand evasively, as if to avoid specifying what he meant by that. He could have added that from a shopping point of view it wasn't exactly Babylone, and that fashion week wasn't about to move to Vanville-la-Rocque. At the same time, I said to myself, all she had to do was marry someone else, the slut.

'Or buy her things, you know, pretty things . . .' he took another drag on his joint; it seemed to me that he was getting a bit lost. He could have added, more to the point, that they'd stopped fucking, and that that was the heart of the problem, women are less bribable than is sometimes claimed, as far as jewellery is concerned you get them an African trinket and that'll do the trick, but if you're not fucking them any more, if you don't even desire them any more, things get worrying, and Aymeric knew that; with sex everything can be resolved, and without sex nothing can, but I knew he wouldn't tell me any more about it, not under any pretext, not even to me and probably especially not to me; he might have talked to a woman, but to tell the truth there would have been no point talking about it and it might even have been counterproductive, and twisting the knife in the wound wasn't a good option – obviously I'd worked out the previous day that his wife had left him and during that day I'd had time to prepare a counter-attack, to develop a positive plan, but it wasn't yet the moment to go there, and I lit another cigarette.

'I should mention that she went off with a guy,' he added after a very long silence. He gave a kind of painful little involuntary groan just after the word 'guy'. There was no answer to that: this was a tough position, masculine humiliation in its raw state, and all I could do in turn was to emit a corresponding painful groan. 'He was a pianist,' he went on, 'a well-known pianist – he gives concerts all over the world, he's made records. He came here to rest, to take a break, and then he ran off with my wife . . .'

There was another silence, but I had plenty of ways of filling it; pouring another glass of Chablis, cracking the joints of my fingers. 'I'm a real idiot, I didn't notice . . .' Aymeric went on at last, in a voice so low that it was getting alarming. 'We've got a very good piano in the château, a Bösendorfer baby grand that belonged to one of my ancestors – she hosted a kind of salon during the Second Empire – but to tell the truth we were never really patrons of the arts, not like the Noailles, but she held a salon anyway, and apparently Berlioz played on that piano; in short, I suggested that he play it if he wanted to, though it had to be restrung of course, but in the end he was spending more and more time in the château, and there you have it: they live in London but they travel around a lot because he gives concerts all over the world, in South Korea, in Japan . . .'

'And what about your daughters?' I sensed it was a good idea to move away from the business with the Bösendorfer; I suspected that things weren't all that great with the daughters, but the Bösendorfer was the kind of detail that literally kills you, that pushes you right towards suicide, and it absolutely had to be banished from his mind; with the girls there was at least the possibility of starting a new conversation.

'I have access in theory, obviously, but in practice they're in London, and so I haven't seen them for two years; what am I supposed to do here, with two little girls of five and seven?'

I glanced around the dining room, with the empty tins of cassoulet and cannelloni lying on the floor, and the battered dresser revealing a shattered china set (and it was probably Aymeric himself who had knocked over the dresser during an outburst of alcoholic fury); in fact it was impossible to disagree with him: it's amazing how quickly men let themselves go. I had noticed the previous day that Aymeric's clothes were frankly filthy, and that they smelled a little; even while he was at Agro he took his clothes back to his mother to wash every weekend – so did I but I'd still learned how to work the washing machines placed at the disposal of the students in the basement of the residence, and I had done it two or three times, but he never had; I don't think he'd even suspected their existence. Perhaps it was better to forget about the little girls, and concentrate on the matter at hand; after all he could always make new little girls.

He poured himself another large glass of vodka, which he drained in one, and concluded soberly: 'My life is fucked.' At that point a kind of click ran through me, and I smiled inwardly because I had known from the start that he would get there, and during the few silences that had interrupted his narrative I had had time to refine my answer, my counter-attack, that positive plan that I had secretly been developing during my afternoon devoted to the observation of seabirds.

'Your fundamental mistake,' I launched in with alacrity, 'was to marry within your own circle. All those chicks, the Rohan-Chabots, the Clermont-Tonnerres, what are they now, really? Just little bitches ready to do anything to get an internship in a weekly cultural magazine, or with an alternative fashion designer.' (There I hit the nail on the head without knowing it, because Cécile was a Faucigny-Lucinge, a family from exactly the same class, the same class of aristocracy, obviously.) 'In short, not farmers' wives. Whereas you've got hundreds, thousands, millions of girls' (I was getting a bit carried away) 'for whom you represent the absolute masculine ideal. Take a Moldovan girl, or a Cameroonian or a Malagasy girl, a Laotian even: they're girls who aren't very rich and they're poor quite honestly; they've come from an absolutely rural background, they've never known another world, they don't even know that another world exists. And then you turn up, in the prime of life, in not bad physical shape, a sturdy, handsome guy in his forties, and you own half the pastures in the area.' (I was exaggerating a bit, but, well, that's the idea.) 'Obviously it brings you in bugger all, but they can't guess that and they will never understand because in their minds land is land, it's land and the herd, so I can assure you that they won't abandon the business; they'll work hard on the task at hand, and never give up, they'll be up and about at five in the morning to do the milking. And also they'll be young, a lot more sexy than all those aristocratic bitches, and they'll fuck forty times better. You'll just have to hold off a bit on the vodka; it risks reminding them of their origins, particularly if it's a girl from an Eastern country, but anyway it can't hurt you to hold off a bit on the vodka. They'll get up at five in the morning to do the milking,' I said enthusiastically, increasingly convinced of my own vision (I could see the Moldovan girl already) 'then they'll wake you up with a blow-job, and breakfast will be ready as well . . .'

I cast a glance at Aymeric; I was convinced he'd been listening to me attentively until then but he was beginning to doze off – he must have started boozing before I got there, probably in the early afternoon. 'Your father would agree with me . . .' I concluded, having somewhat run out of arguments; here I was less sure of myself; I barely knew Aymeric's father, in fact I'd only seen him once, and he'd seemed like a decent type but a bit stiff; the social transformations that had taken place in France after 1794 had probably more or less passed him by. Historically I knew that I wasn't wrong; the aristocracy had never hesitated, when they spotted signs of decadence, to renew the genetics of the flock by going out in search of washer-women or laundry-maids, and now you had to go a bit further to find them, that was all, but was Aymeric in a fit state to demonstrate common sense? Then I had a more general doubt, a more biological one: what was the point of saving a defeated old male? We had both reached more or less the same point; our fates were different, but the ending wasn't dissimilar.

Now he had really fallen asleep. Perhaps I hadn't spoken in vain, perhaps the Moldovan girl could slip inside his dreams. He was asleep, sitting bolt upright on the sofa, his eyes wide open.

I knew I wouldn't see Aymeric the next day, or probably for days after that, and that he would regret his confession – he would come back on the 31st because you can't *do nothing* on the evening of the 31st; well, that had happened to me several times before but I was different from him, I was impervious to convention. I still had four days of solitude and I immediately sensed that the birds wouldn't be enough – neither the television nor the birds, either taken together or separately, could be enough – and it was then that I thought again of the German, so on the morning of the 27th I turned my Schmidt & Bender binoculars on the German; basically I think I would like to have been a cop, insinuating myself into people's lives, penetrating their secrets. I didn't expect anything exciting as far as the German was concerned; I was mistaken. At about five o'clock in the afternoon, a little girl knocked at the door of his bungalow; well, I say a little girl but let's get this straight; she was a brunette of about ten with a childish face, though she was tall for her age. She had cycled there, so she must have lived very close by. Of course, I immediately expected a case of paedophilia: what reason could a little ten-year-old girl have for knocking at the door of a sinister and misanthropic forty-year-old man, and a German to boot? Did she want him to read poems by Schiller to her? It was more likely so he could show her his cock. And he very much had the profile of a paedophile; cultured and in his forties, solitary, incapable of forming relationships with others let alone with women; that was what I said to myself before realising that the same could have been said about me, that I could have been described in exactly the same terms, and I was appalled, so to calm myself I trained my binoculars on the windows of the bungalow, but the curtains were drawn, and I could find out nothing more that evening, except that she came out almost two hours later and consulted the messages on her mobile phone before getting back on her bike.

The next day she returned at about the same time, but this time he forgot to draw the curtains, enabling me to make out a video camera fitted on a tripod; my suspicions were confirmed. Unfortunately, immediately after the girl arrived he noticed that the curtains were open, walked towards the window and hid the room from my view. Those binoculars were extraordinary; I had had a perfect view of his face, and saw he was in an extreme state of arousal, and I even had a sense right then that he was salivating slightly; I'm sure that for his part he didn't suspect my surveillance in the slightest. The little girl left again, like the day before, after just under two hours.

The same scenario played out two days later, apart from the fact that I thought I briefly saw the little girl moving in the background, in a T-shirt, with her bottom bare; but it was vague and fleeting, I'd been focusing on the guy's face and that uncertainty was frankly becoming exasperating.

An opening appeared at last on the morning of the 30th. At about ten o'clock I saw him leaving in his 4x4 (a collector's Defender, probably from 1953 or something; the idiot wasn't only a misanthrope and probably a paedophile, but also a snob of the worst kind – why couldn't he be satisfied with a Mercedes 4x4 like me and everyone else? He would pay for it, he would pay dearly for it); in short, the paedophile (I hadn't noticed earlier, but he had the exact face of a German academic, a German academic on sick leave or more probably on research leave, where he was probably going to observe Arctic terns in the north-west of Cotentin, near Cap de la Hague or something); so he put an ice-box – it must have contained some special Bavarian beers – and a plastic bag probably full of sandwiches in the boot of his Defender; he had enough to keep him going for the morning, and would probably come back just before his ritual five o'clock appointment; it was time to spring into action and unmask him.

I still waited for an hour to be certain he wasn't coming back, then strolled calmly towards his bungalow. I had brought an emergency tool kit, which I always kept in the boot of my Mercedes, but the door wasn't even closed – it's amazing how trusting people are when they get to Manche, they feel that they're entering a foggy, peaceful space, far from the usual human troubles and in a sense far from evil; well, that's the image they have of it. I still had to turn on the computer; he must have been very careful about consuming electricity even in sleep mode – he probably had ecological beliefs – but on the other hand there was no password and that was frankly baffling; everyone has a password these days, even six-year-old children have a password on their tablets, so what kind of person was this guy?

The files were organised by year and by month, and in the file for December there was only one video, entitled 'Nathalie'. I'd never seen a paedophilic video – I knew they existed but nothing more than that – and suddenly I sensed that the amateurish quality of the filming was going to be hard to bear: in the first few seconds he accidentally pointed the camera at the tiles in the bathroom, then returned to the face of the little girl who was busy putting on make-up; she spread a thick layer of vermilion on her lips, too thick a layer and it spilled over, then she put on some blue eyeshadow in great lumps – she wasn't brilliant at doing that either – but the birdwatcher seemed to like it a lot, and I heard him muttering: '*Gut . . . gut . . .* '; so far that was the only slightly disgusting thing about the film. Then he tried a reverse tracking shot – well, to be more precise he pulled back to show the girl at the bathroom mirror, naked apart from a pair of denim mini-shorts, the same she had had on when she arrived. She had hardly any breasts, or rather one could make out a swelling, a promise. He said a few words that I didn't understand and she immediately took off her shorts and sat down on the bathroom stool, spread her legs and started running her middle finger over her pussy; she had a small pussy that was well-formed but perfectly hairless and at that point I suppose a paedophile must have started getting seriously aroused, and in fact I could hear his breathing getting harder and harder, making the camera shake slightly.

Suddenly the shot changed and the girl could be seen in the sitting room. She was already wearing a tartan mini-skirt and was putting on a pair of fishnet stockings which she hooked to a suspender belt – it was all a bit big for her, they must have been XS but for adults; they fit but only just. Then she tied a little top, also in tartan, around her chest, and I thought she got that right, because it gave the idea of breasts even though she had none.

Then came a slightly confused passage during which he looked for an audio cassette that he inserted into a radio cassette player; I didn't know those things still existed, well, it was like the Defender; it was vintage. The girl waited calmly, arms dangling. I had trouble recognising the song when it got going – it sounded like a disco thing from the late seventies or early eighties, maybe something by Corona – but the girl reacted well and immediately started spinning around and dancing and it was then that I really started feeling sick to my stomach, not because of the content but because of the filming; he must have crouched down to get her in a low-angle shot, he must have been hopping around her like an old toad. The girl danced with real enthusiasm, carried away by the rhythm, every now and again she threw up her mini-skirt, enabling the birdwatcher to get some very good angles of her little bum; at other times she froze facing the camera and opened her thighs, putting in one or two fingers, then she put those fingers in her mouth and sucked on them for a long time; either way he was getting more and more aroused, the camera movements became frankly chaotic and I was starting to get a bit bored, when at last he calmed himself, set the camera on its tripod and sat back down on the sofa. The girl went on spinning to the music for some time, while he looked at her with adoration; he had already come – intellectually, you must understand – but there was still a physical dimension, and I suppose he had already started masturbating.

The cassette suddenly stopped, with a distinct click. The girl gave a little bow – she had a kind of ironic rictus – and came over to the German, kneeling down between his thighs: he had lowered his trousers, but without taking them off. He hadn't moved the camera from its plinth, which meant that you could hardly see anything – contrary to all the codes of pornography, amateur included. In spite of her youth, the girl seemed to acquit herself of her task with competence, and every now and again the birdwatcher uttered a groan of satisfaction, which he interrupted with tender words along the lines of '*Mein Liebchen*', well, he seemed extremely fond of that girl, and I never would have believed that of such a cold character.

That was where I had got to, and the video was reaching its end – ejaculation couldn't have been far off in my opinion – when I heard the crunch of footsteps on the gravel. I leapt to my feet, immediately aware that there was no other means of access, no way to avoid confronting him, and that that confrontation could be fatal: he could kill me immediately and hope to get away with it, there wasn't much of a chance but he could still hope. When he came in he gave an almost cataleptic jump – his whole body was trembling and for a moment

I hoped that he would faint but in the end he didn't, he stood there on his feet with his face extraordinarily red. 'I'm not going to report you!' I yelled – I sensed that I had to yell, that only yelling could get me out of this, and then immediately afterwards I worked out that he probably didn't know the word 'report', and started yelling louder than ever: 'I'm not going to talk! I'm not going to say anything to anybody!' and I started yelling several times: 'I'm not going to talk! I'm not going to say anything to anybody!' while moving slowly towards the door. Still yelling, I raised my arms, spread out in front of me in a gesture of innocence. He couldn't have been used to physical violence: that was my hope, my only chance.

I went on gently shuffling forwards, repeating in a lower voice, to a rhythm that I hoped was obsessive: 'I'm not going to talk. I'm not going to say anything to anybody.' And all of a sudden, when I was less than a metre away from him and I had entered his personal physical space, I don't know, but he leapt backwards, giving me access to the door, so I hurried into the gap, ran on to the path and in less than a minute I'd locked myself up in my bungalow.

I poured myself a big glass of Poire Williams and quickly came to my senses: *he* was the one who was in danger, not me; *he* was the one who was risking thirty years' jail without remission, not me; he wasn't about to make a fuss. And in fact, less than five minutes later, I watched him – those binoculars really were remarkable – as he stowed his luggage in the boot of his Defender, sat down at the wheel and disappeared towards an unknown destiny.

On the morning of the 31st I got up in an almost tranquil mood and cast a serene eye over the landscape of bungalows, of which I was now the only tenant; if the birdwatcher had driven well, he would now be somewhere near Mainz or Koblenz, and he was bound to be happy, that brief happiness that comes with having just escaped a considerable misfortune and finding oneself confronted once again with ordinary unhappiness. Even though my attention had been focused on the German, I hadn't neglected the lovers of shore fishing, who had arrived throughout the week in tight bursts; it's true that it was the holiday season. A good little guide, published by Éditions Ouest-France and which I had bought at the Super U in Saint-Nicolas-le-Bréhal, had revealed to me the extent of the phenomenon of shore fishing, as well as the existence of certain animal species such as the pelagic red crab, the various species of surf clam, the saddle oyster and the peppery furrow shell, not to mention the banded wedge shell which is eaten pan-fried in a parsley sauce. There was a kind of conviviality at work there, I was sure of it; I had seen that way of life being celebrated on TF1, and more rarely on France 2; people assembled in families or sometimes in pairs of friends, then they grilled razor shells and clams on hot embers, accompanied by a Muscadet consumed in moderation; here we were dealing with a higher stage of civilisation in which wild appetites were sated by shore fishing. The confrontation was not without its risks: the lesser weaver could inflict unbearable pain, it was the most virulent of fish; if the surf clam was easy to fish, catching the peppery wedge shell required patience and agility; fishing for ear shells was unimaginable without the help of a long-handled grapple; there was no single distinguishing feature, it was important to know, that enabled one to identify a clam. Personally I hadn't reached that stage of civilisation, and neither had the German paedophile, who by now would be somewhere near Dresden, or might even have crossed over to Poland, where extradition was more difficult. At about five in the evening, as she did every day, the little girl stopped her bike outside the birdwatcher's bungalow. She knocked on the door for a long time, walked over to look through the curtains, then went back to the door and knocked again for a long time before giving up. Her expression was difficult to decipher; she didn't really seem truly sad (or at least not yet?), but rather surprised and disappointed. At that moment, I wondered if he paid her; there was no way of knowing, but the answer in my view was probably yes.

At about seven I headed towards the château; it was time to get this year over with. Aymeric wasn't there but he had done some preparation: arranged on the dining room table was an assortment of pork products, along with some *andouille de Vire*, some artisanal black pudding, different kinds of Italian charcuterie and also a variety of cheeses, and there were bound to be drinks – I had no worries on that score.

At night, the byre was a calming place; the herd of three hundred cows made a gentle noise consisting of sighs, light mooing, movement in the straw – because there was straw; he had rejected the ease of racks, and preferred to produce dung to cover his fields; his goal was really to work in the old style. I had a moment of unease as I remembered that in accounting terms he was fucked, and then something else happened: the gentle mooing of the cows, the not entirely disagreeable smell of dung, they all briefly gave me the sense of – I wouldn't say of having a place in the world, let's not overstate the case – but of belonging to a kind of organic continuum, of animal regrouping.

The light was on in the little cubbyhole that served as his office, and Aymeric was sitting at the computer with a microphone headset on his head, fascinated by the contents of the screen, and only noticed me at the last second. He jumped to his feet and made an absurd protective gesture as if trying to hide the image, which I couldn't see in any case. 'Don't worry, take your time, don't worry, I'll go back to the château . . .' I said to him with a vague wave of the hand (I was probably unconsciously trying to imitate Inspector Columbo, Inspector Columbo had had a surprising impact on young people my age), before heading back. I had raised my hands to accompany my words, a bit like I had done the day before with the German paedophile, but sadly this wasn't about paedophilia, it was worse: I was sure he wanted to Skype-call London on this last day of the year, probably not with Cécile but certainly with his daughters; he must have communicated with his daughters by Skype at least once a week. 'And how are you, Dad?' I could see it as if I was there, and I understood the little girls' view: could a classical concert pianist give them a manly paternal image? Absolutely not, obviously (Rachmaninov?) – he was just one more London queer, while their father dealt with adult cows, big mammals, at least five hundred kilos either way. And what could he talk to his little girls about? Just nonsense, obviously; he told them he was fine, the dick, while in fact he was anything but fine, he was being destroyed by their absence, and by the absence of love more generally. So to all intents and purposes he was fucked, I said to myself as I crossed the farmyard again; he would never get out of this business and would suffer from it until the end of his days, and all my patter about the Moldovan girl would have been pointless. I was in a bad mood, and I poured myself a big glass of vodka without waiting for him while devouring slices of artisanal black pudding; you really can't do anything about people's lives, I said to myself, neither friendship nor compassion nor the intelligence of situations is of any use: people manufacture the mechanism of their own misfortune, they wind it right up and the mechanism goes on turning, ineluctably, with the odd mistake, a few errors when there's sickness in the mix, but it goes on turning to the end, to the final second.

Aymeric arrived a quarter of an hour later, trying to seem casual, as if to make me forget the incident, which only confirmed my certainties, and above that my impotence. But I wasn't completely reassured, nor entirely resigned, and I began the conversation by going straight for the most painful topic.

'Are you getting divorced?' I asked very calmly, almost with indifference.

He literally slumped on the sofa, and I poured him a big glass of vodka; it took him at least three minutes to bring it to his lips and for a moment I even thought he was going to start crying, which would have been embarrassing. There was nothing original about what he had to tell me; not only do people torture one another, they torture one another with a complete absence of originality. It's obviously painful to see someone you've been fond of, someone you've spent the night with and woken up with, maybe been sick with or been worried about the health of your children with, turning within a few days into a kind of ghoul, a harpy with bottomless financial greed; it's a painful experience that you never fully get over, but it may in a sense be healthy (obviously to the extent that you think love might be a healthy thing): going through a divorce may be the only effective way of putting an end to love, and if I had married Camille and then divorced her maybe I'd have managed to stop loving her – and it was at that precise moment, as I listened to Aymeric's story, that for the first time, without any kind of protection, falsification or constraint, I allowed my consciousness to be penetrated by the painful, atrocious and fatally obvious fact that I still loved Camille; this New Year's Eve had definitely got off to a bad start.

In Aymeric's case it was even worse; even the end of his

love for Cécile would be of no use to him, there were the little girls, the trap was perfect. And on the financial side his story had some particularly worrying aspects, even though it conformed absolutely to what may commonly be observed in cases of divorce. Community reduced to property, fine, that was the usual deal, but in his case the properties were far from negligible. First of all there was the farm, the new byre, the farming machinery (agriculture is a heavy industry, which freezes major production capital in order to generate a low income, if any; indeed, in Aymeric's case, a negative income): did half of that capital belong to Cécile? Overcoming his revulsion for legal niceties, the members of the bar and probably the law more generally, Aymeric's father had decided to take on a lawyer, recommended to him by a contact at the Jockey Club. The consultant's first conclusions had been relatively reassuring, at least where the farm was concerned: the land still belonged to Aymeric's father, and all the improvements he had carried out – the new byre, the machinery – could also be considered to belong to him; in legal terms, it was possible to support the argument that Aymeric was only a kind of administrator over the land. The bungalows were another story: the hotel business and all the buildings were in his name; only the land had remained the property of his father. If Cécile insisted on demanding half the value of the bungalows, they would have no choice but to put the business in compulsory liquidation and wait for a buyer, which would take time, probably years. All in all, Aymeric concluded with a mixture of despair and disgust, that mixture which becomes your permanent state of mind as the procedure of a divorce falls into place – as the negotiations, the horse-trading, the proposals and counter-proposals of lawyers and notaries, fall into place – all in all, he was nowhere close to seeing the end of this divorce.

'Apart from anything else, for my father there's no question of selling the land that overlooks the sea, the land the bungalows are built on – he could never bring himself to do that . . .' He added: 'For years he's taken it personally every time I've been forced to sell a plot of land to balance the books. I know it hurts him – it hurts him almost physically – but you've got to remember that for a traditional aristocrat – and that's exactly what he is – the most important thing is to pass the family estate on to the next generations, and if possible to enlarge it a little but at the very least not to reduce it, and from the beginning that's what I've been doing; I've been reducing the family estate, but there's no other way I can manage, and so he's starting to get fed up with it all. I wish he'd throw in the towel – the last time he told me openly: "The vocation of the Harcourts has never been as farmers . . ." He said it to me just like that, and maybe it's true but it isn't their vocation to be hoteliers either, and strangely enough he liked Cécile's plan – the plan for the stately-home hotel – but it's probably only because it would have allowed him to restore the château. He doesn't give a damn about the bungalows, you could blow them up with a bazooka tomorrow and he wouldn't care. What's terrible is that he's someone who has hardly ever done anything useful with his life – he's just gone along to weddings, funerals, the occasional fox hunt, a drink at the Jockey Club from time to time; he's also had a few mistresses I think, but nothing excessive – and he's left the inheritance of the Harcourts intact. I'm trying to build something, the work's killing me, I get up at five every day, I spend my evenings doing the accounts – and the end result is that I'm impoverishing my family . . .'

He talked for a long time; this time he really had told me the whole story, and I think it was nearly midnight when I suggested that he put on some music, which had for some time been the right thing to do – the only possible thing in our situation – and he nodded gratefully; I don't remember very clearly what he put on because I was completely pissed myself, pissed and in despair; thinking about Camille again had finished me off in a few seconds; immediately before that I had felt like a strong man, a wise and consoling man, and then all of a sudden I felt like a drifting pile of misery; well, I'm sure that he put on the best music he had, the music he was most fond of. The only precise memory I have is a recording of *Child in Time*, a bootleg made in Duisburg in 1970, and the sound quality of his Klipschorns was truly exceptional; it was perhaps the most aesthetically beautiful moment of my life. I like to mention it in the context of beauty being useful in some way; in fact we must have put it on thirty or forty times, captivated each time it came on by the movement of absolute flight with which Ian Gillan moved from word to song, then from song to cry before, against the background of Jon Lord's calm mastery, returning to word; immediately after that came the majestic break of Ian Paice – admittedly Jon Lord was supporting him with his usual mixture of effectiveness and grandeur, but Ian Paice's break was still sumptuous, probably the most beautiful break in the history of rock, and then Gillan came back and the second part of the sacrifice was performed; Ian Gillan flew off again from word to song, then from song to pure cry, and unfortunately shortly after that the piece came to an end and there was nothing left but to put the needle back to the beginning and we could have lived like that for ever, for ever – I don't know, it was probably an illusion but a beautiful one – I had gone, I remembered, with Aymeric to a Deep Purple concert at the Palais des Sports, and it was a good concert but not as good as the one in Duisburg; we were old, moments like this would become rare from now on, but it would all return when we were in our death throes, both his and mine; there would also be Camille in my case, and probably Kate – I don't know how I managed to get back, but I remember picking up a slice of artisanal black pudding which I chewed for a long time, at the wheel of my 4x4, without really tasting it.

The morning of 1st January broke, like all mornings in the world, on to our problematic lives. I got up, paid a small amount of attention to the morning – which was foggy, but not excessively so, a morning of ordinary fog: there were New Year programmes on the main entertainment channels, but I didn't know any of the singers; however, it did seem to me that the hot Latina babe was yielding ground to the concerned Celt, but I had only an anecdotal and approximate, generally optimistic, vision of that aspect of life: if that was what audiences had decided, then it was fine. At about four o'clock I headed towards the château. Aymeric had returned to his usual state: morose, stubborn and desperate; rather mechanically stripping and reassembling his Schmeisser assault rifle. It was then that I told him I wanted to learn to shoot.

'Shoot how? Shoot to defend yourself, or shoot for sport?' He looked delighted that I was addressing a concrete, technical subject, and most importantly relieved that I wasn't returning to the previous day's conversation.

'A bit of both, I think . . .' In fact, during my confrontation with the birdwatcher, I would have felt more comfortable with a revolver; but there was also something about precision shooting that had attracted me for a long time.

'As a defensive weapon I can give you a short-barrelled Smith & Wesson – a bit less accurate than the long-barrelled one, but a lot easier to transport. It's a 357 Magnum, easily fatal at ten metres, and it's really easy to use, I can explain it to you in five minutes. For sport . . .' His voice had become more sonorous; I heard it quivering with an enthusiasm that I hadn't known him to have for years, since we were twenty, in fact. 'I really love shooting for sport, I've been doing it for years, you know. It's really extraordinary: the moment when you get the target in the centre you take aim, you stop thinking about anything, you forget all your worries. For the first few years after I moved here it was so hard – so much harder than I had imagined – and I don't think I would have managed without my shooting sessions. Now, obviously . . .' He held out his right hand horizontally, and in fact after a few seconds it started trembling, in a faint but unmistakeable way. 'The vodka . . . there's no comparison, you have to choose.' Had he had a choice? Does anyone have a choice? I had my doubts on the matter.

'For sport shooting there's one weapon that I've loved, a Steyr Mannlicher HS50. I can lend it to you if you like but I have to check it, give it a deep clean. I haven't used it for three years, but I'll look into it this evening.'

He staggered slightly as he walked towards his gun cabinet, which was three sliding doors in the hall, and behind them about twenty weapons – rifles, carbines and a few handguns – as well as dozens of piles of boxes of cartridges. The Steyr Mannlicher surprised me: it didn't look like a carbine at all but like a simple dark grey steel cylinder, totally abstract. 'There's everything else, of course, and you have to reassemble it . . . But the machining of the barrel, I assure you, is the most important thing . . .' He held the barrel in the light for a moment to let me admire it; I was prepared to agree that yes, it was a cylinder, probably a perfect cylinder. 'Fine, I'll look into it . . .' he concluded without pressing the point. 'I'll bring it to you tomorrow.'

Sure enough, at eight o'clock the next morning he parked his pick-up outside the bungalow, and really was in an unusual state of excitement. We took a quick look at the Smith & Wesson – they are disconcertingly user-friendly. The Steyr Mannlicher was something else. From the boot he took a rigid polycarbonate protective case, which he set down carefully on the table. Inside, positioned precisely in their foam-rubber housings, lay four dark grey steel parts, machined with extreme precision, none of them immediately suggesting a weapon, which he got me to strip and reassemble several times: apart from the barrel there was a mount, a cartridge clip and a tripod stand; once the whole thing had been assembled it still didn't look like a carbine in the usual sense of the word, but more like a kind of metal spider, a deadly spider in which no aesthetic flourish was permitted, not a gramme of metal was wasted, and I began to understand his enthusiasm: I don't think I'd ever seen a technological object that created such an impression of perfection. At last he added a scope on top of the metal assemblage. 'It's a Swarovski DS5,' he explained. 'It's frowned upon in sport-shooting circles, and even frankly forbidden in competition; what you have to realise is that the trajectory of a bullet isn't a straight line, it's always a parabola, and sport-shooting authorities see that as part of the test, so it's normal for competitors to get used to aiming a bit above the centre to take the parabolic deviation into account. The Swarovski has a built-in laser telemeter, meaning it gauges your distance from the target and automatically corrects it so you don't have to think about it; you just aim at the centre, precisely at the centre. They're quite traditional in sport-shooting circles – they like to add pointless little complications and that's why I gave up competitions pretty quickly. So I had the travel case made to measure, with room for the Swarovski. But the essential thing is still the gun. Let's take it out and try it . . .'

He grabbed a blanket from a box. 'We'll start straight away with the prone firing position – that's the queen of positions, the one that allows you to shoot with the greatest possible precision. But you have to be lying comfortably on the ground, you have to protect yourself against cold and damp, or it could cause trembling.'

We stopped at the top of the slope that fell towards the sea, and he spread the blanket on the grassy ground and pointed to a boat buried in the sand, about a hundred metres away. 'You see the registration painted on the side, BOZ-43? Try and get a bullet in the middle of the O. It's about twenty centimetres in diameter; with a Steyr Mannlicher, a good shooter could probably do it from fifteen hundred metres; but OK, let's try like that.'

I lay down on the blanket. 'Find your position, take your time . . . You must have no reason to move; no other reason but your own breathing.'

I succeeded without great difficulty; the stock was a smooth, curved surface, easy to position in the hollow of my shoulder.

'You'll find these Zen-type guys who will tell you that the important thing is to become one with your target. I don't believe it, it's nonsense, and besides the Japanese are rubbish at sport shooting; they've never won a single international competition. On the other hand, it's true that precision shooting has a lot in common with yoga: you try to be one with your own breathing. So you're going to breathe slowly, more and more slowly, as slowly and deeply as you can. And, when you're ready, you aim your sights at the centre of your target.'

I set about doing as he said: 'Right, have you got it?' I nodded. 'So now what you have to know is that you mustn't try for absolute motionlessness, that's simply impossible. You're inevitably going to be moving, because you're breathing. But what you've got to achieve is a very slow movement, a regular swinging motion, guided by your breathing, that passes through the target. Once you've got it, once you've got the movement, you just have to pull the trigger as you pass the centre. Just a very small motion, nothing more than that; it's on a hypersensitive setting. The HS50 is a single-shot model. If you want to fire again you have to reload; that's why snipers don't use it so much in real wars, because what they want above all is effectiveness, they're there to kill; for me personally, I think it's good to have only one chance.'

I closed my eyes briefly to avoid having to think about the personal implications of that choice, then opened them again; it was going well, as he had told me it would, and the letters BOZ passed slowly back and forth in my sights; I pulled the trigger at what I thought was the right moment, and there was a very faint sound, a faint plop. In fact it was an extraordinary experience; I had just spent a few minutes outside time, in a pure, ballistic space. Standing up again, I saw that Aymeric had trained his binoculars on the boat.

'That's not bad, not bad at all . . .' he said, turning towards me. 'You didn't hit the centre, but you got your bullet in the paint of the O, so you were ten centimetres away from your target. For a first shot, at a distance of a hundred metres, I would even say it's very good.'

As we got ready to leave, he advised me to train for a long time on fixed targets, before progressing on to 'moving targets'. Registration letters were perfect as they allowed you to find your bearings precisely. There was no problem about my damaging the boat, he said in response to my objection, he knew the owner (who, in parentheses, was a real idiot), and it would probably never go out to sea again. He left me ten boxes of fifty cartridges.

During the few weeks that followed, I trained for at least two hours every morning. I can't say I 'forgot all my worries', that would be going too far, but it's true that I passed through a period of calm and relative peace every morning. The Captorix also helped, that was undeniable, and my daily doses of alcohol remained moderate; it was also comforting to note that I was on a dose of 15 mg, slightly below the maximum dosage. Stripped of desires and of reasons to live (were those two terms equivalent? That was a difficult topic on which I didn't have a well-formed opinion), I kept my despair at an acceptable level. You can live and be despairing – most people live like that in fact, although sometimes they wonder whether they can allow themselves a whiff of hope; well, at least they ask themselves the question before answering in the negative. And yet they persist, and it's a touching sight.

My shooting was making rapid progress, at a rate that impressed even me; in less than two weeks I managed to get my shots not only in the centre of the O, but also inside the two closed loops of the B and the triangle of the 5; it was then that I started thinking about 'moving targets'. There was no shortage of them on the beach, the most obvious ones being the seabirds.

I had never killed an animal in my life – it wasn't something that had ever presented itself – but in principle I wasn't hostile to the idea. As repelled as I was by industrial animal breeding, I had never had any principled objection to hunting, which lets animals live in their natural environment, and leaves them free to run and fly until they are killed by a predator higher up the food chain. The Steyr Mannlicher HS50 turned me into a predator very high up the food chain, there was no doubt about that; still, I had never had an animal at the other end of my rifle.

I made my mind up one morning, just after ten o'clock. I was very comfortable on my blanket at the top of the slope, the weather was cool and agreeable, and there was no shortage of targets.

I held a bird in the centre of my sights for a long time; it wasn't a seagull or a tern, nothing so famous, just an undistinguished little bird with long legs which I had seen many times on these beaches, a proletarian of the beaches in some sense; in fact a stupid bird, with a mean staring eye, a little killing machine that moved on its long legs, only interrupting its mechanical and predictable motion when it had spotted its prey. By blowing its head off I could save the lives of numerous gastropods, numerous cephalopods too; well, I was introducing a little variation into the food chain without any personal interest as this baleful little avian was probably inedible. I just had to remember that I was a man, a lord and master, and that the universe had been created for my convenience by a just God.

The confrontation lasted a few minutes, at least three, more probably five or ten, then my hands started trembling and I realised that I was incapable of pulling the trigger, I was nothing but a pussy, a sad and insignificant pussy, and an ageing one at that. 'Anyone without the courage to kill lacks the courage to live': the phrase revolved in my head on a loop without creating anything other than a groove of pain. I went back towards the bungalow to get a dozen empty bottles which I placed at random on the edge of the slope before blowing them to pieces in less than two minutes.

Once all the bottles were shattered, I realised that I had reached the end of my supply of cartridges. I hadn't seen Aymeric for almost two weeks, but I had noticed that since the start of the year he had received various visits – often 4x4s or pick-ups parked in the courtyard of the château, and I had seen him walking back to the vehicles with men of his age, dressed in work clothes like him – other local farmers, probably.

Just as I reached the château he was coming out with a man in his fifties whom I had already seen two days previously – a man with a pale, intelligent, sad face; they were both wearing dark suits, with navy blue ties that clashed with the suits; I was immediately certain that he must have lent the other man a tie. He introduced me as 'a friend, renting a bungalow', without mentioning the fact that I had previously worked at the Ministry of Agriculture, for which I was grateful to him. Frank was 'the union representative for La Manche', he added. I waited a few seconds before he explained: 'The Farmers' Federation.' He nodded, doubtfully, then added: 'Every now and again I wonder if we shouldn't join Rural Cooperation. I don't know, I'm not sure, I'm not sure of anything right now . . .'

'We're on our way to a funeral . . .' Aymeric added. 'We have a colleague in Carteret who shot himself two days ago.'

'That's the third one since the start of the year . . .' Frank added. He had planned to organise a union meeting in two days' time, on Sunday afternoon, in Carteret; I was welcome to come along if I wanted.

'We have to do something either way; we can't accept the new lowering of the milk price – if we let that one through we're all fucked, every last one of us, and we might as well give up on the spot.' Before getting into Frank's pick-up, Aymeric gave me an apologetic look; I hadn't talked to him at all about my own emotional life – I realised at that moment that I hadn't said a word about Camille, but as a rule there's no point in saying much; things are self-explanatory, and he must have suspected that they weren't much better for me right now and that the fate of milk-producers would struggle to arouse my compassion.

I returned at about seven in the evening and Aymeric had already had time to get through half a bottle of vodka. The funeral had been as one might imagine; the man who had killed himself had left family, he had never met the right woman, his father was dead and his mother more or less senile, and she had done nothing but sob, saying over and over again that times had changed. 'And I had to explain a few things to Frank . . .' he apologised. 'I had to confess to him that you knew a bit about agricultural matters; but he won't hold it against you, you mustn't think that, he knows that civil servants don't have much room to manoeuvre . . .'

I wasn't a civil servant, which still, incidentally, didn't give me much room to manoeuvre, and I was tempted to move on to vodka myself; why suffer more than you need to? But something held me back, and I asked Aymeric to open a bottle of white wine. He agreed, and sniffed the beverage with surprise before pouring me a glass, as if remembering happier times. 'Are you coming on Sunday?' he asked me almost lightly, as if talking about a pleasant gathering of friends. I didn't know, I said, yes, probably, but was anything going to come out of this meeting? Had an action been decided upon? In his opinion yes, probably yes; the producers were really furious, at the very least they were going to stop delivering milk to cooperatives and factories. Except when milk tankers arrived two or three days later, from Poland or Ireland, what were they going to do? Block the road with rifles? And even if it came to that, what would they do when the tankers came back protected by CRS units? Open fire?

The notion of 'symbolic actions' sprang to mind, but I was paralysed with shame before even finishing my sentence. 'Pour hectolitres of milk on to the forecourt of police head-quarters in Caen . . .' Aymeric added. 'Obviously we could do that but it would get us a day of media coverage, nothing more, and I don't think I want that. I was one of the ones who emptied milk tankers into the Bay of Mont-Saint-Michel in 2009; I have a bad memory of that. Milking like you do every morning, filling the tankers, and then chucking it all away as if it's worthless . . . I think I'd rather get the rifles out.'

Before I set off again, I took some more boxes of cartridges from his cupboard; I didn't imagine that things would develop into an armed confrontation, well, I didn't imagine anything at all, but there was something disturbing about their state of mind; generally nothing happens but sometimes something happens and you're never really prepared for it. A bit of extra shooting practice couldn't hurt anyway.

The union meeting was held at Le Carteret, a huge brasserie on Place du Terminus, which referred, I think, to the old station just opposite, abandoned and already partly invaded by weeds. In terms of catering, Le Carteret mostly offered pizza. I arrived quite late, I'd missed the speeches, but there were still about a hundred farmers sitting around the tables, most of them drinking beers or glasses of white wine. They weren't talking much – there was nothing cheerful about the atmosphere of the meeting – and gave me suspicious looks when I went towards the table where Aymeric was sitting with Frank and three other men who, like him, had sad and reasonable faces, and gave the impression of having studied at least at an agricultural college; well, they were probably other union members but they didn't talk much either. I have to say that the reduction in the price of dairy (I'd done some research in *La Manche Libre* in the meantime) had been very dramatic around this time, a crushing blow, and I failed to see how they could even imagine a basis for possible negotiations.

'Sorry for bothering you . . .' I said, trying to adopt a light tone. Aymeric looked at me uneasily.

'Not at all, not at all . . .' said Frank, who looked even wearier, even more crestfallen than last time.

'Have you decided on a course of action?' I don't know what led me to ask the question – I didn't want to know the answer.

'We're working on it, we're working on it . . .' Then Frank gave me a strange look from below, a little hostile but above all incredibly sad, even desperate; he was talking to me as if from the other side of an abyss, and I started to feel properly embarrassed; I had no business among them, I wasn't one of them, I couldn't be, I didn't lead the same life as they did – my life was hardly brilliant but it wasn't the same – and that was that. I quickly took my leave, I'd stayed for no more than five minutes, but I think when I left I had already understood that this time things could turn really ugly.

During the two days that followed, I remained cloistered in my bungalow, getting through the last of my supplies and trying out various different channels; I tried to masturbate twice. On Wednesday morning, the landscape was drowning in a huge lake of fog that stretched as far as the eye could see; you couldn't see a thing ten metres away from the bungalow but I needed to go out to get more supplies, or at least go to the Carrefour Market in Barneville-Carteret. It took me about half an hour of driving very cautiously, without going over 40 kilometres an hour; every now and again, vague, yellowish halos indicated the presence of another car. Carteret usually had the look of an elegant little seaside resort, with its marina, its shops selling sailing equipment, its gastronomic restaurant offering lobsters from the bay; it now looked like a ghost town, filled with fog, and I didn't encounter a single car on my way to the supermarket, or even a pedestrian; the Carrefour Market, with its almost deserted aisles, looked like the last vestige of civilisation or human occupation; I supplied myself with cheese, charcuterie and red wine, with a deranged but persistent impression that I was going to have to withstand a siege.

I spent the rest of the day walking along the coast road, in a total and muffled silence, passing from one bank of fog to another, without being able to make out the sea below at any point; my life seemed to me to be as shapeless and uncertain as the landscape.

The next morning, passing in front of the door of the château, I saw Aymeric distributing guns to a small group – there were about ten of them – wearing parkas and hunting jackets. Then they got into their vehicles before setting off towards Valognes.

Passing by again at about five o'clock, I saw that Aymeric's pick-up was parked in the courtyard, and I went straight to the dining room: he was sitting with Frank and a third man, a red-haired giant, uneasy-looking, who was introduced to me as Barnabé. Apparently they had just arrived; they had kept their guns within reach and poured themselves some vodka, but hadn't yet taken off their coats – I noticed then that it was terribly cold in the room as Aymeric seemed to have given up heating the place and I wasn't sure that he got undressed to go to bed either – he seemed to be giving up a fair number of things.

'This morning we stopped the milk tankers coming from the port of Le Havre . . . It was Irish and Brazilian milk. They didn't expect to find themselves face to face with armed men and left without any problems. Except it's almost certain that they went to the police station immediately afterwards. What are we going to do tomorrow, when they come back with a CRS unit? We're still at the same point; we're at the brink.'

'We've got to hold our ground; they won't dare shoot at us, they can't do that,' the red-haired giant pleaded.

'No, they won't fire first . . .' Frank cut in. 'But they'll charge us and try to disarm us; confrontation is inevitable. The question is whether we fire too. In any case, if we resist we'll be spending tomorrow night at the station in Saint-Lô. But if there are dead or wounded it'll be a different story.'

I glanced incredulously at Aymeric who said nothing, turning his glass in his hands; he looked stubborn and morose, avoiding my eye, and I said to myself right then that I really had to intervene, or try to intervene, if it was still possible. 'Listen!' I said at last, raising my voice, without the faintest idea of what I was going to say next.

'Yes . . . ?' This time he raised his head and looked straight into my eyes, with the same open and honest expression that he had had when we were twenty, and which had immediately made me fall for him. 'Tell me, Florent . . .' he continued very gently, 'tell me what you think, I'll listen to your point of view. Are we really fucked, can we really try to do anything? Do I have to try to do anything? Or do I have to behave like my father, sell up the farm, renew my membership at the Jockey

Club and end my life peacefully like that? Tell me what you think.'

It was inevitable from the start that we would end up there; we had put off this conversation for over twenty years since my first visit when he had just set up as a farmer and I was embarking on a more banal career as an executive, but now the time had come, and the other two abruptly fell silent; it was between the two of us now, him and me.

Aymeric waited, straight-backed and candid, his eyes fixed on mine, and I started talking without even being fully aware of what I was saying; I had a sense of sliding down a slope, and it was dizzying and a little bit sickening, like each time you plunge into reality; at the same time, that doesn't happen very often in a life. 'You see,' I said, 'from time to time you shut down a factory or you move a production unit, and let's say there are seventy workers fired, so then there's a report on BFM, there's a picket, they burn some tyres, one or two local politicians speak up, it becomes a news story with an interesting subject and a powerful visual aspect: the steel industry isn't the same as lingerie, and there are pictures to show. Here, for example, you've got hundreds of farmers shutting up shop every year.'

'Or blowing their brains out . . .' Frank intervened then waved his hand as if to apologise for having spoken, and his face became sad and impenetrable again.

'Or blowing their brains out,' I agreed. 'The number of farmers has dropped dramatically over the past fifty years in France, but it still hasn't dropped enough. You still need to divide it by two or three to reach European standards, the standards of Denmark or Holland – well, I mention those because we're talking about dairy products, but for fruit it would be Morocco or Spain. Right now there are just over sixty thousand milk producers; in fifteen years, in my opinion, there will be twenty thousand. In short, what's happening in French agriculture right now is a huge social plan, the biggest social plan in operation, but it's a secret, invisible social plan, in which people disappear individually, in their corners, without ever providing a theme for a news item on BFM.'

Aymeric shook his head with a satisfaction that pained me because at that moment I understood that he didn't expect anything else from me, and was just waiting for objective confirmation of the disaster, and I had nothing, absolutely nothing, to suggest to him, apart from my absurd Moldovan reveries – and the worst thing was that I hadn't finished.

'Once we've divided the number of farmers by three,' I continued, this time sensing that I was at the heart of the failure of my professional life, and destroying myself with every word I uttered; at the same time, if I had had personal success to field, or if I had managed to create the happiness of a woman or at least an animal, but I hadn't even done that, 'We still won't have won when we've reached European standards; we'll be on the brink of definitive defeat, because then we'll really be in contact with the world market and we won't win the battle of global production.'

'And do you think there will never be protectionist measures? Does that strike you as absolutely impossible?' Frank's tone was strangely detached and absent, as if he was enquiring into curious local superstitions.

'Absolutely impossible,' I cut in without hesitation. 'The

ideological pressure is too great.' Thinking back to my professional past, to my years of professional life, I realised that I had been confronted, in fact, with a strange cast of superstitions. My interlocutors weren't fighting for their interests, or even for the interests that they were supposed to defend, and it would have been a mistake to believe as much: they were fighting for ideas; for years, I had been confronted with people who were ready to die for free trade.

'So there you have it,' I said, turning back towards Aymeric, 'if you ask me, it's all fucked, it's really fucked, so what I advise you to do is try to save your own arse. Cécile was a fat slut, let her fuck her pianist, and forget your daughters, move, sell the farm again, forget the whole thing – if you do that straight away you still have a small chance of starting your life again.'

This time I had been clear, I could hardly have been any clearer, and I only stayed for a few minutes. Just as I was getting up to go, Aymeric gave me a weird look in which I thought I could read a hint of amusement – but it was, perhaps, more probably a hint of madness.

The next day I was able to follow the development of the conflict on BFM – a short report. They had finally decided to lift the blockade without resistance and let through the milk tankers coming from the port of Le Havre for the factories in Méautis and Valognes. Frank had been able to give an interview lasting almost a minute, in which he set out – very clearly, succinctly and convincingly, I found, using few numbers – the ways in which the situation of stockbreeders in Normandy had become untenable. He concluded that the battle was just starting, and that the Farmers' Federation and Rural Cooperation were together calling for a big day of action the following Sunday. Aymeric was beside him during the whole interview but he didn't say anything, merely playing mechanically with the firing pin of his assault rifle. I emerged from that report in a probably temporary and paradoxical state of optimism: Frank had been so clear, so moderate and so lucid in his intervention – I thought it would have been impossible to do better in a minute-long interview – that I didn't see how anyone could fail to respond to it, how in the face of such argument anyone could refuse to negotiate. Then I turned off the television, looked out of the window of my bungalow – it was just after six and the swirls of fog were gradually fading as night fell – and I remembered that for almost fifteen years I too had *always* been right in summaries defending the point of view of local farmers; I had *always* produced realistic figures suggesting reasonable protection measures and economically viable short circuits, but I was just an agronomist, a technician, and at the end of the day I had *always* been told I was wrong, things had *always* toppled at the last minute towards the triumph of free trade, towards the race for higher productivity; then I opened a fresh bottle of wine. Night, *Nacht ohne Ende*, had now settled on the landscape – who was I to imagine I could change the course of the world?

The Normandy dairy farmers had been summoned to converge in the centre of Pont-l'Évêque at lunchtime on Sunday. Hearing the news on BFM, I thought at first that it was a symbolic choice, designed to ensure good media coverage for the demonstration – the name of the cheese was known all over France, and even beyond. In fact, as the sequence of events would show, Pont-l'Évêque had been chosen because it was at the intersection of the branch of the A13 coming from Deauville and the A13 Caen–Paris.

When I got up early in the morning the west wind had totally dispersed the fog; the ocean was sparkling, stirred by the most delicate waves, far off into the distance. The perfectly clear light offered a range of vivid shades of very bright blue; for the first time I thought I could make out the shores of an island on the horizon. I went out again with my binoculars: yes, it was amazing, given the distance, but one could just make out a soft green lip of land, which must have been the east coast of Jersey.

In weather like this it seemed as if nothing dramatic could ever happen, and I really had no desire to be confronted by the misery of the farmers; sitting down at the wheel of my 4x4, I more or less felt like going for a walk on the cliffs at Flamanville, perhaps carrying on all the way to the Nez de Jobourg; on a day like this it was very likely that you would be able to see the coasts of Alderney; I briefly thought again of the birdwatcher; perhaps his hopeless quest had taken him much further away, to much darker zones; perhaps at this very moment he was crouching in a prison in Manila, where the other prisoners had already given him a going-over, his swollen and bleeding body covered by a flood of cockroaches, his mouth, with its broken teeth, unable to stem the flow of insects sliding down his throat. That unpleasant image was the first hitch in the progress of the morning. There was a second one when, while passing by the hangar where Aymeric kept his agricultural machinery, I saw him going back and forth, storing jerrycans of fuel on the bed of his pick-up. Why jerrycans of fuel? It didn't bode well. I turned off the engine, hesitating; did I need to go and talk to him? But to say what? What else could I say to him, about our last evening? People never listen to the advice you give them, and when they ask for advice it's specifically with a view to not following it, and have it confirmed by an external voice that they are stuck in a spiral of annihilation and death; the advice one gives them plays exactly the same role for them as that of the tragic choir, confirming to the hero that he has taken the path of destruction and chaos.

But it was a beautiful morning; I couldn't really quite

believe it yet and, after a brief hesitation, I set off again towards Flamanville.

My walk on the cliffs was unfortunately a failure. And yet never had the light been so beautiful, never had the air been so fresh and reinvigorating, never had the green of the meadows been so intense, never had the reflection of the sun on the wavelets of the almost flat ocean been so enchanting; neither, I think, had I ever been so unhappy. I carried on to the Nez de Jobourg and it was even worse; it was probably inevitable that the image of Kate would return to me – the blue of the sky was even deeper, the light more crystalline, it was now a northern light – and I saw again her eyes turned towards me in the park of Schwerin Castle, her expression tolerant and gentle, already forgiving me; and then other memories returned to me from some older days, during a walk we had taken together on the dunes at Sonderborg – that was it, her parents lived in Sonderborg and the light that morning was exactly the same – I took refuge for a few minutes at the wheel of my G 350 and I closed my eyes, weird little shocks ran through my body but I didn't cry; apparently I had no tears left.

At about eleven o'clock in the morning, I headed towards Pont-l'Évêque. The B-road was blocked by tractors parked in the middle of the thoroughfare two kilometres before the entry to the town. There were many of them all the way to the town centre, several hundred; the absence of the forces of law and order was a bit surprising, but that said the farmers seemed rather calm, picnicking and drinking beers near their vehicles. I called Aymeric's mobile without getting a reply, then continued for several minutes on foot before realising: I had no chance of finding him in this crowd. I went back to my car and turned back towards Pierrefitte-en-Auge, before turning off towards a hill overlooking the motorway junction. I had barely parked for two minutes when events escalated. A small group of ten or so pick-ups, among which I recognised Aymeric's Nissan Navara, was coming slowly down the access road of the A13. One last car, slaloming a little, had time to get past them with a roar of its horn, before they blocked the road towards Paris. They had chosen their location well: immediately after a straight line of at least two kilometres, visibility was perfect, and cars had broadly enough time to brake. The traffic was still flowing that early in the morning, but a traffic jam formed quite quickly; there were a few more honks of car horns, more and more infrequent, before silence fell.

The commando unit was made up of about twenty farmers; eight of them had taken up position on the back of their pick-ups, training their guns on the car drivers, and there was a space of about fifty metres between them and the first cars. Aymeric was in the middle, clutching his Schmeisser assault rifle. He was relaxed, very much at ease, and nonchalantly lit what looked to me like a joint – to tell the truth, I had never seen him smoking anything else. Frank was on his right – I sensed that he was a lot more nervous – gripping what looked to me like a simple hunting rifle. The other farmers started unloading the jerrycans of fuel stored on the beds of the pick-ups before carrying them about fifty metres back and arranging them along the whole length of the motorway.

They had more or less finished when the first CRS armoured vehicle appeared on the horizon. The slowness of the intervention would be the subject of numerous controversies; having witnessed what happened, I can say that it was really difficult to get through, even though they frantically activated their sirens, and the car drivers (most of whom had braked at the last minute, meaning various cars had crashed into each other on the road) simply had no way of moving; they would have had to leave their armoured vehicle and continue on foot – it was the only option, and that was the sole rebuke that one could, in my view, honestly make towards the commander of the unit.

At the same time, just as the authorities were arriving in the vicinity of the site of the confrontation, the farming machines came down the access road; they were huge great things, a combine harvester and a maize forager almost as wide as the access road itself, their drivers perched four metres off the ground. The two machines parked heavily, definitively, in the middle of the jerrycans, before their drivers leapt from their seats and came and joined their comrades; now I understood what they were preparing to do, and I had trouble believing it. To get hold of the farming machinery they would have had to contact CUMA, the Agricultural Cooperative, probably the branch in Calvados; the image of the offices of CUMA, a short walk from DRAF; the image of the receptionist (an unhappy old divorcee who had never completely succeeded in giving up sex, and that had given rise to no shortage of distressing incidents) briefly ran through my mind. The farmers must at least have shown their ID to get hold of a combine harvester (and what on earth could they have told them? It wasn't silage season, let alone harvest time), it wasn't possible otherwise – those machines were worth several hundred thousand euros, and they were legally responsible – they wouldn't get out of this one now; it was impossible, they had driven themselves into a cul-de-sac, a shortcut to suicide, *brother*?

Then it all happened at surprising speed, like a perfect sequence repeated at length; as soon as the two drivers of the machines had joined the others, a big, sturdy, red-haired man (I thought I recognised Barnabé, the man I had seen at Aymeric's a short time before) got a rocket-launcher from the back of his pick-up, and calmly loaded it.

There were two rockets fired in the direction of the fuel tanks of the machines. Combustion was instantaneous: two huge fountains of flame shot towards the sky before coming together, and a huge cloud of smoke appeared, blackish and properly Dantesque; I would never have suspected that agricultural fuel could produce such black smoke. It was during those few seconds that most of the photographs were taken, the ones that were then reproduced in newspapers all around the world – and in particular the one of Aymeric, which would make so many front pages, from the *Corriere della Sera* to the *New York Times*. He was already commandingly handsome; the puffiness of his face seemed to have mysteriously disappeared and he looked peaceful, almost amused, his long fair hair floating in the breeze that had just risen at that very second; a joint still hung from the corner of his mouth, and he held his Schmeisser assault rifle half upright against his hip; the setting was one of absolute and abstract violence, a column of flames twisted against a backdrop of black smoke; but at that second Aymeric seemed happy, well, almost happy – he seemed in his place at the very least, his expression and relaxed pose reflected an unbelievable insolence; he was one of the eternal images of rebellion, and that was what led to the image being picked up by so many daily newspapers around the world. Also – and I was certainly one of the only ones who understood – he was the Aymeric I had always known: a nice guy, nice to the core and even good; he had simply wanted to be happy and had devoted himself to a rustic dream of durable, high-value production, and to Cécile, but Cécile had turned out to be a fat slut excited by life in London with a high-society pianist; and the European Union had also been a fat slut with that business about milk quotas; he certainly wouldn't have expected things to end up like this.

In spite of all that, I don't understand, I still don't understand, why things ended up as they did; various respectable configurations of life were still available as options; I didn't think I'd been overdoing it with my story about the Moldovan girl – it was even compatible with the Jockey Club – and there is certainly a Moldovan kind of nobility, nobility exists more or less everywhere – well, we could certainly have cobbled together a scenario, but the fact remains that at some point Aymeric raised his weapon, placed it clearly in the firing position and advanced towards the line of CRS.

They had had time to get into an acceptable combat formation; a second armoured vehicle had arrived in the meantime and had driven a few journalists away without much ceremony; they had protested of course, but had yielded in the face of the simple manly threat of a good truncheon blow to the head; there was no need for them to even show their weapons – though that's easier in any case when you're dealing with a bunch of softies – well, they had withdrawn to a spot some way down from the action (the journalists in question were already tweeting their protests about attacks on press freedom, but that wasn't the job of the CRS – there were spokespeople for that kind of thing).

Either way, the line of CRS men was there, about thirty metres away as far as I could see from the line of farmers. It was a compact, slightly curved line, militarily acceptable, defined by a rampart of reinforced Plexiglas shields.

For a while I thought I was the only witness to what was about to happen, but I wasn't in fact; a BFM cameraman had managed to hide in a bush on the slope of the motorway embankment, escaping the CRS raid, and he would produce perfectly clear images of the event – which were later broadcast for two hours on the channel before it issued a public apology and took them down, but it was too late; the sequence had appeared on social media and by mid-afternoon it had had over a million views; the voyeurism of the television channels was once again, and rightly, stigmatised; it would have been better in fact for that video to have been used at the inquiry, and only the inquiry.

With his assault rifle comfortably resting at hip level, Aymeric began a slow rotating motion, aiming at one CRS man after another. They tightened their formation and the width of the line shortened by at least a metre; there was quite a loud noise when their Plexiglas shields collided, then silence. The other farmers had picked up their rifles and were advancing in front of Aymeric while also aiming their weapons; but they only had hunting rifles, and the CRS obviously understood that Aymeric's Schmeisser, with a calibre of 223, was the only one that could shatter their shields and pierce their bulletproof vests. And in retrospect I think it was that – the extreme slowness of Aymeric's movements – that led to the tragedy, but also the strange expression on his face; he looked as if he was *ready for anything*, and luckily there aren't many men who are *ready for everything*, but they can do considerable damage and those ordinary CRS men, usually based in Caen, knew that in a rather theoretical way; they weren't prepared to confront this danger and the people from GIGN or RAID would probably have kept their cool for longer – that rebuke was levelled often enough at the Minister of the Interior – but how can you predict these things; they weren't international terrorists, they were, at least at first, a bunch of farmers demonstrating. Aymeric seemed amused, sincerely amused and mocking, but very distant too, somewhere else, frankly – I don't think I've ever seen anyone so *far away* – and I remember because I briefly had the idea of going down the slope and running towards him, but at the very moment when it came to me I understood that it was pointless and nothing friendly or human would be able to reach him at that final moment.

He turned slowly, from left to right, aiming individually at each CRS man behind his shield (in any case they couldn't shoot first, I was sure; but that was in fact the only certainty that I had). Then he made the same movement in reverse, from right to left; then, slowing down again, he came back towards the middle and froze for a few seconds – I think less than five. Then a different expression passed across his face, like that of general pain; he turned the barrel around, placed it under his chin and pulled the trigger.

His body collapsed backwards, noisily striking the metal bed of the pick-up; there was no spurt of blood or brain – nothing like that – everything was strangely sober and flat; but nobody apart from me and the BFM cameraman had seen what had just happened. Two metres in front of him, Frank yelled and fired his gun towards the CRS without even aiming; several other farmers immediately imitated him. It was all clearly established in the course of the inquest, by a viewing of the tape: contrary to what his comrades had believed not only had the CRS not killed Aymeric, but they had taken four or five shots before returning fire. The fact remains that in returning fire – and this was the subject of another, more serious controversy – the CRS didn't do half-measures; nine farmers were killed on the spot; and a tenth died during the night at the general hospital in Caen, together with one CRS man, bringing the number of victims to eleven. Nothing like this had been seen in France for a very long time, and certainly not at a farmers' demonstration. I learned that a little later in the media, over the next few days. I don't know how I managed to get back to Canville-la-Rocque the same day; there are automatic reflexes for driving; there are automatic reflexes for pretty much everything, it seems.

I woke up very late the next morning in a state of nausea and disbelief that was close to spasm; none of what had happened seemed possible or real; Aymeric couldn't have shot himself, it couldn't end like that. I had experienced a similar phenomenon once, a very long time ago, coming down from acid, but it was infinitely less serious: no one had died, there was just the matter of a girl who couldn't remember if she'd agreed to be fucked in the arse; well, young people's problems. I turned on the coffee machine, swallowed my Captorix pill and undid the wrapping on a new carton of Philip Morris before turning on BFM, and everything immediately blew up in my face. I hadn't dreamt the previous day; BFM was showing exactly the same pictures that I remembered – which they tried to match with appropriate political comments – but either way the previous day's events really had happened: the ambient noise among the dairy farmers of Manche and Calvados had crystallised into drama, a local disagreement had solidified into a short sequence of extreme violence, and a historical configuration matched with a mini-narrative had been organised immediately. That configuration was local, but it would plainly have global repercussions: political commentaries were gradually appearing on the news channel, and I was surprised by their general tenor: everyone as usual condemned the violence, deplored the tragedy and the extremism of certain agitators; but among senior politicians there was an unease, an embarrassment rarely associated with them, and they all emphasised that one had to understand the distress and anger of the farmers up to a certain point, the dairy farmers in particular; the scandal of the abolition of milk quotas returned like an obsessive, guilty, unspoken question that nobody could quite shake off: only the National Assembly seemed to be entirely clear on the subject. The unbearable conditions that large-scale distribution was placing on producers was also a shameful subject that everyone, apart from the communists perhaps – I learned on this occasion that there was still a Communist Party, and that it even had Members of Parliament – preferred to try and avoid. I realised with a mixture of alarm and disgust that Aymeric's suicide might have a political effect where nothing else had. For my part there was only one certainty – I had to leave, I had to find a new place to stay. I thought about the Internet connection in the byre; it was bound to function, there was no reason why it wouldn't.

A police van was parked in the courtyard of the château. I drove in as well. Two *gendarmes*, one maybe fifty and the other about thirty-five, had stopped by the cupboard where Aymeric kept his guns, and were examining them carefully. They were plainly captivated by this arsenal; they were exchanging comments in low voices which I imagine were judicious – that was more or less their job, after all – and I had to say 'Hello!' loudly for them to pay me any attention. I had a brief moment of panic when the older man turned towards me – I thought again of the Steyr Mannlicher – but I immediately came to my senses; I said to myself that it must have been the first time they had seen Aymeric's guns, so they had no reason to suspect that one was missing – two even, with the Smith & Wesson. Obviously if they checked the gun licences and cross-checked, there was the risk of a problem, but tomorrow takes care of tomorrow as Ecclesiastes says, more or less. I explained to them that I was staying in one of the bungalows, but didn't add that I knew Aymeric. I wasn't worried in the slightest: for them I was an insignificant element, a kind of tourist; they had no reason to complicate their lives with me and their task couldn't have been easy anyway: it was a peaceful department, where criminality barely existed – Aymeric had told me that people often left their doors open when they went away during the day, which was rare these days even in a rural area – in short, they had probably never encountered a situation like this before.

'Ah yes, the bungalows . . .' the older officer said as if emerging from a long daydream, seemingly having forgotten the very existence of the bungalows.

'I've got to leave now,' I went on. 'That's all I've got to do.'

'Yes, you've got to leave,' the older man confirmed. 'That's all you have to do.'

'You were supposed to be on holiday,' the younger man said. 'That's a shame for you.'

All three of us nodded, satisfied that our analyses converged. 'I'll be back straight away,' I concluded, slightly strangely, to bring the conversation to an end. As I passed through the door I turned round: they were already immersed once more in their examination of the rifles and carbines.

In the byre, I was welcomed by long, worried, plaintive moos; of course, I said to myself, they haven't been fed or milked this morning, and they should probably also have been fed last night; did cows have regular mealtimes? I had no idea.

I went back up to the château and joined the *gendarmes* in front of the gun rack; they still seemed to be immersed in impenetrable meditations, probably of a ballistic and technical nature; they must also have been saying to themselves that if all the local farmers were similarly armed they risked having difficulties in case of serious trouble. I informed them of the cows' situation. 'Ah yes, the cows . . .' the older man sad sadly. 'What are we going to do with the cows?' Well, I don't know, feed them, or call someone who can – in the end it was their problem, not mine. 'I'm going to leave straight away,' I went on. 'Yes, of course, you're going to leave straight away,' the younger man agreed, as if it was clearly the only thing to do, as if he was wishing me to go. It was as I thought: the police officers seemed to be trying to tell me they really didn't need any additional problems, in fact they seemed completely overwhelmed by the scale of what would happen, and by the minute detail with which the police hierarchy would be picking apart their report into the 'aristocratic martyr to the farmers' cause', as they were starting to call him in certain newspapers, and I returned to my 4x4 without another word being exchanged.

In the end I didn't have the will to look on the Internet for a place to stay, particularly as I was accompanied by the plaintive mooing of the cows; to tell the truth, I didn't have the will to do anything so I drove around completely at random for a few kilometres, in an almost totally blank mental state, with my last perceptual faculties entirely devoted to looking for a hotel. The first one I noticed was called Hostellerie de la Baie; I hadn't even noticed the name of the village, but the landlord would later tell me it was Regnéville-sur-Mer. For two days I lay prostrate in my room, still taking my Captorix but unable to get up, wash or even unpack my suitcase. I was incapable of thinking of the future, or indeed of the past, and not the present either, but the immediate future in particular posed a problem. To avoid alarming the landlord, I explained that I was a friend of one of the farmers killed in the demonstration, that I had been there when it had happened. His rather pleasant face darkened all of a sudden; clearly, like everyone who lived in the region, he was on the side of the farmers. 'I say they did the right thing!' he stated firmly. 'Things couldn't go on like that – there are things that can't be allowed, there are times when you have to react . . .' I wasn't tempted to contradict him, not least because deep down I felt more or less the same.

On the evening of the second day I got up to go shopping. On the way out of the village there was a little restaurant called Chez Maryvonne. The rumour that I was a friend of 'Monsieur d'Harcourt' must have spread around the village, and I was given a kind and respectful welcome by the owner:

she asked with concern several times if I didn't need anything else, if I was sitting in a draught, etc. The few other
customers were local farmers drinking glasses of white wine
at the bar; I was the only one eating. From time to time they
swapped a few words in a low voice and I recognised the
word 'CRS' several times, uttered with rage. I sensed a
strange atmosphere around me in this café, almost *ancien
régime*, as if 1789 had only left superficial traces; from one
moment to the next I expected a farmer to mention Aymeric
and call him 'our gentleman'.

The next day I went to Coutance, which was immersed in fog;
you could hardly make out the spires of the cathedral which,
having said that, seemed to be very elegant. The town in
general was peaceful, leafy and beautiful. I bought a *Figaro*
in the bar that doubled as a newsagent's and tobacconist's,
and set about reading it in the Taverne du Parvis, a huge
brasserie that stood right in the cathedral square, and which
was also a restaurant and a hotel, with early 1900s decor, all
wood and leather chairs, and some art nouveau lamps; well,
it was visibly *the place to be* in Coutances. I was in search of
some background analysis, or at least the official position of
the Republicans, but there was nothing of the kind; instead,
there was a long article devoted to Aymeric, whose funeral
had been held the previous day – the ceremony had been
celebrated in Bayeux cathedral in the presence of a 'dense
and contemplative crowd', the paper explained. 'The tragic
end of a great French family' seemed excessive – he did have
two sisters, after all, though that might pose a problem in

passing on the aristocratic title, but such things were outside my area of expertise.

I found a cybercafé two streets further on, run by two Arabs who looked so similar that they must have been twins, and whose Salafist look was so extreme that they were probably harmless. I imagined they must be bachelors living together, or perhaps they were married to twin sisters and lived in adjacent houses; anyway, it was that kind of relationship.

There were a fair few websites – there are websites for everything these days – and I struck lucky with *aristocrates. org*, or perhaps it was *noblesse.net*, I can't remember now. I knew that Aymeric had come from an old family but I didn't know how old, and I was quite impressed. The founder of the dynasty was one Bernard the Dane, companion to Rollon, the Viking chief who had gained possession of Normandy in 911 with the treaty of Saint-Clair-sur-Epte. Then the three brothers, Errand, Robert and Anquetil d'Harcourt, had taken part in the conquest of England beside William the Conqueror. By way of reward they had received suzerainty over vast domains on either side of the Channel, and had consequently experienced certain difficulties in choosing which side to take during the Hundred Years War; however, they ended up opting for the Capetians to the detriment of the Plantagenets – well, apart from Geoffroy d'Harcourt, known as 'the Lame', who played quite an ambiguous role in the 1340s for which he was emphatically reproached by Chateaubriand, but with that one exception they became loyal servants of the French crown and provided a considerable number of ambassadors, priests and senior military officers to the country. There was still, however, an

English branch whose motto, 'The good time will come', was far from appropriate in the circumstances. Aymeric's violent death on the bed of his Nissan Navara pick-up seemed to me to be both in line with and contrary to the vocation of his family, and I wondered what his father would have thought of it; Aymeric had died with his gun in his hand protecting the French peasantry, which had always been the mission of the aristocracy; on the other hand, he had committed suicide, which did not look like the passing of a Christian knight; it would have been preferable, all in all, for him to have taken two or three CRS men with him.

My research had taken me some time, and one of the two brothers offered me a mint tea, which I refused – I had always hated the stuff – but I did accept a fizzy drink. As I sipped my Sprite Orange, I was aware once again that my initial plan had been to find somewhere to stay, preferably in the region and preferably that very night – I didn't yet feel up to going back to Paris, where there was nothing calling me back in any case. My idea had been to find a holiday cottage to rent somewhere near Falaise; it took me just over an hour of additional research to find the appropriate spot, between Flers and Falaise, in a village answering to the strange name of Putanges, which sounded like a combination of *pute* (whore) and *ange* (angel) and inevitably led to Pascalian circumlocutions, such as 'Woman is neither angel nor whore', 'They who wish to behave like angels behave like whores', etc. Having said that, it didn't mean very much, but the meaning of the original had always escaped me anyway – what could Pascal have been trying to say? My lack of sex drive probably brought me closer to the angel, at least that's what my small knowledge of angelology told me, but how did that lead me to behave like a beast as suggested by the original? I didn't get it.

Either way, the owner of the cottage was easy to get hold of and, yes, the place was available for an indeterminate amount of time, available that very evening if I wished; it was quite difficult to find, he warned me, isolated in the middle of the woods, and so we agreed to meet at 6.00 p.m. at the foot of Putanges church.

Isolated in the middle of the woods, I would need to buy some food. Various posters had informed me of the existence of a Centre Leclerc in Coutances, with a Leclerc Drive, a Leclerc filling station, a Leclerc bookshop and a travel agent's – also Leclerc. There was no Leclerc undertaker's, but that seemed to be the only service missing.

I had never, at that point, set foot in a Leclerc Centre. I was dazzled. Never would I have imagined the existence of such a well-stocked shop – that kind of thing was inconceivable in Paris. Apart from that, I had spent my childhood in Senlis, an outmoded, bourgeois town, even anachronistic in some respects – and my parents had insisted, until their death, on supporting the existence of local shops through their purchases. As to Méribel, let's not even mention it: it was an artificial, re-created place, far from the authentic flux of global trade, a pure piece of touristic play-acting. The Centre Leclerc in Coutances was something else; there, you were really in the presence of large-scale, massive-scale, retail distribution. Foodstuffs from every continent were displayed along interminable shelves, and I felt almost dizzy as I thought of the mobilised logistics, the vast container vessels crossing uncertain oceans.

> *See on these canals*
> *The vessels slumber*
> *With their vagabond mood;*
> *It is to satisfy*
> *Your every desire*
> *That they come from the ends of the earth.*

After an hour of strolling, and with my trolley already more than half full, I couldn't help thinking once again about the imaginary Moldovan girl to whom Aymeric could and should have brought happiness, and who would now be dying in an obscure corner of the Moldova of her birth, without even suspecting the existence of this paradise. Order and beauty – that was the least one could say. Luxury, calm and delight, really. Poor Moldovan girl; and poor Aymeric.

The house was in Saint-Aubert-sur-Orne; it was a hamlet dependent on Putanges, but it didn't appear on every GPS, the owner explained. He was in his forties, like me, his grey hair cut very short, almost shorn, like mine, and he had the air of someone quite sinister, the kind of man that scares me; he drove a Mercedes G class, a point in common between middle-aged men that helps a germ of communication come to life. Even better than that, he had a G 500 and I had a G 350, which established an acceptable mini-hierarchy between us. He came from Caen; I wondered what he did for a living, I couldn't quite place him. He was an architect, he told me. A failed architect, he said by way of clarification. Well, like most architects, he added. Amongst other things he was responsible for Appart'City in the urban redevelopment zone in Caen Nord where Camille had lived for a week before really entering my life; that wasn't anything to brag about, he observed; no, it really wasn't.

He obviously wanted to know how long I planned to stay;

that was a good question, it could have been three days or three years. We agreed quite easily on a one-month lease, automatically renewable; I would pay him rent at the beginning of every month, a cheque was probably OK as he could put them through his business account. It wasn't even to save on taxes, he added with disgust, it's just that it was boring filling in the tax declaration – he never knew if he was supposed to put it under BZ or BY, so it was simpler not to put anything at all; I wasn't surprised, I had spotted that casual attitude among independent professionals before. He never came back to the house, and he was beginning to have a sense that he never would; since his divorce two years previously he had lost a lot of his motivation with regard to property, and lots of other things too. Our lives were so similar that it was almost becoming oppressive.

He had few tenants, and anyway none before the summer months, and would see about taking the notice off the website. And even in the summer, business wasn't very good. 'There's no Internet,' he said to me, suddenly anxious, 'I hope you knew that – I'm pretty sure I mentioned it on the website.' I told him I did know and that I had accepted the idea. I then saw a brief movement of fear in his eyes. There can be no shortage of depressives who want to isolate themselves, spend a few months in the woods to 'come to terms with themselves'; but people who agree to cut themselves off from the Internet for an indefinite period without even wincing are up to no good – I read that in his anxious expression. 'I'm not going to kill myself,' I said with a smile that I hoped was disarming, but which must in reality have been quite creepy. 'Well, not right now,' I added by way of confession.

He groaned and concentrated on the technical aspects of the house, which were incidentally quite simple. The electric radiators were regulated by a thermostat and I just had to turn a button to get the desired temperature; hot water came directly from the boiler; I had absolutely nothing to do. I could make a wood fire if I wanted; he showed me the fire-lighters, the store of logs. Mobile phones worked more or less, SFR not at all, Bouygues quite well, Orange he had forgotten about. Otherwise there was a landline, but he hadn't put in a metering system because he preferred to trust people, he added with a wave of his arm that he seemed to use to mock his own attitude, he just hoped I wasn't going to spend my nights calling Japan. 'Certainly not Japan,' I cut in with an abruptness that I hadn't premeditated; he frowned and I sensed that he wanted to ask me some questions to try to find out more, but after a few seconds he gave up, turned around and headed for his 4x4. I thought we would see each other again, that this was the start of a relationship, but before setting off he handed me a business card: 'My address, for the rent . . .'

So now I was on earth, as Rousseau writes in his *Reveries*, without any brother, neighbour, friend, or society but myself. That was accurate enough, but the resemblance stopped there: in the following sentence Rousseau proclaimed himself 'the most sociable and the most loving of humans'. I didn't fall under that category; I have mentioned Aymeric, I have mentioned certain women, the final list is short. Unlike Rousseau, neither could I say that I had been 'banished from human society by unanimous agreement'; humanity was not at all in league against me; it was simply that there hadn't been anything, that my connection with the world, which had already been limited, had gradually dwindled to zero, until nothing could halt that slide.

I turned up the thermostat before deciding to go to sleep, or at least to lie down on the bed – sleeping was something else – it was the heart of winter, the days had started to lengthen but the nights were still long, and in the middle of the woods they would be impenetrable.

I finally slipped into fitful sleep, not without repeated recourse to an aged calvados from the Centre Leclerc in Coutances. There had not been a single dream before it, but I was woken abruptly in the dead of night by the sense of something brushing or caressing my shoulders. I got back up and paced around the room to calm down, and went to the window: the darkness was total, it must have been during that phase of the moon when it is completely concealed and not a single star could be seen, the cloud cover was too low. It was two o'clock in the morning, only halfway through the night, in monasteries it was the hour when the vigils are held; I turned on every available light without really feeling reassured: I had dreamt about Camille, that was certain, in my dream it was Camille who had caressed my shoulders, as she used to do every night a few years ago, many years ago in fact. I hardly expected that I would still be happy, but I still hoped to escape dementia, pure and simple.

I lay down and glanced around the room in a circle: it

formed a perfect equilateral triangle, the two sloping walls met in the middle where the roof beam was. Then I understood the trap that had closed on me: it was in a bedroom precisely identical to this one that I had slept with Camille every night in Clécy during the first three months of our life together. There was nothing surprising about coincidences as such, all Norman houses are built on more or less the same lines, and we were only twenty kilometres from Clécy; but I hadn't anticipated this: the two houses didn't look similar from the outside as the one in Clécy was half-timbered, while the walls of this one were rough stone – probably sandstone. I got dressed hastily and went back down to the dining room; it was freezing and the fire hadn't taken; I had never been good at lighting fires. I didn't understand the assembly of logs and kindling that you were supposed to build – so in many respects I was a long way from being the model of masculinity – Harrison Ford, let's say – that I would have liked to be; well, for now that wasn't the issue and an excruciating pain twisted my heart while memories came back in a steady flow; it isn't the future but the past that kills you, that comes back to torment and undermine you, and effectively ends up killing you. The dining room was also identical to the one in which I had dined for three months with Camille after shopping at the artisanal *boucherie-charcuterie* in Clécy, at the equally artisanal *boulangerie–patisserie*, at various greengrocers' shops as well, and after she had *set to work at the stove* with that enthusiasm that is so painful in retrospect. I recognised the row of copper saucepans, which gleamed gently on the stone wall. I recognised the massive walnut dresser, its shelves perforated to show off the Rouen porcelain, with its colourful and naive pattern, to its best advantage. I recognised the oak grandfather clock, stopped forever at some point in the past at one o'clock – some people stopped them at the death of a son or a close relative; others at the time of France's declaration of war on Germany in 1914; others at the time when the vote was taken for absolute power to be granted to Marshal Pétain.

I couldn't stay there like that, and picked up a big metal key that gave access to the other wing; it wasn't very habitable right now, the architect had warned me, and was impossible to heat, but well, if I stayed until the summer I'd be able to enjoy it. I found myself in an enormous room, which in other times must have been the main room in the house, and which was now filled with a stack of armchairs and garden furniture, but a whole wall was occupied by bookshelves on which I was surprised to discover a complete works of the Marquis de Sade. It must have been from the 19th century; it was fully leather-bound with various gilded flourishes on the boards and the edge – fuck, that must have cost an arm and a leg, I said to myself briefly, flicking through the book which was illustrated with numerous engravings; well, I lingered particularly over the engravings and the curious point was that I didn't understand them at all: different sexual positions were represented involving varying numbers of protagonists, but I couldn't locate myself among them, or imagine the place that I might have occupied in the whole thing; it got me nowhere and so I headed towards the mezzanine – it must once have been more funky and cool up there, but what remained was disembowelled sofas with mouldy fabric, half upside-down on the floor. There was also a record player and a collection of discs, mostly 45s, which I identified after a few moments as twist records – you could tell by the postures of the dancers on the covers, while the singers and musicians had fallen into oblivion once and for all.

I remembered the architect had seemed uneasy throughout the visit, he had stayed only long enough to explain to me how things worked – ten minutes at the absolute maximum – and he had told me several times that he would be better off selling this house if the legal formalities weren't so complicated, and more particularly if he had a chance of finding a buyer. In fact he must have had a past in this house, a past whose outlines I struggled to define – somewhere between the Marquis de Sade and the twist – a past that he needed to get rid of, even though that wouldn't open up the possibility of a future; but in any case the contents of that wing evoked nothing for me that I could have encountered in the house in Clécy: it was a different pathology, a different history, and I went back to bed almost comforted, since it's true that in the middle of our own dramas we are reassured by the existence of others that we have been spared.

The following morning, a half-hour stroll took me to the banks of the Orne. The route wasn't very interesting, except for people who are interested in the transformation of dead leaves into humus – which I had been in the past, more than twenty years ago now; I had even carried out various calculations on the quantity of humus produced as a function of the density of forest cover. Other half-memories, extremely imprecise, returned to me from my studies: for example I thought that I noticed this forest was badly kept – the density of vines and parasitic plants was too great and must have hindered the growth of the trees; it is wrong to imagine that nature left to its own devices produces splendid plantations with powerfully well-proportioned trees, plantations that people have compared to cathedrals, and have also prompted religious emotions of a pantheistic kind; nature left to its own devices generally produces nothing but a shapeless and chaotic mess, made up of various plants, and is as a whole quite ugly; that was more or less the spectacle presented to me by my stroll to the banks of the Orne.

The landlord had advised me to avoid feeding the deer if I happened to come across any. Not that such an operation struck him as contrary to their dignity as wild animals (he shrugged impatiently as if to stress how ridiculous that objection was) – deer, like most wild animals, are opportunistic omnivores and eat more or less anything, nothing brings them more joy than happening upon the leftovers of a picnic, or a disembowelled bin bag; it was just that if I started feeding them they would come back every day and then I wouldn't be able to get rid of them – they can be real limpets when they put their minds to it, deer. If, on the other hand, the grace of their leaps stirred an animal-loving emotion in me, he advised *pains au chocolat*, an almost incredible predilection – in that respect they were very different from wolves, whose tastes inclined more towards cheese, but in any case there were no wolves, so for now the deer had nothing to worry about; it would be a few years before wolves came up from the Alps, or even from the Gévaudan.

Either way I didn't encounter a single deer. More generally I didn't encounter anything that could justify my presence in this house stranded in the middle of the woods, and it seemed almost inevitable to me that I should have laid my hand on the sheet of paper on which I had jotted down the address and telephone number of Camille's veterinary practice after searching for it on the computer in the corner office in Aymeric's byre, at a time that seemed very long ago, which seemed almost to belong to a previous life; a time that was in fact less than two months ago.

*

It was only about twenty kilometres to Falaise, but the journey took me almost two hours. I stayed parked in the main square in Putanges for a long time, fascinated by the Hôtel du Lion Verd for no perceptible reason other than its strangely spelled name – but would a correctly spelled green lion have been any more acceptable? With even less reason I then stopped in Bazoches-au-Houlme. After that the road left the Suisse Normande with its dips and bends, and the last ten kilometres of the road to Falaise were perfectly straight; I felt as if I was sliding along an inclined plane and noticed that I had involuntarily gone up to 160 kilometres per hour: a stupid mistake as this was exactly the kind of area where they put up speed cameras and, more importantly, the easy glide was probably leading me towards the void; Camille would inevitably have remade her life, she would inevitably have found a guy, it was seven years ago now – how could I have imagined anything else?

I parked at the foot of the fortifications surrounding Falaise, overlooked by the castle where William the Conqueror was born. Falaise's street plan was simple and I found Camille's veterinary practice without any difficulty: it was on Place du Docteur Paul-Germain, at the end of Rue Saint-Gervais – clearly one of the main shopping streets in the town – and near the church of the same name – whose foundations, in the primitive gothic style, had suffered a great deal in the siege laid by Philippe Auguste. At that point I could have gone straight in, spoken to the receptionist and asked to see her. That was what other people would have done, and perhaps what I would end up doing after various pointless and boring prevarications. I had also ruled out the option of making a phone call; the idea of writing a letter had held my interest for longer – personal letters are now so rare that they always have an impact – but it was mostly my sense of incompetence that had led me to abandon the idea.

There was a bar directly opposite, Au Duc Normand, and in the end that was the solution I chose, expecting that my strength or my desire to live or anything else of that kind would gain the upper hand. I ordered a beer, which I sensed would be the first of a long series; it was only eleven o'clock in the morning. The bar was tiny, there were no more than five tables and I was the only guest. I had a perfect view of the veterinary clinic; people turned up occasionally with a pet – most often a dog, sometimes in a basket – and exchanged the appropriate words with the receptionist. From time to time, people also came into the bar, sat down a few metres away from me and ordered a coffee with a shot – old men for the most part, but they didn't sit down, preferring to have their drinks at the counter; I understood and admired their choice: these were spirited old men who wanted to show they weren't finished yet, whose hamstrings still held them upright; it wouldn't have been a good idea to slap with the back of your hand. While his regular customers indulged in this mini-display of strength, the landlord continued, with almost priestly slowness, his reading of *Paris-Normandie*.

I was on my third beer, and my attention had slightly lost its focus, when Camille appeared in front of me. She came out of the room where she saw her patients, and exchanged a few words with the receptionist – it was plainly time for a lunch break. She was about twenty metres away from me, no more, and she hadn't changed, physically she hadn't changed at all; it was frightening, she was over thirty-five now and she still had the appearance of a nineteen-year-old girl. I had changed physically – I was aware that I had *put on a bit of mileage* – I knew that from occasionally catching sight of myself in the mirror without any real satisfaction but without any real displeasure either, a bit like bumping into a very awkward neighbour from across the hall.

To make matters worse, she was wearing a pair of jeans and a light grey sweatshirt, exactly the same outfit as she had worn when she got off the train from Paris one Monday morning in November, with her bag over her shoulder, just before we looked deep into each other's eyes for a few seconds or a few minutes – well, for an indeterminate amount of time – and she said to me: 'I'm Camille,' thus starting a new sequence of circumstances, a new existential configuration which I had not left, which I would probably never leave, and which, to tell the truth, I had no intention of leaving. I had a brief moment of terror when the two women, while leaving the veterinary clinic, chatted on the pavement: were they going for lunch at the Duc Normand? Finding myself face to face with Camille by chance seemed to me like the worst possible solution, certain failure. But no, they went back up Rue Saint-Gervais, and to tell the truth, taking a closer look at the Duc Normand, I understood that my worry had been in vain; the landlord offered no food of any kind, not even sandwiches, and the lunchtime rush wasn't his style; instead he continued with his exhaustive reading of *Paris-Normandie*, in which he seemed to take an exaggerated and morbid interest.

I didn't wait for Camille to come back, paid for my beers

straight away and returned in a state of slight intoxication to the house in Saint-Aubert-sur-Orne where I found myself confronted with the triangular walls of the bedroom, the copper pans on the walls and my memories; I still had a bottle of Grand Marnier but it wasn't enough; my anxiety was mounting by the hour in abrupt little gradations, and the episodes of tachycardia began at about eleven in the evening, immediately followed by night sweats and nausea. At about two in the morning, I realised that it was a night from which I would never fully recover.

In fact, it's from that moment that my behaviour starts to escape me, that I am reluctant to assign a meaning to it, and that it manifestly begins to part company from ordinary morality and from ordinary reason, which I thought I shared until then. I hope I have explained clearly enough that I have never had what is called a strong personality; I wasn't one of those people who leave indelible traces in history, or even in the memories of their contemporaries. For a few weeks I had started reading again – well, if you can put it that way; my curiosity as a reader was not very extensive, in fact I was only reading *Dead Souls* by Gogol, and I wasn't even reading that very much, no more than one or two pages a day, and I was often rereading the same ones for several days in a row. That reading gave me boundless pleasure – perhaps I had never felt as close to another man as I had to that rather forgotten Russian author – but unlike Gogol, I couldn't have said that God had given me a complex nature. God had given me a simple nature, infinitely simple in my opinion – it was more the world around me that had become complex, and now I could no longer deal with the complexity of the world, could no longer deal with the complexity of the world into which I had been plunged, and so my behaviour – and I'm not trying to justify it – became incomprehensible, shocking and erratic.

I went to the Duc Normand at five the next afternoon; the landlord had already got used to my presence, and while he had seemed a little surprised the previous day, today he wasn't at all, and already had his hand on the handle of the beer pump before I even gave him my order, and I took a seat in exactly the same place. At around a quarter past seven, a girl of about fifteen opened the door of the veterinary clinic; she was holding a child by the hand, a very small boy – he might have been three or four. Camille rushed into the room and took him in her arms, spinning around several times and covering him with kisses.

A child, then, she had a child; it's what you call a new fact. I could have anticipated that – women do sometimes have children – but the fact is that I had thought about everything except that. And to tell the truth my first thoughts were not for the child itself: it usually takes two people to make a child, that's what I said to myself, generally but not always; I'd heard of different medical possibilities these days, and in fact I would rather that the child had been the product of artificial insemination, he would have seemed somehow *less real* then, but that wasn't the case: five years earlier, Camille had bought a train ticket and a ticket for the Festival des Vieilles Charrues when she was at the height of her fertility, and she slept with a guy she met at a concert – she didn't remember the name of the band. She hadn't exactly picked the first person she came across: the guy wasn't too ugly or too stupid, and he was a business school student. The only slightly suspect point about him was that he was a heavy metal fan, but nobody's perfect, and for a heavy metal fan he was polite and clean. The thing had happened in the guy's tent, erected in a field a few kilometres from the concert stages; it had been neither good nor bad, but simply correct; the question of condoms had been avoided without much difficulty, as it always is with men. She had woken up first and left a page from her Rhodia notebook with a fake mobile phone number for him to find; it was a somewhat pointless precaution as there wasn't much chance of him calling her back. The station was a five-kilometre walk away – that was the only downside – but otherwise it was fine, a bright and pleasant summer morning.

Her parents had received the news with resignation; they were aware that the world had changed, not necessarily for the better they thought deep down, but it had changed, and the new generation had to go through strange detours to achieve their reproductive function. So they had shaken their heads, but each in a slightly different way: her father's predominant response was one of shame, the feeling that he had at least partially failed in his child-rearing task, and that things should have happened differently; while her mother was delighted by the arrival of her grandson – because she knew that it would be a little boy, she had known for certain straight away, and it was in fact a little boy in the end.

*

At about seven o'clock, Camille came outside with the receptionist who walked off down Rue Saint-Gervais, after which Camille closed the clinic and sat down behind the wheel of her Nissan Micra. I had more or less assumed that I would follow her – or, rather, the idea of doing so had passed through my mind earlier in the day – but I had parked my car near the ramparts; it was too far away, I didn't have time to go and get it, and anyway I didn't feel strong enough, at least not that evening, and there was the child to think about; the whole situation needed to be rethought but for now it made more sense to go to the Carrefour Market in Falaise and buy a bottle of Grand Marnier, or maybe even two.

The next day was a Saturday, and Camille's veterinary clinic couldn't be closed, I said to myself, it was even probably her busiest day – people wait when their dog is dead, they wait until they have some free time, that's how people's lives work in general. On the other hand, her son's school or crèche or nursery would be closed, so she would probably need a child-minder for today, well, she would probably be on her own and that struck me as a favourable circumstance. I got there at half past eleven, in case of the very unlikely event that she closed on Saturday afternoons. The owner of the café had already finished *Paris-Normandie* but had embarked on an equally exhaustive reading of *France Football*; he was an exhaustive reader – they really exist – and I had known people like that, people who don't just settle for the big stories, the statements of prime minister Édouard Philippe or the sum of Neymar's transfer payment, but instead want to get to the bottom of things; they are the foundation of enlightened opinion, the pillars of representative democracy.

A steady stream of customers went in and out of the veterinary clinic, but Camille closed earlier than she had the previous day, at about five. This time I had parked my car on the parallel road, a few metres away from hers; I was worried for a moment that she would recognise it, but that wasn't very likely. When I bought it twenty years ago, the Mercedes G-Class wasn't a very popular car; people bought it when they wanted to drive across Africa, or at least Sardinia; now it was fashionable, people had been charmed by its vintage side, and these days it was seen as a bit of a gangster car.

She turned off at Bazoches-au-Houlme, and at the precise moment when her car headed towards Rabodanges I became sure that she must live alone with her son. It wasn't just the expression of a desire; it was an intuitive certainty, powerful although unjustifiable.

We were alone on the road to Rabodanges and I slowed down pointedly to let her get ahead; the fog was rising and I could hardly make out her rear lights.

Reaching the shores of Lake Rabodanges, on which the sun was beginning to set, made an impression on me; it stretched for kilometres, on either side of a bridge, in the middle of dense forests of oaks and elms; it was probably a reservoir; there was hardly any sign of human occupation, and the landscape didn't remind me of anything I had ever seen in France – it felt more like being in Norway or Canada.

I parked at the top of a hill to the rear of a restaurant, shut for the season, whose terrace offered 'panoramic views of the lakes', and which claimed to be willing to provide banquets on request, as well as serving ice cream at all times of day. Camille's car drove on to the bridge; I took my Schmidt & Bender binoculars out of the glove compartment, but was no longer worried about losing her because I'd already guessed where she was going: it was a little wooden chalet on the other side of the bridge, a few hundred metres away; a terrace at the front looked out over the lake. Stranded halfway up the slope in the middle of the woods, the chalet really looked like a doll's house, surrounded by ogres.

And in fact, after leaving the bridge, the Nissan Micra turned up a steep path and stopped just below the terrace. A girl of about fifteen greeted Camille – the same one that I had seen the day before. They talked for a moment, then the girl set off on a scooter.

So Camille lived there, in an isolated house in the middle of the woods, several kilometres away from her nearest neighbours – well, I was exaggerating, there was another house, a bit bigger and further to the north, one or two kilometres away, but it was clearly a holiday home: the shutters were closed. There was also the panoramic restaurant La Rotonde, the one I had parked behind, and closer examination revealed that it would reopen at the start of the Easter holidays in April (there was even a water-skiing club just beside it, which would resume its activities at more or less the same time). The entrance to the restaurant was protected by an alarm – a little red warning light flashed at the bottom of a digital receiver – but further along there was a service entrance for deliveries, and I forced the lock without difficulty. The temperature inside was quite mild, more pleasant than the one outside; there must have been a thermostat system, probably for the cellar – a very fine cellar, with hundreds of bottles. In terms of food, it was less impressive, there were a few shelves of preserves – tinned vegetables and fruit in syrup; I also discovered a thin mattress on a little iron bed in a utility room; it must have been intended for the employees, for use during high season when they were allowed a break. I easily carried it upstairs into the hall of the panoramic restaurant, and sat down with my binoculars beside me. The mattress was far from comfortable, but the bar was filled with aperitif bottles that had already been partly drunk; well, I can't explain the whole situation, but for the first time in months – or years, rather – I felt I was in exactly the place where I was supposed to be, and to put it simply, I was happy.

She was sitting on the sofa in her living room with her son beside her, and they were immersed in a DVD that I struggled to identify, probably *The Lion King*; then the child fell asleep, and she picked him up and headed towards the stairs. A short time later the lights went out all over the house. I had nothing but a torch, and hardly any other solution: I was sure that at this distance she wouldn't be able to see me, but if, on the other hand, I had turned on the lights in the restaurant she would have suspected something unusual. I ate quickly in the storeroom – a tin of peas and another of peaches in syrup, which I accompanied with a bottle of Saint-Émilion – and I went to sleep almost immediately.

At about eleven the next day, Camille came out, strapped the child into a baby seat and drove off, taking the bridge in the other direction; her car passed about ten metres in front of the restaurant; she would be in Bagnoles-de-l'Orne before midday.

Everything exists or asks to exist, which is why situations come together, sometimes bringing powerful emotional configurations, and a destiny is fulfilled. The situation that I have just described continued for almost three weeks. I generally arrived at about five o'clock and immediately took up position in my observation post; I was well organised now: I had my ashtray and my torch; sometimes I brought slices of ham to go with the tinned vegetables from the storeroom; once I even brought some garlic sausage. As to the alcohol reserves, they could have kept me going for months.

Now it was clear not only that Camille lived alone, that she had no lovers, but also that she didn't have many friends either; over those three weeks she didn't have a single visitor. How had she ended up like that? How had we both ended up like that? And to borrow from the communist bard: is this how men live?

Well, yes: the answer, Léo Ferré, is yes – I was gradually becoming aware of that. And I was also becoming aware that things weren't going to work out. Camille was now involved in a deep and exclusive relationship with her son; it would last for at least another ten years, but more probably fifteen, before he left her to study – and because he would work hard at school, he would be followed with attentive devotion by his mother, and he would go to university – I had no doubt about that. Gradually things would get less simple; there would be girls and then, even worse, there would be *a* girl, who would not be well received; then Camille would become an embarrassment, an obstruction (and even if it wasn't a girl but a boy the situation would hardly be any better; we were no longer living in a time when mothers were relieved to accept their son's homosexuality – now they form couples, the little faggots, and still manage to escape maternal domination). Then she would fight, she would fight to keep the only love of her life, and the situation would be painful for a time, but she would face the facts in the end and she would bend to 'natural laws'. Then she would be free, free again and alone – but she would also be fifty, and obviously it would be too late for her; as for me don't even think about it: I was already barely alive now and in fifteen years I would be richly dead.

It was two months since I had used the Steyr Mannlicher, but the pieces fit together smoothly and precisely, the machining was truly admirable. I spent the rest of the afternoon practising on an abandoned house, a little further off in the woods, where there were still a few windows to break: I hadn't forgotten anything, my precision from five hundred metres was still excellent.

Was it imaginable that Camille would endanger that perfect symbiotic relationship that she had with her son for me? And was it imaginable that he, the child, would agree to share his mother's affection with another male? The answer to those questions was fairly obvious, and the conclusion ineluctable: it was him or me.

The murder of a four-year-old inevitably provokes an intense emotion in the media so I could expect considerable investigative resources to be deployed. The panoramic restaurant would quickly be identified as the source of the shot, but I had never at any moment taken off my latex gloves in this establishment and I was sure I had left no prints. As to DNA, I didn't know exactly what DNA could be taken from: blood, sperm, hair, saliva? I'd had the foresight to bring a plastic bag into which I poured the cigarette butts that I had held between my teeth; at the last moment I added the cutlery I had put in my mouth, although I had a sense that I was taking slightly unnecessary precautions; to tell the truth, my DNA had never been taken – the systematic recording of DNA in the absence of a crime had never been voted for so in some respects we lived in a free country – well, I didn't have the sense of being in any great danger. The key to success seemed to me to lie in rapid execution: in less than a minute after firing, I could have left La Rotonde once and for all; in less than an hour, I could be on the motorway to Paris.

One evening, while I was running through the parameters of the murder in my mind, I was pierced by the memory of an evening in Morzine, one 31st December, the first New Year's Eve that my parents had let me stay up till midnight, and they were having some friends over – it was probably a small party but I have no memory of that aspect; what I remembered, on the other hand, was my absolute intoxication at the idea that we were entering a new year, an absolutely new year in which every action, however anodyne – even drinking a bowl of Nesquik – would in a sense be accomplished for the first time; I might have been five years old then, a bit older than Camille's son, but at the time I saw life as a succession of joys that could only get greater – only give rise in the future to more varied and bigger joys – and it was as that memory came into my mind that I understood Camille's son, that I was able to put myself in his place, and that identification gave me the right to kill him. To tell the truth, if I had been a stag or a Brazilian macaque, the question wouldn't even have arisen: the first action of a male mammal when he conquers a female is to destroy all her previous offspring to ensure the pre-eminence of his genotype. This attitude had been maintained for a long time in the first human populations.

Now I had all the time in the world to think back to those few hours, and even those few minutes; I have little else in my life but to think about them again: I don't think that contrary forces, the forces that tried to keep me on track for murder, had much to do with morality; it was more an anthropological matter, a matter of belonging to a late species, and of adhering to the code of that late species – a matter of conformity, in other words.

If I managed to pass beyond those limits, the rewards would of course not be immediate. Camille would suffer, she would suffer enormously; I would have to wait at least six months before resuming contact. And then I would come back, and she would love me again because she had never stopped loving me – it was as simple as that – and she would simply want another child, would want it very quickly; and that's what would happen. A big swerve had occurred some years before and we had deviated atrociously from our normal destinies; I had made the first mistake, but Camille had done her bit to make things worse; now it was time to make things better, it was exactly the right time – now was our last chance, and I was the only one who could do it, I was the only one with the cards in my hand, and the solution was at the end of my Steyr Mannlicher.

An opportunity arose the following Saturday, mid-morning. It was the beginning of March and there was already a spring-like mildness in the air, and when I opened one of the windows overlooking the lake by a few centimetres to slide out the barrel of my gun, I didn't feel a cold breath, or anything that could compromise the stability of my aim. The child was sitting at the table on the terrace, in front of a big cardboard box containing the pieces of a Disney jigsaw puzzle – Snow White, my binoculars told me, but only the face and torso of the heroine had been reconstructed so far. I adjusted the scope to maximum before positioning my gun, my breathing becoming regular and slow. The child's head, in profile, occupied the whole of my sights; he wasn't moving at all, he was concentrating entirely on his jigsaw puzzle – it's an exercise, it's true, that requires great concentration. A few minutes before, I had seen the babysitter disappearing towards the upstairs bedrooms – I had noticed that when the child immersed himself in a book or a game, she took advantage of the fact to go and surf the Internet after putting on headphones; she would probably do that for a few hours so I didn't think she would come down before the child's lunch.

He remained completely motionless for ten minutes, apart from slow movements of his hands as they rummaged through the pile of cardboard pieces – Snow White's neckline was gradually being completed. His motionlessness was matched only by my own – never had I breathed so slowly, never had my hands trembled so little, never had I had such total mastery of my gun; I felt I was about to accomplish the perfect liberating and unique shot, the most important shot in my life, the only goal underlying my months of training.

What felt like ten motionless minutes passed like that, though more likely fifteen or twenty, before my fingers began to tremble and I collapsed on the ground, my cheeks scraped the carpet and I understood that it was over, that I wouldn't shoot, that I wouldn't manage to alter the course of things, that the mechanism of unhappiness was the strongest of all, that I would never regain Camille and that we would both die alone, unhappy and alone, each in our own way. I was trembling violently when I got to my feet, my vision blurred with tears, and I pulled the trigger at random making the picture window of the panoramic room explode into hundreds of fragments of glass; the noise was so loud that I thought somebody might have heard it in the house opposite. I trained my binoculars on the child: no, he hadn't moved, he was still concentrating on his puzzle; Snow White's dress was gradually taking shape.

Slowly, very slowly, funereally slowly, I unscrewed the pieces of the Steyr Mannlicher, which fit neatly into their foam rubber holdings. When the polycarbonate case was closed again, I had for a moment the idea of throwing it in the lake, then that demonstration of ostentatious failure struck me as useless; I had failed anyway and to emphasise it any further would have been unfair to this trusty carbine, which for its part had asked only to serve its user, to accomplish his purposes with precision and excellence.

Then, in a second phase it occurred to me to cross the bridge and introduce myself to the child. I juggled the plan in my head for two or three minutes, then finished a bottle of Guignolet kirsch, and it was the return of reason or at least a normal form of reason; in any case, I could only have been a father or a substitute figure, and what would the child have done with a father? What need could he have had of any kind of father? No need at all: I had a sense of turning over in my head the parameters of an equation that had already been resolved, and resolved to my disadvantage; it was him or me, as I've said, and in the end it was him.

More reasonably, in the third phase, I stowed the gun in the boot of my G 350 and set off without turning back in the direction of Saint-Aubert. In a bit less than a month people would come and open the restaurant again, would note the traces of human occupation, probably blame a homeless man, decide to install an extra alarm below to protect the delivery entrance – the police wouldn't necessarily even open an inquiry or go looking for prints.

As far as I was concerned, there seemed to be nothing now that could halt my path towards annihilation. But I didn't leave the house in Saint-Aubert-sur-Orne – at least not immediately, something which struck me as hard to explain in retrospect. I had no hopes and I was fully aware that I had nothing to hope for. My analysis of the situation seemed complete and certain. There are areas of the human psyche that remain little-known because they haven't been much explored, because luckily few people have found themselves in a situation of needing to explore them, and those who have done so have, as a general rule, preserved too little of their reason to produce an acceptable description of them. Those areas can hardly be approached except by the use of paradoxical and even absurd formulas, of which the phrase *hope beyond all hope* is the only one that really comes to mind. It's not like night, it's worse than that; and without having personally known that experience I have a sense that even when you plunge into true night, polar night – the one that lasts for six months in a row – the concept or the memory of the sun remains. I had entered an *endless night,* and yet there remained, deep within me, there remained something less than a hope, let's say an uncertainty. One might also say that even when one has personally lost the game, when one has played one's last card, for some people – not all, not all – the idea remains that *something in heaven* will pick up the hand, will arbitrarily decide to deal again, to throw the dice again, even when one has never at any moment in one's life sensed the intervention or even the presence of any kind of deity, even when one is aware of not especially deserving the intervention of a favourable deity, and even when one realises, bearing in mind the accumulation of mistakes and errors that constitute one's life, that one deserves it less than anyone.

There was still a three-month lease to go on the house, which at least had the advantage of imposing a concrete limit on my insanity – even if it was rather unlikely that I would remain in that situation for more than a few days. In any case there was one immediate necessity: a return trip to Paris to raise my dose of Captorix to 20 mg, an elementary survival precaution which I couldn't ignore. I made an appointment with Dr Azote for the day after next, for shortly after my train got in to Saint-Lazare, leaving just enough time to cover any possible delay.

Strangely, the journey did me good in a way, allowing my thoughts to drift towards reflections which, while they might have been negative, were also impersonal. The train got in to Saint-Lazare thirty-five minutes late, which was more or less what I had anticipated. The ancestral pride of the railway workers, the ancestral pride of respect for the timetable, so powerful and so rooted in the early twentieth century that villagers in the fields used to set their clocks by the running of the trains, had disappeared once and for all. SNCF was one of the companies whose complete failure and degeneracy I had witnessed in my lifetime. Not only had the indicative timetable become a big joke in the present day, but also any notion of catering seemed to have vanished from intercity trains, together with any plan to maintain materials – the slashed seats spewed opaque fluff, and the toilets – at least the ones that weren't locked and which had probably been forgotten – were in such a filthy condition that I didn't dare enter them, and preferred to relieve myself on the platform between two carriages.

An atmosphere of general catastrophe always alleviates individual catastrophe – that's probably why suicides are so rare in wartime – and I headed towards Rue d'Athènes almost with a spring in my step. Having said that, Dr Azote's first glance quickly disillusioned me. It contained a mixture of unease, compassion and pure professional concern. 'It doesn't really seem to be working . . .' he observed briefly. I couldn't contradict him because he hadn't seen me for several months, so he inevitably had a point of reference that I lacked.

'Obviously I'll move you up to 20 mg,' he went on, 'but OK, 15 mg or 20 . . . Antidepressants can't do everything; I imagine you're aware of that.' I was aware of that. 'And besides, 20 mg you must understand is still the maximum dose on the market. Obviously you could take two pills, you could move on to 25, 30 and then 35, and then where do you stop? Frankly, I would advise against it. The truth is that it's been tested at 20, nothing beyond that, and I don't really want to take the risk. How are things where sex is concerned?'

The question left me flummoxed. But it wasn't a bad one, I had to agree, it had a connection with my situation, a connection that seemed remote and vague, but was still a connection. I didn't reply, but I probably spread my hands, I opened my mouth a little: well, my face must quite eloquently have conveyed an idea of the void because he said: 'OK, OK, I see . . .

'You're still going to have to give me a blood sample to check your testosterone level. I'd expect it to be very low:

unlike natural serotonin, serotonin produced through the medium of Captorix inhibits the synthesis of testosterone, don't ask me why, nobody has a clue. Normally speaking – I'm saying normally speaking – the effect should be completely reversible; as soon as you stop the Captorix it'll kick in again; well, that's what studies have shown but you can never be a hundred per cent certain – if they had to wait to have absolute scientific certainty they'd never have put out a single drug on the market, you understand all that?' I nodded.

'However, however . . .' he went on, 'we're not just going to check testosterone; I'm going to give you an overall hormonal check-up. It's just that I'm not an endocrinologist – there may be things that are beyond me – wouldn't you rather see a specialist? I know one who's not bad.'

'I'd rather not.'

'You'd rather not . . . Well, I suppose I have to take that as a sign of trust. Well, fine then, we'll try and carry on. Basically hormones aren't as complicated as all that, just ten or so and you've pretty much covered the lot. Also I enjoyed endocrinology when I was a student; it was one of my favourite subjects, I'd like to do a bit more of that again . . .' He seemed to fall into a vaguely nostalgic reverie, as is probably inevitable after a certain age when you think about your student years; I understood that all the better since I'd liked biochemistry a lot and had felt a strange pleasure studying the properties of complex molecules; the difference is that I was more interested in vegetable molecules such as chlorophyll or anthocyanins, but in the end they were broadly the same – I had a good idea what he was getting at.

*

So I left with two prescriptions and picked up the 20 mg of Captorix from a chemist's close to Gare Saint-Lazare; the hormonal analysis would have to wait till I came back to Paris and it was inevitable that I would be coming back to Paris; it was inevitable, perfect solitude is even more normal there, more appropriate to the environment.

But I did return to the shores of Lake Rabodanges one last time. I had chosen a Sunday morning; a time when I was sure that Camille wouldn't be there, that she would be having lunch with her parents in Bagnoles-de-l'Orne. I think it would have been almost impossible if Camille had been there to say my final farewells. Final farewells? Did I really believe that? Yes, I really believed it – after all I had seen people die and I was going to die shortly myself – we constantly encounter final farewells, all through our lives unless our lives are fortunately brief; we encounter them practically every day. The weather was absurdly fine; a bright, warm sun lit the water of the lake, making the woods sparkle. The wind didn't moan, the waves didn't murmur either – nature demonstrated an almost impossible lack of empathy. Everything was peaceful, majestic and calm. Could I have lived for years alone with Camille, in this isolated house in the middle of the woods, and been happy?

Yes, I knew I could. My need for social relationships (if by that we mean relationships other than romantic relationships), which started very weak, had declined to nothing over the years. Was that normal? It's true that humanity's unpalatable ancestors lived in tribes of a few dozen individuals, about the size of a hamlet, and that that formula pertained for a long time – both among hunter-gatherers and among the first farming populations. But time had moved on since then; there had been the invention of the city and its natural corollary – loneliness – to which only the couple could offer an alternative; we would never return to the tribal stage – though some unintelligent sociologists claim to be able to distinguish new tribes in 'reconstructed families', that was possible – but for my part I had never seen reconstructed families, deconstructed yes; in fact those were the only ones I'd ever seen at close quarters, apart of course from the many cases in which the deconstructing process had already begun at the couple stage, before the production of children. As to the reconstructing process, I had never had the opportunity to see it in action. 'Once our heart has harvested its grapes/To live is torment', Baudelaire wrote more accurately; this business of reconstructed families was, in my eyes, nothing but revolting hot air – although it wasn't a piece of pure propaganda, optimistic and postmodern, unworldly and dedicated to the ABC+ and the ABC++ economic groups, already inaudible beyond the Porte de Charenton. So, yes, I could have lived alone with Camille, in that isolated house in the middle of the woods, and I would have seen the sun rise over the lake every morning, and I think that, in so far as such a thing had been granted to me, I could have been happy. But life, as they say, had decided otherwise: my bags were packed and I could be in Paris by early afternoon.

I easily recognised the receptionist at the Hôtel Mercure, and she recognised me too. 'So you're back?' she asked, and I agreed that I was, with a hint of emotion, because I had heard – I had definitely heard – that she had been about to say: 'You're back *among us*?', but a qualm had held her back at the last minute; she must have had very precise notions of the level of familiarity that could acceptably be used with a customer, even a loyal customer. The next thing she said, 'You're our guest for a week?', seemed to me to be exactly the same phrase that she had uttered several months before, the first time I had stayed there.

I returned with childish and even pathetic satisfaction to my tiny hotel room, with its functional and ingenious furnishings, and the following day I resumed my daily circuits which took me from Brasserie O'Jules to Carrefour City, via Rue Abel-Hovelacque which I followed with a quick stroll up Avenue des Gobelins, turning off at the end towards Avenue de la Soeur-Rosalie. But something had changed in the general atmosphere; we were a year, or nearly a year, on and it was the beginning of May, an exceptionally mild May, a true prefiguration of the summer. I should normally have felt something along the lines of lust, or at least of simple desire, in finding myself side by side with those girls in short skirts or tight leggings, sitting at tables not far from me in Brasserie O'Jules, ordering coffees and maybe swapping stories about their love lives; more probably they were comparing their respective life insurance policies. But I felt nothing, radically nothing, even though we theoretically belonged to the same species; I had to address that business of my hormone levels and Dr Azote had asked me to ensure he was sent a copy of the results.

I called him three days later; he seemed embarrassed. 'Listen, this is weird . . . If you don't mind I'd like to consult a colleague. Shall we meet up again in a week?' I noted the appointment in my diary without comment. When a doctor tells you he's spotted something strange in your results, you should at least feel slightly worried; not so in my case. Immediately after hanging up, I said to myself that I could at least have pretended to be worried – well, taken a bit of an interest – that was probably what he expected of me. Unless perhaps – I went on to reflect – he hadn't really understood what point I had reached; that was an awkward idea.

My appointment was at 7.30 the following Monday evening; I imagine it was his last appointment of the day, and wonder whether he hadn't even stayed on a bit late. He looked exhausted, and lit a Camel before offering me one – I felt a bit like a condemned man. I saw that he had scribbled some numbers on my results. 'Right . . .' he said, 'the testosterone level is clearly low, I expected that, it's the Captorix. But there is also a very high level of cortisol – the quantities of cortisol that you're secreting are incredible. In fact . . . can I speak frankly?' I said he could, that had been more or less the tone of our exchanges until now – frankness. 'Well, in fact . . .' He hesitated even so, his lips trembled slightly before he said: 'I have the sense that you are, very simply, dying of sorrow.'

'Is there such a thing as dying of sorrow; does that mean anything?' was the only answer that came to mind.

'Well, it's not very scientific from the point of view of terminology, but we might as well call a spade a spade. In the end it's not sorrow that will kill you, not directly. I imagine you've already started putting on weight?'

'Yes, I think so, I haven't really noticed, but I guess so.'

'That's inevitable with cortisol: you're going to get fatter and fatter, you will frankly become obese. And once you are obese, there's no shortage of fatal illnesses: you'll be spoilt for choice. What made me change my opinion about your treatment was the cortisol. I was reluctant to advise you to stop taking Captorix, for fear that your cortisol rate might increase; but now, quite frankly, I don't see how it could go any higher.'

'So you're advising me to stop taking Captorix?'

'Well . . . that's not an easy choice either. Because if you stop, your depression will come back, it'll come back even more powerfully; you're going to become a real zombie. On the other hand, if you go on, you can write off the idea of sex. What you need to do is keep your serotonin at the correct level – right now it's OK, you're fine – but lowering the cortisol, and maybe increasing dopamine and endorphins, that would be ideal. But I have a sense that I'm not being very clear, is that OK, you're still following me?'

'Not entirely, to tell you the truth.'

'Well . . .' He glanced at the page again with a slightly dazed look, giving me the impression that he no longer really believed in his own calculations, before looking back up at me and saying: 'Have you thought of visiting prostitutes?' I was open-mouthed, my mouth probably did actually fall open, and I must have looked completely flummoxed, because he went on:

'OK, these days we call them escorts, but it comes down to the same thing. Financially, I don't think you're in too bad a way?'

I agreed that things were fine for now from that point of view at least.

'Right . . .' He seemed quite cheered by my reaction. 'Some of them aren't too bad, you know. In fact, to be honest, they're the exception; most of them are cash machines in a raw state, and they feel obliged to play out a drama of desire – pleasure and love and whatever you like – and though it might work with people who are very young and very stupid, it doesn't with people like us.' (He had probably meant 'like you', but the fact is that he said 'like us'; he was quite a remarkable doctor.) 'In short, it can only increase despair in our case. But still, you get to fuck, that's not to be sniffed at, and it's better if you can fuck suitable girls; well, I guess you know that.

'In short,' he went on, 'in short, I've drawn you up a little list . . .' From a drawer in his desk he took out an A4 sheet with three names written on it: Samantha, Tim and Alice; each name was followed by a mobile phone number. 'You don't need to tell them I sent you. Although hang on, it might be better to say so, they're suspicious girls; you need to understand them, their job's not an easy one.'

It took me a while to get over my surprise. I understood that doctors can't do everything, that you have to put one foot in front of another as they say, but, well, escorts was still quite surprising, so I said nothing, and it took him a few minutes to continue (there was no traffic in Rue d'Athènes by now; the silence in the room was complete).

'I'm not on the side of death. As a general rule, I don't care for death. Well, obviously, there are cases . . .' (He waved his arm vaguely, impatiently, as if to sweep away a recurring and stupid objection.) 'There are some cases when it's the best solution, but they're very rare cases, much rarer than people say; morphine works almost every time, and in those very rare cases of intolerance to morphine there's hypnosis, but you haven't got there – my God, you're not even fifty! There's one thing you've got to know, which is that if you were in Belgium or Holland and you asked to be euthanised with the depression that you've got, they'd let you go ahead without any difficulties. But I'm a doctor. And if a guy comes to see me: "I'm depressed, I want to top myself," am I going to say: "OK, top away, let me give you a hand . . . "? Well, no, sorry but no, that's not why I studied medicine.'

*

I assured him that, for now, I had no intention of going to Belgium or Holland. He seemed reassured; in fact, I think he was waiting for me to give him an assurance along these lines – was I really in such a bad way, and visibly so? I had more or less understood his explanations, but there was still one point that escaped me, and I asked him the question: was sex the only way to reduce the excessive secretion of cortisol?

'No, not at all. Cortisol is often called the stress hormone, and not without reason. I'm sure that monks, for example, secrete very little cortisol; but that's not really my field. So I know, it may seem weird to call you stressed when essentially you do nothing all day, but the figures are there!' He gave the sheet with my results a vigorous tap: 'You're stressed; you're stressed to a terrifying degree and it's as if you were having a static burn-out, as if it was consuming you from within. Well, this kind of thing isn't easy to explain. And besides, it's getting late . . .' I looked at my watch; in fact it was after nine, I'd really taken up too much of his time, and I was also starting to get a bit hungry – a thought occurred to me for a moment that I could go and eat at Brasserie Mollard, as I had done back in Camille's day, and it was immediately dispelled by a feeling of pure terror; there is no doubt that I really was an idiot.

'What I'm going to do,' he said at last, 'is give you a prescription for Captorix 10 mg, in case you decide to stop – because, I repeat, stopping abruptly is a bad idea. At the same time it's not worth making things too complicated: you stay at 10 mg for two weeks, then zero. I won't lie to you, there's a risk that it'll be hard, because you've been on antidepressants for a long time. It'll be hard, but I think it's the thing to do . . .'

He shook my hand for a long time in the doorway of his surgery. I would have liked to say something, find a phrase that expressed my gratitude and admiration; I searched frantically for something during the thirty seconds that it took me to put on my coat and walk to the door; but yet again words failed me.

Two or maybe three months passed and I often found myself looking at the prescription for 10 mg, the one that was supposed to help me give up; I also had the A4 sheet with the numbers of the three escorts; and I did nothing apart from watch television. I turned it on after my little stroll at a few minutes past midday, and I never turned it off – there was an ecological energy-saving measure that meant you had to press the OK button every hour, so I pressed it every hour, until sleep brought me temporary deliverance. I turned it on again shortly after eight o'clock; the debates on *Politique matin* undoubtedly helped me to wash; to tell the truth, I couldn't claim to understand them perfectly and was forever getting *La République en marche* and *La France insoumise* confused; in fact, they were a bit alike; what they shared was the fact that they emanated a sense of almost unbearable energy, but that was precisely what helped me: rather than attacking the bottle of Grand Marnier straight away, I ran the soapy glove over my body, and soon I was ready for my little stroll.

The rest of the schedule was more of a blur: I slowly got drunk, zapping moderately under the predominant impression of moving from one cooking programme to the next; the number of cooking programmes had proliferated considerably – while at the same time eroticism was vanishing from most channels. France, and perhaps the whole of the West, was probably regressing to the *oral stage*, to use the terminology of the Austrian clown. Without a doubt, I was following the same path: I was gradually getting fatter, and a sexual alternative no longer presented itself clearly to me. I was far from being alone in this – there were probably still *cocksmen* and *screws*, but it had become a hobby, more particularly a minority hobby, reserved for the elite (the elite to which Yuzu had belonged, I briefly remembered one morning at the O'Jules, and it was probably the last time I thought of her); in a sense we had returned to the nineteenth century, when libertinism was reserved for a composite aristocracy: a mixture of birth, luck and beauty.

Perhaps there were also young people – well, certain young people – who belonged to the aristocracy of beauty simply by virtue of their youth, and who maybe went on believing it for a few years, between two and five but certainly less than ten; it was early June, and as I went to the café every morning I was forced to admit it: it wasn't the girls' fault – the girls were still there while women in their thirties and forties had largely given up – that the 'chic and sexy' Parisienne was no longer anything but a myth without substance; well, in the middle of the disappearance of the Western libido, girls, I imagine obeying some irrepressible hormonal impulse, went on reminding men of the need to reproduce the species;

objectively there was nothing to reproach them for: they crossed their legs at the appropriate moment when they sat at the O'Jules, a few metres away from me; sometimes they indulged in delicious little playlets, licking their fingers as they savoured a pistachio and vanilla ice-cream cone; well, they were doing their job of eroticising life more than adequately; they were there, but I was the one who was no longer there, not for them or for anyone else, and had ceased to imagine being so.

In the early evening, at more or less the same time as *Questions for a Champion*, I was seized by painful moments of self-pity. Then I thought once again of Dr Azote, and whether he behaved similarly with all his patients? I didn't know, but if he did he was a saint, and also I thought again of Aymeric – but things had changed, I had certainly got older and wasn't about to invite Dr Azote over to mine to listen to records; no friendship would spring into being between the two of us, the time for human relationships was over, for me in any case.

So I was in that state, stable but morose, when the reception-ist gave me a piece of bad news. It was a Monday morning, and I was preparing as I did every day to set off for O'Jules; I was upbeat and even felt a certain satisfaction at the idea of starting a new week, when the receptionist stopped me with a discreet: 'Excuse me, sir . . .' She wished to inform me, she had to inform me, it was her sad duty to inform me, that the hotel would soon become 100 per cent non-smoking; it was the new rules she told me, the decision had been taken at group level, they had no way of getting out of it. It was annoying, I told her, I would have to buy an apartment, but even if I bought the first one I viewed it would take time to go through all the formalities – there are lots of checks these days, greenhouse gas energy performance or whatever; well, it takes months, two or three at the very least, before you can really move in.

She looked at me in bewilderment, as if she hadn't under-stood, before asking for confirmation: I was going to buy an apartment because I could no longer stay in the hotel, was that it? Were things that bad?

Well, yes, they were that bad, what else could I tell her? There are times when modesty has to give because one is simply no longer able to maintain it. Things were that bad. She looked me straight in the eyes; I read the compassion rising to her face, gradually distorting her features; I just hoped that she wasn't going to start crying – I could tell she was a nice girl and I'm sure she made her boyfriend very happy, but what could she do? What can we do, any of us, about anything?

She would go and talk to her superior, she told me, she would go and talk to him this very morning, she was sure they would be able to find a solution. I gave her a broad smile as I left, an entirely sincere smile as a sign of friendship, but one which was at the same time intended to convey an impression of heroic optimism – it'll be fine, I'll manage – that was frankly dishonest. It wouldn't be all right, I wouldn't manage, I knew that very well.

I was busy watching Gérard Depardieu marvelling at the manufacture of artisanal sausages in the Pouilles when the superior in question called me in. I was surprised by his physique: he looked more like Bernard Kouchner, or let's say generally more like a humanitarian doctor, than the manager of a Mercure hotel; I couldn't work out how his day-to-day work could have created those crows' feet or that tan. He must have gone survival-trekking in hostile environments at the weekend, that was probably the explanation. He welcomed me while lighting a Gitane and offered me one. 'Audrey explained your situation to me . . .' he began; so her name was Audrey. He seemed embarrassed in my presence and he had trouble looking me in the eye – that's normal when you're dealing with a condemned man; you never know how to approach him, well, men never know, women sometimes do, but rarely.

'We'll work something out,' he went on. 'I'll have to carry out an inspection, but not straight away; I'd say in six months at the most, but more likely in a year. That'll give you time to find a solution . . .'

I nodded and confirmed that I would leave in three or four months at the most. There, it was over, and we had nothing left to say to each other. He had helped me. I thanked him before leaving his office; he assured me that it was nothing, that it was really the least he could do; I sensed that he wanted to launch into a diatribe about those idiots who spoil our lives but in the end he said nothing – he had probably launched into that diatribe too many times, and he knew it was pointless and the idiots always won in the end. For my part, before I left his office I apologised for the bother, and just as I uttered those banal words I understood that that would sum up my life from now on: apologising for the bother.

So I was now at the stage where the ageing animal, wounded and aware of being fatally injured, seeks a den in which to end its life. Furniture requirements are limited: a bed is enough, you know you're hardly ever going to have to leave it; there's no need for tables, sofas or armchairs, they would be useless accessories – superfluous or indeed painful remnants of a social life that will no longer exist. A television is necessary: television diverts. It all tended to guide me in the direction of a studio flat – quite a big studio, you might as well be able to move about a little, if at all possible.

The question of district turned out to be more difficult. Over time I had built up a little network of medical practitioners, each one assigned the task of keeping an eye on a different organ, so that I would not, before the time of my actual death, face exaggerated levels of pain. Most of them had practices in the fifth arrondissement in Paris; for my last life, my medical life, my real life, I remained faithful to the area of my studies, my youth, my dream life. It was natural that I should try and get close to my medical practitioners, who were now my main partners in conversation. Those trips to their surgeries were disinfected in a sense, rendered harmless by their medical nature. On the other hand, living in the same district would, I realised as I began my search for an apartment, have been a terrible mistake.

The first studio that I viewed, on Rue Laromiguière, was very pleasant: high ceiling, light, with a view of a large tree-lined courtyard; the price was high, of course, but I might be able to afford it – well, I wasn't absolutely sure, but I had still more or less decided to conclude the deal when I turned into Rue Lhomond and was swept away by a wave of terrible, crippling sadness that winded me; I struggled to breathe and my legs barely supported me; I had to take refuge in the first café I came to, which didn't help at all, quite the contrary, and I immediately recognised one of the cafés that I had frequented during my studies at the Agro – I had probably even gone to that café with Kate and the interior had barely changed. I ordered something to eat: a potato omelette and three glasses of Leffe gradually helped me recover – oh, yes, the West was regressing to the oral stage, and I understood why it was doing so – I thought I had more or less recovered as I left the bar but it all kicked in again as soon I came out into Rue Mouffetard; the journey was turning into a *via dolorosa*, and this time it was the image of Camille that came back to me; her childish joy at going to the market on Sunday morning, her wonder at the asparagus, the cheese, the exotic vegetables, the live lobsters; it took me over twenty minutes to get back to Monge metro station, tottering like an old man and panting with pain, with that incomprehensible pain that sometimes

afflicts old men, and which is nothing but the weight of life –
no, the fifth arrondissement was out of the question, completely out of the question.

So I began a gradual descent along metro line 7 – a
descent accompanied by a corresponding drop in price – and
in early July, I was surprised to find myself viewing a studio
flat on Avenue de la Soeur-Rosalie, almost opposite the Hôtel
Mercure. I gave up when I realised that I was, somewhere
deep inside, fostering a plan to stay in contact with Audrey;
my God, hope is hard to conquer, so sly and tenacious – are
all men like that?

I had to descend, descend further south, abandoning all
hope of a possible life, otherwise I wouldn't manage, and it
was in that state of mind that I visited the numerous tower
blocks that stretch between the Porte de Choisy and the
Porte d'Ivry. I had to go in search of empty, white and bare:
the environment corresponded almost perfectly to my quest:
living in one of those tower blocks meant living nowhere,
completely nowhere, or let's say in the immediate vicinity of
nowhere. Besides, in these areas populated by office workers,
the price per square metre was very accessible; with my
budget I could have planned to acquire a two- or indeed a
three-room apartment, but who would I have put up in it?

All of those towers looked the same, and all of those
studio flats looked the same too; I think I chose the empti-
est, the quietest and the barest, in one of the most anonymous
tower blocks – there at least I was sure that my move would
go unnoticed, would prompt no comment – and neither
would my death. The neighbourhood, largely Chinese, was a
guarantee of neutrality and politeness. The view from my

window was pointlessly broad across the southern suburbs – in the distance one could make out Massy, and probably Corbeil-Essonnes; that didn't matter much, because there were roller blinds which I planned to close for ever the day after I moved in. There was a rubbish chute, which I think was what won me over once and for all; with the use of the rubbish chute together with the new food delivery service that Amazon had just launched, I could attain almost perfect autonomy.

Strangely, my departure from the Hôtel Mercure was a difficult moment, particularly because of little Audrey; she had tears in her eyes, but at the same time what could I do? If she couldn't bear this she wouldn't be able to bear anything in her life – she was twenty-five at most but she was going to have to toughen up. All of a sudden, I gave her a kiss, and then two, and then four; she threw herself into those kisses with real abandon, even fleetingly held me in her arms, and then that was it; my taxi was at the door.

Moving was easy: I quickly got hold of some furniture and renewed my subscription to an SFR box – I had decided to remain loyal to this supplier, loyal until the end of my days, that was one of the things that life had taught me. But I was less interested in their sports package; I realised after a few weeks that I was getting older, so it was normal that I was becoming less sporty. But there were some gems in the SFR mix, particularly in terms of cookery programmes; I was now turning into a really fat old man – an Epicurean philosophy, why not; what else did Epicurus have in mind in the end? At the same time, a crust of dry bread with a drop of olive oil was really a bit limiting – what I needed were lobster medallions and scallops with garden vegetables; I was a decadent, not a rural Greek queer.

In about mid-October, I started getting bored with cookery programmes – however faultless they might have been – and that was the real start of my decline. I tried to take an interest in social debates, but that period was disappointing and brief: the extremely conformist nature of the speakers, the dreadful uniformity of their outrage and enthusiasm, had become such that I could now predict what they were going to say, not only in terms of their broad lines, but even the details, to the word in fact; columnists and major witnesses passed by like pointless European puppets, cretin after cretin, congratulating themselves on the pertinence and morality of their views – I could have written their dialogue for them and in the end I turned off my television for good; it would only have made me sadder if I had had the strength to carry on.

For a long time I had planned to read *The Magic Mountain* by Thomas Mann; I had a sense that it was a gloomy book, but that suited my situation and it was probably time. So I dived into it, at first with admiration, then with mounting reservations. Even though its range and ambitions were considerably greater, the ultimate meaning of the work was basically the same as *Death in Venice*. No more than that old imbecile Goethe (the German humanist with a Mediterranean inclination, one of the most sinister dotards in the whole of world literature), no more than his hero Aschenbach (broadly more sympathetic, however), Thomas Mann, Thomas Mann himself – and this was extremely serious – had been incapable of escaping the fascination of youth and beauty, which he had in the end placed above everything, above all intellectual and moral qualities, and in which, at the end of the day, he too, without the slightest restraint, had abjectly wallowed. So the whole of the world's culture was pointless – the whole of the world's culture provided no moral benefit and no advantage – because during those same years, exactly those same years, Marcel Proust, at the end of *Time Regained*, concluded with remarkable frankness that it was not only social relationships that supplied nothing substantial, friendships didn't either, they were quite simply a waste of time; and that what the writer needed was not intellectual conversations, contrary to popular belief, but 'light affairs with young girls in bloom'. At this stage of the argument, I am keen to replace 'young girls in bloom' with 'young wet pussies'; that would, it seems to me, contribute to the clarity of the debate without detracting from its poetry. (What could be more beautiful, more poetic, than a pussy that is starting to get wet? I ask you to think about that seriously before giving me an answer. A cock beginning its vertical ascent? There are arguments in favour. It all depends, like so many things in this world, on the sexual point of view that one adopts.)

Marcel Proust and Thomas Mann, to return to my subject, might have had all the culture in the world, they might (in those impressive early years of the twentieth century, which summarised eight centuries and even a bit of European culture all by themselves) have been at the head of all the knowledge and intelligence in the world, they might respectively have represented the peak of French and German civilisation – that is to say, the most brilliant, the most profound and the most refined cultures of their time – but they were at the mercy of, and ready to prostrate themselves before, any wet young pussy or any valiantly upright cock – according to their personal preferences, Thomas Mann remaining undecided in this respect, and Proust being somewhat vague as well. The end of *The Magic Mountain* was thus even sadder than a first reading suggested; it didn't just signify, with the two highest civilisations of the day rushing, in 1914, into a war as absurd as it was bloody, the failure of the very idea of European culture; it signified the final victory of animal attraction, the definitive end of all civilisation and of all culture. A Lolita could have made Thomas Mann *lose his marbles*; Marcel Proust would have *crushed* on Rihanna; these two authors, the crowns of their respective literary cultures, were not, to put it another way, honourable men, and we would have had to go further back, probably to the start of the nineteenth century, to the days of early Romanticism, to breathe a healthier and a purer air.

That was still open to debate, that purity; Lamartine was basically only a kind of Elvis Presley; he had the ability to *make the chicks melt* with his lyricism, but at least those conquests were made in the name of pure lyricism – Lamartine gyrated his hips with greater moderation than Elvis, well, I assume he did; we would need to be able to examine television footage which didn't exist at the time, but that didn't matter hugely: that world was dead in any case, it was dead for me and not only for me; it was simply dead. In the end, I found certain comfort in the more accessible reading of Sir Arthur Conan Doyle. Apart from the Sherlock Holmes series, Conan Doyle was the author of an impressive number of short stories, all agreeable to read and often enthralling; throughout his life he had been an exceptional *page turner*, perhaps the best in the history of world literature, but that probably didn't count for much in his own eyes – that wasn't his message – rather, Conan Doyle's message was that each page had to vibrate with the protestations of a noble soul, of a sincere and good heart. The most touching aspect of this was probably his personal attitude towards death: separated from the Christian faith by his gruesomely materialistic medical studies, confronted all through his life with cruel and repeated loss – including the loss of his own sons, who were sacrificed to England's warlike plans – his last resort was to turn towards spiritualism; the last hope, the final consolation of all those who can neither accept the deaths of their loved ones nor remain attached to Christianity.

For my part, without loved ones, it seemed to me that I was accepting the idea of death more and more easily; of course I would have liked to be happy, to be part of a happy community – all humans want that – but, well, it was really out of the question at this stage. In early December, I bought a photographic printer and a hundred boxes of Epson matt paper, 10 x 15 cm. Of the four walls of my studio flat, one was occupied by a picture window at waist height whose roller blinds I kept closed, with a big radiator below it. The available space of the second was limited by my bed, a bedside table and two half-height bookshelves. The third wall was almost entirely free, apart from a doorway leading to the bathroom area on the right and the kitchenette on the left. Only the fourth wall, facing my bed, was fully available. Limiting myself for the sake of ease to the two last walls, I had an exhibition space of 16 square metres; taking into account a printing format of 10 x 15 cm, I could exhibit a little over a thousand photographs. There were just over three thousand on my laptop, representing the whole of my life. Choosing one out of three struck me as reasonable, very reasonable, and gave me the impression of having lived rather well.

(Although looking at it closely, it had followed a strange course. Basically, for several years after my separation from Camille, I had told myself that we would find one another again sooner or later, that it was inevitable since we loved each other, that we just needed to let the wounds heal, as they say, but we were still young and had our whole lives ahead of us. Now, I turned around and noticed that life was over, that it had passed us by without really giving us any clear signs, then it had quietly, discreetly and elegantly taken its cards back and simply turned away from us; really, if you looked at it closely, it hadn't been very long, our life.)

In a sense I wanted to make a Facebook wall, but for my own personal use: a Facebook wall that would never be seen by anyone but me – and, very briefly, by the estate agent who would have to value my apartment after my death; he would be a bit surprised, then would throw everything in the bin and bring in a cleaning company to remove the traces of glue from the walls.

The task was an easy one thanks to modern cameras; each of my pictures was linked to the time and date when it was taken, so there was nothing simpler than filtering them all according to those criteria. If I had activated the GPS function on each of my cameras, I could also have identified the locations beyond any doubt; but in fact there was no point in that – I remembered all the places of my life, I remembered them perfectly, with surgical and pointless precision. My memory of dates was more vague, but dates were unimportant; everything that had happened had happened for all eternity, I knew that now, but it was an eternity that was closed and inaccessible.

In the course of this story, I have mentioned a number of photographs; two with Camille, one with Kate. There were others, just over three thousand others, of much less interest; it was surprising to note how mediocre my photographs were: tourist snapshots in Venice or Florence, exactly like the ones taken by thousands of other tourists; why had I thought it was a good idea to take them? And what had led me to have these banal images developed? Now, however, I was going to stick them on the wall, each one in its place, not in the hope that they would exude any kind of beauty or meaning; but I would still carry on to the end, because I could, I could in material terms; it was a task physically within my range.

So I did.

In the end, I developed an interest in service charges too. They were extraordinarily high in the tower blocks in the thirteenth arrondissement – that was something which I hadn't anticipated, and which would interfere with my plan for my life. A few months previously (only a few months? A whole year, even two? I could no longer give my life a chronology and only a few images survived in the midst of a confused nothingness, but the attentive reader will fill in the gaps), well, in short, when I decided to disappear, to leave the Ministry of Agriculture and Yuzu once and for all, I still had a sense that I was rich, and that the inheritance from my parents would give me a limitless amount of time.

Now I had just over two hundred thousand euros left in my account. Of course going on holiday was out of the question. (A holiday to do what? Funboarding, skiing in the Alps? And in what context? Once, in some club in Fuerteventura I had gone to with Camille, I had come across a guy who had gone there on his own: he had dinner on his own, and as far as one could tell he would go on having dinner on his own until the end of his stay; he was in his thirties, Spanish I thought, not in bad physical shape and probably of an acceptable social status – he might have been a cashier in a bank; the courage he had to display every day, particularly during mealtimes, had startled me, had almost plunged me into a state of terror.) I wouldn't be going away for the weekend either; I was finished with country-house hotels: if you're going to a country-house hotel on your own you might as well blow your brains out; I had had a moment of genuine sadness as I parked my G 350 on the third underground level of this grim car park that came with my apartment; the floor was repellent and oily, the atmosphere nauseating, there were vegetable peelings lying around here and there: it was a very sad end for my old G 350, shut away in this dirty and sordid car park after devouring mountain roads, crossing swamps, passing through fords and racking up just over 380,000 kilometres on the clock, and never for one moment disappointing me.

Neither did I think of calling escorts, and besides I had lost the piece of paper that Dr Azote had given me. When I noticed that and reflected that I had probably left it in my room at the Hôtel Mercure, I was worried for a moment that Audrey might have happened upon it, that it might have affected her esteem for me. (But why on earth would I have cared? My mind was all over the place.) I could obviously ask Azote again, or do a search of my own – there was no shortage of websites – but it seemed pointless: nothing resembling an erection seemed imaginable for now – my sporadic attempts at masturbation left me in no doubt about that – so the world had become a neutral surface without relief or attraction and my working expenses were considerably reduced; but the sum of charges was so indecently high that even with restricting myself to the moderate joys of food and wine, I could only afford ten years at most before my bank account dwindled to zero and brought the process to an end.

I planned to work at night so as not to be put off by the sight of the concrete forecourt; I didn't have much faith in my own courage. In the sequence I had planned, the order of events was brief and perfect: a switch by the door to the main room let me raise the roller blinds in a few seconds. Trying to avoid thinking, I would walk to the window, slide the picture window open, lean out and it would be over.

For a long time, I was restrained by the thought of falling: I imagined myself floating in space for several minutes, becoming increasingly aware of the inevitable bursting of my organs at the moment of impact, the absolute agony that would run through me, and I filled more and more, with each second of my fall, with a terrible state of total terror that would not be softened even by the blessed mercy of unconsciousness.

This was the problem of having studied science for a long time: height, h, travelled by a body in free fall for a time, t, was in fact given precisely by the formula $h = 1/2gt^2$, with g being the gravitational constant, giving a falling time, for height h, of $\sqrt{2h/g}$. Taking into account the height of my building (almost exactly one hundred metres), and the fact that air resistance could be neglected for a fall from such an altitude, that meant a falling time of four and a half seconds – five seconds at most if one absolutely insisted on including air resistance; nothing, as we can see, to get worked up about; with a few glasses of calvados under one's belt, it wasn't even certain that one would have time to think clearly. There would certainly be more suicides if people knew that simple figure: four and a half seconds. I would hit the ground at a speed of 159 kilometres per hour, which was a bit less pleasant to imagine; but all right, it wasn't the impact that I was afraid of but the flight, and physics established with certainty that my flight would be brief.

Ten years was much too much – my spiritual suffering would have reached an unbearable and fatal level long before then – but at the same time, I couldn't see myself leaving an inheritance (and anyway who to, the state? The prospect was extraordinarily disagreeable), so I had to increase the rhythm of my expenditure – it was worse than mean, it was frankly stingy – but I couldn't bear the prospect of dying with any money in my account. I could have given it away, shown generosity, but to whom? I wasn't about to hand over my cash to a bunch of Romanians. I hadn't been given much, and I didn't have much desire to give anything myself; goodness had not developed in me, the psychological process had not taken place and human beings as a whole had, on the contrary, become increasingly indifferent to me; not to mention the cases of hostility pure and simple. I had tried to get close to certain human beings (and female human beings in particular, first of all because they were more attractive to me, but

I've already mentioned that), well, I think I'd made a number of normal, standard, average attempts, but for different reasons (which I have also mentioned) nothing concrete had come of them – nothing had given me the feeling that I had a place to live, or a context, let alone a reason.

The only solution to reduce my sum in the bank was to carry on eating, to try and cultivate an interest in expensive and refined foods (Alba truffles? Maine lobsters?); I had just passed eighty kilos, but that wouldn't influence the duration of my fall, as the remarkable experiments of Galileo had already confirmed, carried out, legend has it, from the top of the Tower of Pisa; but more probably from the top of a tower in Padua.

My own tower block also had the name of an Italian city. (Ravenna? Ancona? Rimini?) There was nothing comical about that coincidence, but it didn't strike me as absurd to try and develop a humorous attitude, to imagine the moment when I would lean out of the window, when I would abandon myself to the force of gravity, as a joke; after all, the jocular spirit concerning death was entirely possible: lots of people died every second and they managed to do so perfectly, first time, without making a fuss; some had even taken advantage of the situation to deliver *one-liners*.

I would get there, I felt I was about to get there: it was the home stretch. I still had prescriptions for two months' worth of Captorix and would probably have to see Dr Azote for one last appointment; this time I would have to lie to him, pretend that my condition had improved to make sure that he didn't attempt a rescue operation, an emergency hospitalisation or whatever; I would have to appear optimistic and carefree, but without overdoing it; my abilities as an actor were limited. It wouldn't be easy, and he was far from stupid; but giving up Captorix, even for a single day, was unthinkable. You can't let pain go beyond a certain level or you start doing crazy things: you swallow some Destop Turbo and your internal organs, composed of the same substances that usually block sinks, break down amidst horrible pain; or else you throw yourself under a metro and find yourself two legs short and with your balls crushed to bits, but still not dead.

It's a small white, oval, scored tablet.

It doesn't create or transform; it interprets. It renders fleeting what was definitive; it renders contingent what was ineluctable. It supplies a new interpretation of life – less rich, less artificial, and marked by a certain rigidity. It provides no form of happiness, or even of real relief; its action is of a different kind: by transforming life into a sequence of formalities it allows you to fool yourself. On this basis, it helps people to live, or at least to not die – for a certain period of time.

But death imposes itself in the end: the molecular armour cracks, the process of decomposition resumes its course. It probably happens more quickly for those who have never belonged to the world, who have never imagined living, or loving, or being loved; those who have always known that life was not within their reach. Those people, and there are many of them, have, as they say, nothing to regret; I am not in that situation.

I could have made a woman happy. Well, two; I have said which ones. Everything was clear, extremely clear from the beginning, but we didn't realise. Did we yield to the illusion of individual freedom, of an open life, of infinite possibilities? It's possible; those ideas were part of the spirit of the age; we didn't formalise them, we didn't have the taste to do that; we merely conformed and allowed ourselves to be destroyed by them; and then, for a very long time, to suffer as a result.

God takes care of us; he thinks of us every minute, and he gives us instructions that are sometimes very precise. Those surges of love that flow into our chests and take our breath away – those illuminations, those ecstasies, inexplicable if we consider our biological nature, our status as simple primates – are extremely clear signs.

And today I understand Christ's point of view and his repeated horror at the hardening of people's hearts: all of these things are signs, and they don't realise it. Must I really, on top of everything, give my life for these wretches? Do I really have to be explicit on that point?

Apparently so.